What the critics are saying:

GOLD STAR AWARD...Just Erotic Romance Reviews.... "Ms. Kelly has long been called the queen of the erotic Regency romance. The Gypsy Lovers gets the Gold Star Award because she proves it; with her full rich characters, the scorching HOT sex, an ending that makes you want to stand up and cheer and a story so touching you'll need a few tissues." *Amber Taylor*

Romance Reviews Today... "a wonderful, engaging, and erotic read that will surely attract fans of this author or this genre...a book not to be missed, and I recommend it to everyone for anytime, anyplace..." - *Enya Adrian*

Sensual Romance/The Best Reviews... "Rather like an intricate composition, Kelly weaves threads and lives with care and grace. Her themes of rescue and protection are carefully and touchingly rendered. THE GYPSY LOVERS is a gem of a collection that simply should not be missed." *Ann Leveille*

Discover for yourself why readers can't get enough of the multiple award-winning publisher Ellora's Cave. Whether you prefer e-books or paperbacks, be sure to visit EC on the web at www.ellorascave.com for an erotic reading experience that will leave you breathless.

www.ellorascave.com

THE GYPSY LOVERS
An Ellora's Cave Publication, July 2004

Ellora's Cave Publishing, Inc.
PO Box 787
Hudson, OH 44236-0787

ISBN #1-84360-953-3

ISBN MS Reader (LIT) ISBN # 1-84360-820-0
Other available formats (no ISBNs are assigned):
Adobe (PDF), Rocketbook (RB), Mobipocket (PRC) & HTML

Edited by *Briana St. James.*
Cover art by *Syneca.*

THE GYPSY LOVERS

Sahara Kelly

Chapter 1
Count Karoly's Conquest

Viktor Istvan Karoly was bored.

He glanced around the elegant salon and noted that the same could not be said for his fellow entertainers. The dark eyes, white teeth and flashing smiles of the five other men who had accompanied him this evening gave evidence of their enjoyment.

Cigar smoke hung thickly near the high ceiling, the candlelight flashed brilliantly from the crystal decanters that held the finest port, and the conversation was mellow and punctuated with rich laughter.

Their host for the evening, Lord Alfred Eventyde, slouched lazily in his tall chair, enjoying the after-dinner conversation with the band of "Gypsies" he'd invited to his home for the weekend.

Viktor knew they were "all the rage" with London society at the moment, and his lips twisted wryly. Six months ago, they'd been a penniless troupe of dancers and musicians traveling in one cramped caravan, and earning pennies or trading work for food wherever and whenever they could on the Continent. The ravages of war had left little for anyone, let alone wandering minstrels.

Then his father had died and in a series of unexpected coincidences, he had become Count Karoly, man of wealth and property, with a name that could be traced back at least seven centuries. Most of them bloody and riddled with treachery, debauchery and murder. The name was valid and the wealth accessible, but the property almost non-existent. Napoleon's army had seen to that.

He'd return to Karoly soon. But not yet. He wasn't ready.

His friends had cheered his good fortune, and he saw no reason not to share some of it with them. They had bought the finest clothing in Paris, the best musical instruments available, ordered custom caravans, and now traveled in a degree of luxury they could only have dreamed of up until recently. But they were, at heart, still Gypsies.

Still wild, unpredictable, in love with their music and the women it charmed for them.

Women that Viktor knew were waiting in the parlor across the hall. Fluttering over their teacups, pulling their gowns down over their inadequate breasts, hoping to attract the attentions of one or other of the half-dozen amazingly handsome foreigners who had invaded their genteel English houses and set a spark to their virginally proper English souls.

The pastime had paled on Viktor. Very rapidly.

"But Vik," wailed Pyotr. "I have two lovelies just waiting for me to fuck them into heaven after we leave here."

Several others had echoed the complaint when Viktor had announced that they would accept Lord Eventyde's invitation for the weekend.

"They will survive, Pyotr," answered Viktor. "As will you."

In truth, Viktor needed to escape from London. He was uncomfortable in the noise, unhappy with the amount of attention they were receiving, and frustrated that his audiences demanded the same round of music—traditional, characteristic of what the English imagined Gypsy music to be, and stuff he could have played in his sleep with his eyes closed.

He was tired of the same seductive game, and frankly disgusted with the way it was so blatantly played by married women whose husbands were on the opposite side of the room.

He felt hunted, haunted, and stifled.

A servant opened the long windows to let in the soft night air and Viktor felt his soul wander outside.

With a muttered apology to his host, Viktor followed his soul, pausing only to grab his violin on the way.

"Ah, there goes Viktor." He heard Gyorgy's deep voice as he left. "Off to make more music to charm the hearts of your so beautiful English roses."

Bless Gyorgy, he thought. There was a man who would always cover one's back.

He walked slowly across the carefully manicured lawns and down a slope towards the forest that bordered Lord Eventyde's gardens.

He spared little thought for his host. The man had been all that was acceptable and gentlemanly in London, and had offered a pleasant respite from the hustle and bustle of Society's demands on them.

But here in his home, he had changed slightly, and the change made Viktor uncomfortable. He couldn't quite put his finger on what it was, but a shiver had crossed his skin when Lord Eventyde welcomed them yesterday afternoon, and the premonition had not gone away.

Perhaps it was a look in his eye as he introduced his guests to the ladies, none of whom, Viktor guessed, were ladies by birth or by nature. They had been effortlessly elegant during today's round of strolls, polite conversation, lunch *al fresco* on the terrace, and their impromptu outdoor concert in the late afternoon.

But there was something. An undercurrent, perhaps, an unsettling air of unfinished business that set his teeth on edge and made him wary of the evening to come.

It spoke volumes that Lord Eventyde's family, comprised of his wife and daughter, were not present at this weekend in the country. Or if they were, they had not joined the guests.

Viktor was no saint. But he'd grown up with some basic values instilled in his heart and his soul. He had a nasty feeling that Lord Eventyde had no such scruples to moderate his behavior, and Viktor really was not in the mood for an evening of debauchery.

Pyotr was insatiable and would love it. Gyorgy would go along with the games out of curiosity, and Lukasz and Matyas like the brothers they were, would probably share.

And then of course, there was Fabyan. Oldest of the six, Fabyan had really been the one who had brought them together from their diverse roots. Only Fabyan knew the truth of who each man was, what secrets he hid, and what sorrows he had left behind to join their little band of Gypsies.

And Fabyan would never tell. For Fabyan never spoke.

He was, in Viktor's opinion, the best looking one of them all, with his tall, lean body honed to muscular perfection by years of dancing the energetic Hungarian *Csardas* or dances. His eyes were an unusual shade of dark blue, and his hair was as shining and as black as that of his friends. But there were silver threads showing now around his ears, and his eyes occasionally looked weary instead of joyful.

Viktor had no idea whether Fabyan's silence was self-imposed or physical, but he'd also never felt the need to ask. The older man had a presence, a level of control, which radiated from him and made conversation redundant.

He, like Viktor, found solace in his music, although he was not as bold as to leave a host's table in pursuit of his muse.

Viktor was. And at this moment he was very glad of it.

The night air washed over him, blowing away the scent of stale tobacco and refreshing his mind.

A nightingale sang plaintively from the depths of the woods and its liquid voice lured Viktor on.

He was happiest when alone, and surrounded by nature. After some of his experiences, this sort of isolation was the next best thing to heaven. Clean and pure, the forest offered solace and peace and Viktor took pleasure in both.

He raised his violin to his chest and nestled his chin into place, feeling as comfortable walking with the instrument as another man might have felt with a cane. It was an extension of him, a part of his being, and he knew that life without it was almost unbearable.

The first notes he played echoed the song of the nightingale and he paused as he walked to listen to the rest of the clear piping sounds produced from the throat of one tiny bird.

Once again he mimicked the melody, letting his imagination free to soar into the night sky with the strains of his violin. A flurry of notes followed and Viktor walked on slowly, playing from his heart rather than from some carefully transcribed score.

It was moments like these that reaffirmed his decisions, his determination to let the music in him flow freely, to create something unique, special and essentially *him*.

He was quite used to playing and walking, since many of their performances had followed the old traditions of music around a crackling campfire. Guests adored the strolling minstrels, and Viktor had developed a sixth sense for stepping carefully over whatever might be in his path as his bow urged its plaintive song from the strings.

The night swallowed him, the forest seemed to pause and listen, and Viktor breathed deeply, filled with the magic that such moments always produced. How the others could stay in the stifling, smoke-filled rooms of Eventyde Manor, he didn't know. *This* was paradise for him.

There was only one thing missing. The right person with whom to share it.

Viktor had loved and left as many women as his fellow gypsies, but none as yet had touched his heart.

He sighed and the strings echoed the sound, the melody turning plaintive as he considered the possibility that no such woman existed. That he would be alone for the rest of his life. Destined for years of hopping from one willing woman to the next, satisfying his physical needs, but leaving his inner desires unsated.

His steps took him down a path that was less well-tended, but a flicker of moonlight on water beckoned him. His music was pulsing now, throbbing from his instrument and filling the silence around him with a yearning, wild song. A plea to the gods, as it were, for someone to *understand*.

To take him as he was, not for his title, or the fact that he was a new and fascinating bump in their ordinary aristocratic lives. To look beneath the handsome face and tall, well-muscled body, and see the man within. The man who held such deep and lingering scars. Marks that bore witness to the cruelty humans could inflict upon each other.

Marks that only the right person could erase.

Moving steadily now, he reached the opening at the end of the path and with a final sorrowful chord, he lifted his violin away from his chin and let his hands relax at his sides.

It was beautiful.

A small lake stretched away from him, banked by overhanging willows shining silver in the moonlight. The water rippled as it was fed by a stream bubbling off to his left, and gurgled again as the lake narrowed to a small waterfall of stones and made its way on its never-ending journey.

An artful arrangement of rocks had been set next to the bubbling falls, and a movement from one of them caught his eye.

Viktor blinked. And blinked again.

It must be a water sprite, or a nymph. Or a goddess.

For once, his brain emptied of music and his heart beat in an irregular rhythm.

She was neither nymph nor sprite. She was real.

* * * * *

Madelyne Eventyde struggled to catch her breath. For the last few minutes, she'd been held captive by the sound of an incredible and heart-wrenching melody, drifting through the night to where she sat perched next to the waterfall.

The chattering waters had been a counterpoint to the soaring chords and almost painfully beautiful sounds, and had frozen her to the spot as she listened to the music.

And now he was here. Standing a few yards away from her, violin in one hand, bow in the other.

She knew who he was, of course. One of the Gypsies she'd been forbidden to meet. Along with everyone else her father invited to Eventyde Manor these days.

No one ever had the chance to greet the daughter of the house. The shamed daughter. The one who had brought such social scandal down upon the Eventyde name. The one who had nearly dishonored them all, and sent five hundred years of proud heritage tumbling downstream along with the river that burbled at her feet.

Or so her father had told her, anyway.

The man was watching her, and she knew she had to move. To leave before he could speak to her and bring down even more of her father's wrath upon her head.

But as she stood, he neared her, his footsteps light and almost silent as he crossed the grass towards her.

"You are real," he breathed.

Madelyne couldn't help herself. She chuckled. "Indeed yes. But perhaps your music wasn't. Nothing that beautiful could be of earthly origin. I am thinking you must have an angel dancing on your bow."

He smiled, teeth flashing white against his dark complexion. "Perhaps it was you."

Madelyne drew back a little, unsure of herself now that he was so close to her. "I'm no angel, sir."

One dark eyebrow lifted a little. "Are you sure? You are here, in the moonlight, as silver as the rays that light our paths. Insubstantial as the mist, beautiful as the flowers I passed along the way...I think that qualifies for the title of 'angel'?"

Madelyne felt an unusual sensation flood through her as this tall man swept bold eyes up her body.

"Forgive me for disturbing your composition, sir. I will take my leave and let you return to the pursuit of your muse."

Her brain was telling her to get away from him *now*, before the damage was done. Her heart was telling her other things.

"I find I no longer need pursue my muse, lady. She is here. In front of me."

Madelyne's eyes opened wide as he lifted his violin once more to his chin. The bow stroked across the strings, producing a joyous sound, and one that found an answering pleasure deep within her.

He played carelessly, wildly, circling her as he did so and entrapping her in the sound of his music.

Her feet began to twitch. The rhythm of his melody sank into her very bones, and she found herself swaying in time to the notes.

She couldn't help herself—or stop herself. She raised her arms and began to dance.

As if held in thrall by some magical spell woven by the strings of his violin, Madelyne swayed slowly at first. She felt her skirts brush around her legs as she took cautious steps, letting the music dictate her movements.

She turned and spread her arms wide, responding to an increase in the tempo of his playing. The nature of the music changed, becoming wilder and more primitive and finding an echo inside Madelyne.

She picked up the speed of her steps and her heart began to pound. His liquid notes flooded her ears, the vibrant melody resounded throughout her body, and she found herself restricted by her gown.

How she would have loved to be free to dance the way she really wanted. To let her arms fly high and her legs follow her soul. To jump and spin and lose herself in this moment, this music. To fly higher than was humanly possible and leave all her earthly troubles behind.

Once again the music changed, becoming faster, but darker now, more seductive.

She raised her eyes as she danced and met his. They were glowing at her over the dark mass of his violin, and never left her face as she responded to his every chord.

His bow was bringing more than music to her heart. It was as if he stroked her body with that piece of wood and catgut. Her nipples tightened beneath her fichu and her breath came in little gasps as she surrendered to his musical seduction.

For that was indeed what it was. His playing seduced her, reaching deep within her to places she'd buried long ago. Making her blood pound fiercely in her ears and her belly ache with some fundamental need. She twirled again, trying hard to stop herself from crying out with the pleasure of it.

His nimble fingers flew over the strings and Madelyne's nimble feet answered the call. She spun and leaped as if possessed, finally coming to a stop as his last notes trailed off into the silence of the night.

They faced each other, Madelyne's heart pounding as she stood before him staring into those dark eyes.

He bent and let the violin rest on the grass, rising again to take a step nearer.

Madelyne held her breath at the expression in his eyes, and for a long moment it seemed the whole world stood quite still.

Then he took her in his arms and kissed her.

Chapter 2

At the first touch of her mouth to his, Viktor's mind had emptied of music and filled with need.

She was sweet and sensual, and as his tongue swept her lips demanding they part for him, she'd answered with her own desires.

She'd opened for him, welcoming him, and touching her tongue to his, as eagerly and wantonly as any woman he'd ever kissed.

But she wasn't *any* woman.

He could feel her heart pounding through her breasts as he pressed their bodies together, and he hoped it was from his touch not her recent dance.

His cock was rock hard and ready, and she met it with a slight parting of her thighs along with a little moan as he slid his hands to her buttocks and clutched her even tighter against him.

Her hands were at his neck, tugging at his hair and holding his head captive against her mouth.

She gave him back as much as he gave her, and Viktor nearly gasped at the pleasure of it. Their lips crushed together, mouths learning, tongues exploring, and through it all she let her body speak to his.

She was arousing him to the point of pain, and her increasingly bold pressure against him told him she was as affected as he by their embrace.

Finally he drew apart from her, opening his eyes and savoring her taste on his lips.

"Who are you?" he breathed.

Her eyelids flickered, then rose slowly as she tried to pull herself out of the sensual haze they'd created together.

"I...I'm...nobody," she whispered.

She wasn't running away, however. She wasn't screaming or panicking, or doing anything she should have done after being kissed like that by a total stranger.

Viktor couldn't help but be glad.

He smiled. "I don't usually find myself like this…" He pressed his cock against her softness again watching her eyes widen. "From kissing *nobody*."

With a little sigh she moved from his arms and resumed her seat on the rock. "I am nobody you should know, sir."

The words were sad—almost plaintive.

"Suppose you let me make that decision? Oh, and you probably shouldn't know me, either," he added.

A quick smile lit her face. "Perhaps we are two of a kind, in that case."

Viktor settled himself on another rock, wincing a little as his cock reminded him that two such hardnesses didn't necessarily make for a comfortable seating position.

"So what is an angel like you doing out here at this hour of the night?"

He watched her face as she stared into the water, trying to gauge the color of her eyes. Blue perhaps? Her hair was silvery in the moonlight, so it was quite possible.

But it was hard to tell.

The magic of the night was casting a spell over her, turning her from flesh and blood woman into some mythical and sensual illusion. But he could still taste her on his lips. That kiss had been no illusion.

He moved, easing the hardness of his cock once again.

"Escaping," she murmured.

"From heaven?"

She snorted. "From hell, more like."

Viktor raised one eyebrow in question.

"I should not bore you, sir. Forgive me." She moved a little as if to stand, but Viktor stopped her with a gesture.

"You could not bore me. Ever. Boring is what I too am escaping from. Back there." He tipped his head over his shoulder.

"You did not enjoy Lord Eventyde's dinner party?"

"No." His answer was short, but he wasn't about to go into details. He wanted to listen to her speak, to tell him anything and everything about herself.

"You really want to know who I am?" There was a degree of amazement in her tone.

"Yes. I really want to know."

She sighed, and folded her hands together in her lap. "It's a silly story, and one I'm sure will give you a distaste of me. The path is behind you, sir, should you wish to leave."

"My name is Viktor," he said quietly. "What's yours?"

"Madelyne. Madelyne...Eventyde."

Viktor blinked. "You are my host's daughter?"

She nodded. "For my sins, yes."

"I should think it's his sins, not yours."

Madelyne looked at him. "Unfortunately, it's probably a little of both."

Viktor reached out and briefly caught a lacy frill from the hem of her gown with his hand. He held it tight, as if to anchor her right where she was.

"Tell me." It was a command for all the politeness in his tone.

"Very well. But remember—you asked." She smiled a little. "I am, as you said, Lord Eventyde's daughter. His only child. And you've met my father, so I don't need to go into much about him. I have no illusions about his affection for me, since he made it clear from the start that he was disappointed not to have a son." Her smile disappeared. "I don't think he ever forgave my mother. He never speaks of her."

"Where is she?" asked Viktor. The lace ran through his fingers as he played with it, not unlike the strings of his violin.

"I don't know. Paris perhaps. She travels a lot nowadays. Sometimes she'll write, but not often."

"She left you alone?"

"Not while I was growing up, of course. She was only eighteen when I was born, and I remember the good times we had together. Alone. Here in the country while my father was in London. But once I got old enough to manage on my own, well, she sort of drifted away. And...then she left. Permanently. Just before..." Madelyne stopped.

"Before what, sweet Madelyne?"

Her eyes closed. "Before—I ruined myself and my family."

* * * * *

There. It was out.

Madelyne couldn't believe she'd actually spoken those terrible words to someone, and a man at that.

It must be something about the moonlight and the magic of his music. Or perhaps the warmth she felt radiating from this wildly good-looking man who had appeared from the darkness and swept her into his spell.

"You don't look very ruined to me," he said quietly.

She swallowed past a lump in her throat. "Appearances can be deceiving, sir."

He moved closer, almost too close, sliding his hips onto the rock next to her. She swore she could feel the heat of his flesh as he closed the distance between them.

"I am not easily deceived, Madelyne, and my name is Viktor. It would give me pleasure to hear you use it as you tell me your story."

Dear God—the man was appealing.

How she'd love to lay her head down on that shoulder and let go of all her pain. Just for a minute or two.

But once he'd heard her story, she knew he'd leave. No one she'd known had been able to understand.

She hardened her resolution and prepared herself for his departure.

"Very well…Viktor. I shall tell you, then you can go. Three years ago, I fell in love with a young man who lived near my home. He was a second son, from a respected local family, although not possessing anything near the wealth of my father. I wanted to marry Daniel. To spend my life with him, bear his children, and make a home for us all. Just the normal things any girl in love would want."

She took a deep breath.

"Go on," encouraged Viktor softly.

"We were so young. So in love." Madelyne swallowed. "And of course, my father found out about us. He was furious."

"He had other plans for you, I suppose?"

"I don't know. He'd never spoken to me of such matters. I just knew that when he found out about Daniel and myself he went mad.

Threatened me with the strap, and Daniel with all kinds of dreadful things if we ever saw each other again."

"Did he beat you?"

"Not then. He probably thought the threats would be enough. But to be on the safe side, he went to London, and the next thing we knew Daniel had been 'recruited' into a regiment bound for France. He'd expressed an interest in joining the military before, but had never pursued it since I'd...we'd started making plans for the future."

"I understand. Go on." The gentle kindness in Viktor's voice encouraged Madelyne.

"It was the night before Daniel was supposed to leave for his regiment. We had arranged a meeting in the stables to say goodbye. And we were both...distraught, heartbroken, in love..." Her voice faltered and she stopped as memories flooded back.

Memories she'd held successfully at bay for so long.

"Let me guess," said Viktor smoothly. "Things went farther than they should have, and your father caught you both."

Madelyne barely repressed a shudder. "Quite correct, sir. He caught us at the worst possible moment."

"'Tis not an unusual story, Madelyne. And surely your father must have demanded Daniel wed you?"

Madelyne bit back a sob. "On the contrary, Viktor. My father tore me out of Daniel's embrace. He gave me to his groom and told him to hold me."

Oh God, this was so hard. "I was...I was naked at the time."

Viktor's hand moved and covered Madelyne's, offering a supporting grasp and warmth, and giving her the courage to continue.

"Then...then he proceeded to beat Daniel to within an inch of his life. My father has always been a strong man, and Daniel had no chance. There was so much blood..."

The tears fell then, and she realized she was in Viktor's arms, being held tight against his chest.

"Tell me all of it, sweetheart," he urged. "Let it all out."

She swallowed harshly. "After he'd finished with Daniel, he made him watch while his groom...his groom..."

"Ssshh...it's all right." Viktor stroked her arms and soothed her.

"My father said..." The words still rang clearly in her ears, and Madelyne shuddered. "He said that seeing as I was ruined anyway, Daniel might just as well see the sort of woman he'd turned me into. He told his groom to finish what Daniel had started."

Viktor's arms tightened roughly around her, but she relished the comfort they offered.

She finished her tale with her face tucked beneath his chin. "He let his groom take me there on a bale of hay, while Daniel was forced to watch."

There was silence after she'd finished, but Viktor showed no signs of disengaging from their embrace.

A few moments passed, and Madelyne struggled to brush the tears away.

"What happened to Daniel?"

She sighed. "He was killed in his first engagement. All my father's fury was for naught. We'd never have married. A French bullet saw to that."

"I'm sorry."

Madelyne felt a soft kiss drop onto her hair, and strangely, her pain eased. "Thank you. It was a long time ago, and although I shall never forget Daniel, he's now a memory. A wonderful one, but still just a memory. I'm only sorry that I was responsible for causing such dreadful things to happen to him. He was a good man, Viktor."

"He must have been, for you to love him. And you do realize, of course, that you weren't responsible. Your father was."

Madelyne thought about that. "I suppose so. But if I hadn't...if we hadn't..."

Viktor's chest moved slightly beneath her head as he breathed in a quick lungful of air. "Madelyne, if you hadn't *then*, you would have sooner or later. It's a natural thing to want to give everything you have to the one you love."

"Is it?" She couldn't help turning and looking into the darkness of his eyes. His words were the first ones of comfort she'd heard in so long.

"Indeed it is," he answered. "Our bodies are made that way." His lips dropped to her forehead and dropped little kisses there.

She closed her eyes. "Oh that feels nice."

"I'm glad. It feels nice to me too."

"Are you sure you don't mind being here with me? After all, I'm a ruined woman now. My father made that clear to everybody."

Viktor paused. "I would have thought he'd try to keep everything quiet."

"Not him. It was his temper and his pride. He made it plain that I was not a virgin, and that he wouldn't now consider marrying me to any of the matches he'd apparently had in mind before this happened. He was furious. Unbelievably furious. He'd lost his chance to secure more land, and possibly a title for me. He'd let his temper drive him into a rather unwise course of action, I'd say, and when he realized it, I had to bear the brunt of his displeasure."

She pursed her mouth into an expression of distaste. "He made it clear that I was to consider myself a social outcast. No man would want me for myself. When the time was right, he told me he'd procure me a husband, but until then…I was sent to the Dower House and I've stayed there ever since. I've seen hardly anyone, and certainly not met any young men…until…"

"Until me?"

Viktor's lips were back, tracing her eyebrows with feather light touches, and smoothing away the traces of her tears.

"Until you. Until your music flew through the night and touched me…" Her hand rose to her heart.

Viktor's followed, covering hers and pressing their combined warmth into her breast.

She felt her nipple rise as a surprising pleasure flooded her body.

"Viktor," she breathed.

His lips found hers again, and once more she welcomed them. This time, she opened readily for him, and let his tongue plunder where it would, straining to meet it with her own.

It was a joyous kiss, the first she'd given freely in years, the first to be shared with someone who *knew*. Who knew her darkest secrets, and apparently didn't care.

She snuggled closer, sighing a little as his hand cupped her breast and kneaded it gently through the light fabric of her gown.

She ached.

"Viktor," she said again.

"Mmm?"

"Help me."

He pulled back slightly. "How, Madelyne?"

"By...by touching me. By doing what you're doing. Stay for a while, please?"

"Do you know what you're asking?" His voice was rough, but his hands gentle.

"Yes. I know. But I also know that I need something...someone to let me know I'm still alive. That two people can share pleasure and not have it end in horror. I need...new memories, Viktor."

Madelyne raised her hand to his cheek and touched it, smiling a little at the hint of stubble that tugged on her skin.

"It's too much to ask..." She sighed.

Viktor chuckled. "It's not too much to ask, sweet one. But I'm just a lowly gypsy. I should not even aspire to lay my hands on you."

"I *want* your hands on me. I want...I don't know *what* I want." She paused. "But something tells me that you do."

Chapter 3

Viktor knew.

He knew that the woman he held bore scars on her soul. Scars that had been put there by the one person she should have been able to trust—her father.

He quenched his fury, knowing that now was not the time or place for such emotions. Although he promised himself that there would be a settling of accounts. Soon.

She was so still in his arms, waiting for him to speak, watching him as best she could in the darkness of the night.

Such a warm soul, such a loving woman, and so badly abused.

He understood.

He understood more than she could ever comprehend. For he too bore such scars. And he too had needed the touch of another to help heal the deeply hidden pain of betrayal.

He picked her up in his arms and moved with his precious burden to a soft patch of grass by the river. Pushing willow branches aside, he laid her gently down and followed her, letting the leaves fall back into place and curtain them from the rest of the world.

"Madelyne," he breathed. "I want you."

"Even though you know—"

He touched his finger to her lips. "Sshh. The past is just that. The past. We are here, now, tonight. And we're together. Something special is happening between us."

"You feel it too?" Her question contained amazement, and an undercurrent of longing.

He lowered his lips to hers in a gentle kiss. "How can I not? You entranced me with your dancing, bewitched me with your voice and trusted me with your secrets."

"I...I entranced you?"

He smiled and reached for her hand, sliding it between their bodies and holding it to his cock. "I am entranced."

Madelyne's fingers flexed curiously against his hardness, bringing a shudder to his balls.

"This…this is entranced?"

Viktor's smile was somewhat painful as he let her run her hand up his rock hard length. "It certainly is."

Perhaps he should return the favor. And maybe distract her a little before she caused an explosion in his breeches. He lowered his head to her breasts, and nuzzled them, listening with pleasure as her breath hitched in her lungs.

"Do you like that?" he asked.

"Oh yes," she breathed.

His hand slid to the laces that secured her bodice and loosened them, easing her sleeves from her shoulders. "Then you might like this too."

He let his mouth tug the gown down, pulling the fabric with his teeth, and keeping her hand pressed against him so that she could feel his pleasure. His cock stirred hungrily as he freed her breasts, and her fingers tightened around it.

He clamped down on the urge to thrust himself into her hand, and let her soft fragrance seep into his nostrils as he explored her nakedness with his tongue.

Her breasts were full and firm, and the nipples were already peaking, just begging to be suckled and nibbled.

He answered their call and slowly lowered his open mouth over one taut peak.

She gasped as his tongue found the sensitive bud and played with it, arching her back and thrusting herself into his touch.

He suckled her, relishing the way his attentions were bringing an enthusiastic response from this sweet angel beneath him.

"Viktor," she sighed. "Viktor. I want to touch you, too."

He pulled away from her nipple and quickly shrugged off his jacket and shirt, as anxious to have her hands on him as she was to get them there.

It did mean she'd have to release his cock, but all things considered that might not be a bad idea at this moment. It would certainly still be there when the time came for her to resume her touches.

And Viktor intended that she would resume her touches. And a whole lot more.

With a little moan of pleasure, Madelyne welcomed his bare flesh against hers, rubbing herself like a cat over his chest.

She wasted no time in freeing her arms from her dress and sliding her hands up his spine to rest at the back of his neck, tangled in his hair.

"Oh God, so good, Viktor. You feel so solid, so warm…"

She had no idea how *solid* he was.

Viktor gently slid her from her dress, pulling it over her hips and tossing it aside. Her soft chemise was wrinkled to her waist, and her legs long and bare. She was no society woman, corseted into several layers of whalebone and gartered to the eyeballs.

She was an unfettered angel and she was heating up to a mass of fire beneath his hands.

He was not immune to the furnace himself.

The scent of her arousal bloomed from her mound, and Viktor pulled away from her body to strip her naked.

A generous tuft of silvery hair hid her secrets, but he knew it would be no impairment to his intentions. He'd find her softness, and the places that gave her special pleasure.

Gently, he stroked her mound, the hot and swollen flesh dampening his fingers.

She cried out a little, and tossed her head as he touched her. "Viktor."

"Easy, Madelyne. 'Tis just a glimpse of things to come." He smiled to himself. *You amongst them.*

A significant pain around his balls told Viktor that he needed to release the pressure exerted by his breeches, or he might not survive to accomplish his goals.

With the speed and dexterity born of many years of fending for himself, he stripped bare within moments and finally touched her.

Really touched her.

Lying at her side, he pulled her to face him, breast to chest, cock to belly and thigh to thigh.

He pillowed her head on his arm and pressed them together, feeling her nipples stabbing into his muscles and letting his hand stroke down her spine to fondle her buttocks.

The grass cushioned them, a soft mattress for their loving, and the willows gave them the privacy of a natural bower.

Madelyne's soft sighs of pleasure were echoed by the distant sound of the water as it tumbled over the small waterfall, and Viktor's senses swam with it all.

Magic surrounded them, nature lulled them, and the heat of the woman in his arms seduced him beyond anything he'd ever imagined.

She was kissing him now, letting her lips roam over his throat and down onto his chest.

He bit back a gasp as she found his nipple and teased it with her tongue. "I didn't know men enjoyed that," she whispered.

"Oh we do," groaned Viktor. "We do, very much."

He slipped his fingers between her buttocks and stroked down, feeling her tremble as he reached deep between her legs for her cunt.

Almost unconsciously, she parted her thighs and rested one leg on top of his. She had opened herself to him.

He moved the arm beneath her head and gripped a handful of her tumbling hair, pulling her face back to his.

"Madelyne," he breathed.

Her answer was choked by his kiss.

He plunged his tongue into her mouth just as his fingers found her cunt and one made its way into her body.

He tasted her moan and moved in a rhythm, tongue and finger syncopated to each other, driving Madelyne wild.

Another finger entered her, stretching her, teasing her, and still echoing the possession of his mouth on hers.

His thumb moved and found the hard bud of her clit, soaked and sensitive to the slightest brush of his flesh.

She jerked beneath him and moaned into his mouth once more as he circled it, caressingly, keeping up the pressure of his fingers and the movement of his tongue.

She was trembling and gasping and igniting beneath him, and Viktor was burning from her heat and his need. He moved away slightly, peeling their lips apart.

Slowly, he rolled her onto her back and ran his hands up and down her body, bathing her in her own moisture and making her sigh.

He nibbled her breasts and licked around her navel with his tongue, then eased himself between her thighs and spread them wide.

She propped herself up on her elbows. "Viktor...what are you doing?"

"Hush, darling. I'm just loving you, that's all."

"But...*there*?"

The hesitancy in her voice brought a satisfied smile to Viktor's lips. She may not have been a virgin, but there were many things she had yet to learn. And he was going to be her teacher.

"Yes. Most especially here."

"Oh."

She slumped back down on her back as Viktor touched her clit gently. "And here, too," he added.

"Oooh." Her hips wriggled.

"Do you like that?"

She moaned as he once again stroked around her clit. "Yesss..."

He grinned.

If she liked *that*, then she'd just love *this*.

* * * * *

Madelyne's breath left her lungs in a great whoosh as Viktor slid his hands beneath her buttocks and lifted her to his mouth.

Never could she have imagined anything like *this*.

His tongue was touching her. In a place where she'd never imagined anyone's mouth should be. And oh God, it was *wonderful*. He seemed to know instinctively where to apply pressure, where to stroke and how to send thrilling shudders of pleasure deep into her womb.

Her thoughts shattered as he pressed deep, breathing out against her hot skin and magnifying the experience with each and every part of him.

She wanted to scream, to cry out her feelings, but her throat was closing on her as she struggled to deal with the flood of arousal that swept over her. His tongue was hot, flickering like fire over those places between her legs that were shedding tears of excitement.

He seemed to like it. He was licking her, tasting her, burying his face in her and driving her up to some dizzying level of madness. And just when she thought she would die from it, he moved a little and found another place to touch.

She had no idea that a tongue could be such a sensual weapon. She'd been kissed, certainly, but never in a million years would she have expected a man to use his mouth on her like this.

Nor could she believe how much she was enjoying it. His fingers were clamped into her buttocks, and the pressure added to Madelyne's bliss.

She let herself go. Her hips thrust up, demanding all that his mouth could give, and her thighs spread apart even more in an attempt to tell him without words how wonderful this was.

He answered with the most devastating move yet—he pushed his tongue inside her.

Viktor's face was buried hard against her and his tongue swirled around her most sensitive inner surfaces.

She couldn't help it—she cried out. Her muscles responded to his movements by tightening, her whole body began to shake, and Viktor slowly withdrew, keeping her trembling with long slow licks as he did so.

Madelyne held her breath.

The world had stopped, vanished, disappeared somewhere else. She was taut as a bowstring, waiting, anticipating, knowing that she was on the brink of...of *something*.

"Madelyne."

She heard his voice through a fog, and did her best to open her eyes.

He was there, hovering over her, surrounding her with himself, holding himself above her and looking down at her with eyes shadowed by the night and by desire.

"Watch me," he whispered.

She was unable to do anything else. She was a tool for him to use, a puppet dancing at the command of his fingers on her strings.

She felt his cock, velvety hard, as it sought her entrance, slipping through the wet folds of her flesh and entering her.

God, he was big. He was stretching her already softened passage, but she felt no pain.

He was filling her, completing her, finding those empty places that she'd thought would never be sated.

She shuddered again as he slid all the way inside, touching her core, and bringing a sigh of surprise to her lips. His eyes stayed on hers, as if willing her to experience every single second, every movement he made within her.

She was completely and utterly helpless to break their eye contact. There was something compelling her to watch him, to drown in those dark eyes, to go wherever he bade her.

He pulled back, and her whole body trembled.

Then he thrust into her—a forceful and desperate move as if claiming her for eternity.

That was all it took.

Something incredible was happening to her. Lights flashed inside her brain, dazzling her, and she felt her buttocks harden in Viktor's hands.

He thrust again and her soul exploded.

She screamed his name as she fell apart into a million twinkling stars. Her legs shook, her womb contracted, and her gut clenched down on him as if to pull him along with her. Great shudders swept her, dragging what little breath there was from her lungs and lighting fires all over her skin.

She was vaguely aware of Viktor as he thrust into her again and again, tumbling her into this divine insanity with his hard cock.

As her mind slowed, and the trembling eased, he thrust one last time with a groan and then slipped from her body.

Spellbound, she watched his face as it contorted with passion. His cock lay on her belly and she sensed the savage twitches as he spent himself on her smooth flesh.

Jets of warm liquid bathed her, and she smiled in amazement as Viktor's face reflected his own pleasure.

My God. That she could bring such a man to this point. It was incredible.

And exhausting.

She was sweating, sticky, and content as Viktor eased himself down beside her.

Neither spoke, content for a few moments to let their hearts settle, their bodies rest, and the beauty of the night drift over them.

Finally Viktor spoke.

"Can you replace those old memories now, Madelyne?"

Chapter 4

Viktor tugged a handkerchief from his discarded jacket, and gently wiped Madelyne's belly clean of his seed. Her skin still quivered beneath his hands, or maybe it was his hands that were quivering.

At this point he wasn't quite sure.

Perhaps it was the magic of this forest glade, or the mysteries in the eyes of the woman next to him, or the fact that he'd been jaded by the London seductresses who'd shared his bed.

He didn't know, nor did he care.

This…this incredible night was different.

He heard her hair move as she turned her head towards him. "I think you've obliterated any conscious thoughts, let alone bad memories, Viktor."

He could sense the smile in her voice and answered it with one of his own.

The moon was setting, and she was scarcely more than a silver shadow next to him, but he smiled at her anyway.

"Thank you," she whispered. "Thank you from the bottom of my heart."

An owl hooted nearby and Madelyne jumped.

The spell had been broken.

"I must go. If they find me gone…" Her voice trailed off as she stirred and began to dress.

"I will see you home." Viktor tugged on his breeches and found his boots, dressing by touch alone.

"No…" she sputtered. "That would be most unwise. If we were seen together…"

"We will not be. Trust me, Madelyne. I'm a gypsy, remember?"

She fiddled with her laces. "I'm afraid, Viktor. Afraid that something will spoil this…what we shared. Let me go alone, please. It's for the best."

He paused, thinking carefully. He had no intention of allowing this sprite to travel through the woods alone at this time of night, but he could respect her fears.

"Very well, sweetheart. It shall be as you wish. But I reserve the right to object strenuously."

Madelyne chuckled as she slipped her feet into her shoes. "I'm surprised you have energy enough for anything strenuous at this point. I know I haven't."

Viktor's lips curled up into a wry grin. If she only knew what he still had energy for.

"You'd be surprised how hard we gypsies work, Madelyne. We're well used to *long* physical endeavors."

He heard the rough laugh erupt huskily from Madelyne's throat and his cock stirred. God, he wanted this woman. Again. And again.

"I'll see you tomorrow," he promised.

Madelyne froze. He could sense her stillness across the small distance between them.

"You're leaving tomorrow. Had you forgotten this was just a weekend party?"

It was Viktor's turn to stop still. He had indeed forgotten that they were scheduled to take their leave of Eventyde Manor the next afternoon.

"Damn it to hell," he muttered.

A small hand rested on his sleeve. "Viktor...please...I shall never forget this night, or what happened between us. But it's best that we part now. It will be less painful that way. If we were to see each other again, I don't know if I could bear to say goodbye."

Viktor narrowed his eyes.

The tone of her voice was pleading and God knew he didn't want to cause her pain.

But the thought of never seeing her again was completely untenable. His mind turned over the problem, and began to work furiously.

For the moment, however, he'd allow her to go. It wouldn't be goodbye. Never. Not between them. He knew it as sure as he knew the melodies that flew from his violin.

Some things were just meant to be.

He leaned forward and brushed his lips against her face. "Madelyne..." he whispered. "You are so special."

A hand reached up and stroked his cheek. "Thank you for making me feel that way, Viktor."

Soft lips pressed against his and she turned and left him.

He could have sworn he tasted her tears.

Viktor counted to twenty and then set off after her. His time as a soldier served him well, and he followed Madelyne silently through the forest, setting his feet cautiously on the soft moss and picking his path with care.

She was hurrying, but he had no difficulty keeping the gleam of her white dress in sight.

Within minutes a dim light showed through the trees ahead, and Viktor slowed as the outline of a small house appeared against the night sky. He held himself close to the shadows of a spreading chestnut tree and watched as Madelyne slipped silently over the lawn to a small door set apart from the main entrance.

This must be the Eventyde Dower House she'd mentioned.

The door shut behind her, and Viktor sighed with relief. He knew who she was, where she was, and that she was meant for him.

The matter was closed for discussion.

He turned to leave for Eventyde Manor when the sounds of an approaching carriage made him pause.

It was an odd time of night for visitors.

Viktor quirked a mental eyebrow at this development and moved closer to the drive, finding plenty of concealment amongst the huge shrubs that bordered the gravel covered courtyard.

The front door was flung open and light poured out, silhouetting the impressive figure of Viktor's host. Lord Alfred Eventyde must have deserted the main party to welcome this visitor.

Viktor's curiosity was now well and truly piqued. He crouched low and eased himself to within earshot of the carriage and the four sweating horses.

Their harness jangled and their breathing was heavy. They'd been pushed hard this night.

A footman appeared and ran to their heads, and another opened the carriage door while Lord Eventyde watched silently from the doorway.

A woman fell out and tumbled into a pile of frothing petticoats. Her hair was hanging loosely and her gown barely covering her breasts.

She muttered a curse as her hands struck the gravel.

It was ignored by the man who followed her.

He was fastening the laces on his evening breeches as he carelessly stepped over her and strode to the door.

"So Alfred, where is this wench? I'm of a mind to wed. You've got a bitch to dispose of. Seems we can do business?"

Viktor's heart all but stopped in his chest, and the blood pounded in his ears.

"Glad you could make it, Hucknall." Eventyde's voice pierced the night, redolent with an evil overtone that sent chills down Viktor's spine.

"She's quite ready for you." He looked over the huge man's shoulder. "What about the whore?"

Hucknall glanced down at the woman struggling with her clothing. "Give her a couple of coins and send her on her way. Took her forever to suck me off, useless slut. I hope yours is better."

Eventyde's eyes narrowed. "I have a better idea. Bring her inside." He turned sharply and led the other man into the house as the footman attempted to pull the woman to her feet and was met with a barrage of gutter epithets for his trouble.

With a flounce of her head, she gathered her skirts and stalked up the steps into the Dower House.

The door closed and Viktor was left outside in a state of shock.

He knew the name "Hucknall".

It was a byword for every licentious act and foul perversion in the streets of London. Only the fact that the man had a title he could trace back to William the Conqueror made him tolerable.

He was not admitted to any of the Ton parties, of course, not that he'd have gone if invited.

Gyorgy had run into the man once at a brothel, and returned that night sickened by what he'd seen and heard.

And it took a lot to sicken Gyorgy.

Viktor took a savage breath. If Eventyde was thinking of marrying off Madelyne to the monster he knew Sir Francis Hucknall to be, then Eventyde was in for a big surprise.

He only hoped he could come up with a decent plan before Madelyne got an even bigger surprise.

His heart chilled at the thought of Hucknall's hands anywhere near her. He'd kill that gross piece of filthy flesh before he'd let him touch her.

Once again Viktor began to plan, and easing back into the shadows of the night, he hurried along the path to Eventyde Manor.

This was a job that was too big for one man to handle.

Even a gypsy like himself.

* * * * *

Madelyne slipped hurriedly into her nightgown in the darkness of her room, grateful for the pitcher of water that had allowed her to clean herself up. She'd hated to wash away the scent of Viktor's body from hers, but knew the risk of *anyone* even suspecting she'd been out of the house, let alone lain with a man, was unacceptable.

Her father would kill her. Of that she had no doubt.

And then he'd go after Viktor.

Her body trembled as she lay down on her pillow and let her mind remember. His voice, the touch of his hands, his mouth—it was almost too much. Her eyes filled with tears as she struggled to come to terms with what had happened.

She'd been *loved*. For the first time in so long a man had loved her. Had offered himself freely, giving so much more than he could ever guess by just the brush of his lips.

Madelyne smiled through her tears. She'd never forget this night. She'd hold it close, cherish it, pull it out and remember it on those days when life seemed bleak and pointless. And there had been too many of those lately.

Lord Eventyde had recently appointed guards on the Dower House, telling them that it was because of a string of robberies in the area.

But Madelyne knew better. It was because she was getting older, and more likely to do something drastic. He was not about to let that happen, not if he could find a way to get rid of her and profit from it.

She lived each day in fear of his whims—not his beatings any more, since he'd tired of that pastime. But there was always the knowledge that even though she was of age, she was still at his mercy.

He'd seen to that.

Where could she go with few clothes and no money? Her nearest relative was in Scotland, her mother off who-knew-where, and she was isolated, buried in the forest, a shameful secret hidden by the branches of the trees that grew so thickly around the Dower House.

A blot on the Eventyde escutcheon. A disgrace to the ancient name. A name which she'd like to rid herself of at the earliest opportunity.

Madelyne snuggled her head into her pillow and realized with chagrin that she didn't even know Viktor's last name.

Close upon that thought came another. She didn't care.

It didn't matter if he was royalty or a stable boy. He'd given her a gift tonight. A loving touch and a memory she'd have for the rest of her life.

She sighed and turned over, restless still, even though the hour had grown late.

What would it be like to be free? To roam the world in a caravan, bound by no one's rules, living life as one wished, taking pleasure without worrying about the consequences?

Madelyne couldn't begin to imagine, she just knew she'd love the chance to find out. Preferably with Viktor at her side.

Of course, he probably had a line of women waiting for his favors. Someone as attractive as him would have to beat them away with his violin.

But somehow, deep inside, Madelyne believed that he too had been affected by their loving. Some tone in his voice, some scent, some need she'd sensed within him, all combined to tell her that Viktor had not taken the night lightly.

She snorted. She was dreaming her dreams and creating situations that didn't exist.

But a little smile crossed her lips. Where was the harm in it?

Closing her eyes, she prepared to sleep and kept Viktor in the forefront of her mind. Perhaps he'd appear in her dreams as he had at the lake.

She was almost slipping over the edge into her fantasies when a loud banging on her door made her jump.

Oh God. Her father. No one else hammered at the old wooden panels like that.

"Get out of bed, Madelyne. Now. Don't bother getting dressed. Get down to the Salon within five minutes or I'll come back and get you myself."

His harsh voice jerked Madelyne from her thoughts and sent her heartbeat into chaos. What the devil did he want with her in the middle of the night?

Thanking her guardian angel that she'd made it back to her room in time, she scrambled into her old robe and cautiously opened the door.

There were lights and voices downstairs, and it was with some trepidation that she silently made her way towards the Salon.

Lord Eventyde's footman sneered at her as she paused before the doors, running his eyes up and down her tightly swathed body. "Get on with you, then. They want you inside."

He flung open the door and shoved her through.

✳ ✳ ✳ ✳ ✳

Viktor's pulse was pounding as he dashed into Eventyde Manor in search of his friends.

Lights from the library drew him and he offered up a prayer of thanks to St. Stephan when he found Pyotr and Gyorgy inside, sprawled around a half-empty decanter.

"I need you. Now."

Two pairs of eyes sharpened, and two bodies snapped from their lethargy.

"Where are the others?"

Pyotr tapped his fingers on the table. "The boys are playing billiards and Fabyan is in the music room."

"Thank God. There's a woman in trouble, and it's up to us to stop it from getting any worse than it already is."

Gyorgy's eyebrows rose. "A woman?"

"Madelyne Eventyde. Our host's daughter. He's about to give her to Francis Hucknall."

Pyotr choked. "That piece of filth?"

"Exactly," snapped Viktor. " I won't let that happen. I need your help."

The two men were already on their feet and reaching for their jackets.

"Don't bother...I have an idea. I need a distraction, a believable one, and I think we can provide it."

"Let me get the others," said Gyorgy, already on his way out the door.

Pyotr gazed at Viktor. "You met Madelyne Eventyde?"

Viktor gazed back steadily, understanding the undertones of the question. "Yes, Pyotr. I met her, and...and she's the *one*."

Pyotr's handsome face curled into a smile beneath his mustache. "Enough said, my friend. How can we help?"

The door burst open and Gyorgy returned, with Lukasz, Matyas and Fabyan close behind.

"What's afoot Viktor?" asked Lukasz.

"Where's the fight? Do I need my sword?" Matyas tensed in readiness.

Fabyan crossed the room and stared at Viktor, then placed his hand firmly on Viktor's shoulder.

The pressure of his fingers spoke as loudly as the words of his companions.

"We won't need our swords, just our music and two horses. Here's the plan."

With rapid-fire military precision, Viktor outlined his ideas and accepted suggestions and modifications from the other five men in the room.

It would work, and the devil take the consequences.

It had to. He would never let Hucknall lay a finger on Madelyne.

Chapter 5

Madelyne found herself hard-pressed to take in the tableau that met her eyes as she stumbled into the Salon of the Dower House.

Her father was stretched out in a chair by the fireplace with a glass of brandy in his hand and a fierce glitter in his eyes. But for once, it wasn't her father that demanded her attention. It was the second man in the room.

Huge and imposing, this tall man with greying hair was standing casually in front of a woman in a shockingly red gown. Most of which was around her waist.

Her breasts hung free and swayed as she sucked on the huge man's cock.

Madelyne's eyes widened and she felt a chill of shock sear her body.

"Get in here, you dolt, and close the door," snapped Lord Eventyde.

Numbly, Madelyne did as she was bid.

"This is Sir Francis Hucknall. Your future husband."

The huge man eyed Madelyne. "She's not much to look at, Alfred," he said dismissively. "She any good in bed?"

"How the fuck should I know? She's not my type. Ask my groom."

Both men chuckled and Madelyne felt the color drain from her cheeks. Torn between horror at her father's announcement and shock at what the woman was doing to Hucknall, she felt herself sway.

"Oh for God's sake, girl, get hold of yourself." Her father's voice pulled her back into reality. "Watch this whore, take notes, and don't fucking disgrace me any further than you already have. At least try to keep Francis happy 'til he gets you with child, will you?"

Madelyne swallowed. "I'll do no such thing."

Eventyde was out of his chair in a flash, and had his hands grasping Madelyne's hair before she could breathe.

"You'll do as you're fucking told, bitch. You couldn't keep your legs together for that weakling boy, so what's the problem now?"

He dragged her over to where Hucknall stood, breeches open, cock sliding wetly in and out of the whore's mouth.

She slid her eyes sideways to Madelyne and sneered. "Wanna try some, honey? Not that you look like you'd be any good at it."

"That's what you're here for, bitch. Teach her."

Eventyde's hands ripped Madelyne's hair from her scalp as he forced her to her knees next to the whore and held her there.

She had a close up view of what was taking place and she didn't like it. Not one bit.

Hucknall glanced down. "I shall expect you to suck me off several times a day. Whenever I wish it. So learn fast, girl. I shall teach you about fucking, of course, but this is something more easily learned by showing than doing, don't you think?"

Madelyne blinked back the tears her father's hold on her hair was causing, and clamped down on her hot retort.

There were two large men in the room. She had no chance of avoiding a beating or worse if she made a wrong move. She wished, and not for the first time in her life, for a dueling pistol.

She tried to breathe, to control her temper and her fear, and to *think*.

But the scene before her was so outrageous that it was hard to concentrate on anything else.

Francis Hucknall had a huge cock. It was red and engorged, and the woman seemed to want to swallow it whole. She was reaching between his legs for his balls as she sucked, using one hand to fondle him and the other to slip through the moisture her mouth left on him.

Madelyne felt her bile rise as she saw the woman's tongue flicking around the head and pulling a sticky strand of moisture from it.

Hucknall grunted as the tongue apparently found a particularly sensitive spot.

"Enough," he said harshly. "Turn around and bend over."

Oh God. Please God no.

The hand in her hair pulled savagely again, moving her to a low stool and out of Hucknall's way.

She could hear her father's breathing rasping behind her.

Hucknall casually dropped his breeches around his ankles, revealing hairy buttocks and a nasty scar. Madelyne wished she could give him a few more.

Her mind roamed the room searching for something, *anything*, she could use as a weapon.

Red skirts went tumbling over the whore's head as she rested on all fours. "Spread 'em," grunted Hucknall.

The whore reached behind her and pulled her buttock cheeks apart.

Madelyne closed her eyes. If there was a weapon in the room she was going to use it on herself. Never would she submit to this.

She opened a little door in her heart and pulled out a mental image of Viktor's face. It calmed her, and focused her thoughts.

Her father's grip had eased a little, fingers loosening the strands of hair, and she heard him fumbling with his breeches.

Oh God. It was getting worse and worse.

Hucknall was positioning the whore right where he wanted her. He lowered himself to his knees and found her arse.

He thrust deep.

The whore's cry was muffled by her skirts, but Madelyne's wasn't. This was agonizing.

Her father let go her hair, and she eased away from him very slowly. She refused to look at him, concentrating instead on moving silently out of his reach.

Hucknall continued his abuse of the whore. "Oh yes, tight. Just the way I like 'em. Oooh, yesss…"

Little cries were coming from the woman, but Madelyne had no idea if it was pain or pleasure. Nor did she care.

She just wanted to get out of there before one of these animals got the bright idea that she should anticipate her wedding vows and join in.

As if her thoughts had been spoken aloud, Hucknall raised his eyes and stared at her.

"Get over here, girl. I fancy some pussy. You look clean. You'll do."

Madelyne froze. "I'll die first."

"You'll die if you don't," hissed her father, reaching for her. He was still close enough to grab her head again.

Madelyne's temper boiled, but she was helpless against that firm grip on her hair. She swore she'd cut every last lock if she ever got out of this nightmare. No man should be able to control a woman that way.

Eventyde dragged her over to the couple kneeling on the carpet, and tore her robe from her, evading her nails and her heels as she kicked backwards into his shins.

An especially savage tug made her cry out in pain. "Stop it, you stupid bitch. He's not going to fuck you. This time it'll wait until after you're wed. Now pull up your skirts and let him see what he's getting."

Madelyne went rigid.

"Do it, I said."

Her head was cruelly yanked backwards making her yelp with pain.

"Or shall I do it for you?"

Unbelievably, her father's hands grabbed for her skirts and began to pull them upwards.

This couldn't be happening. It was a nightmare. None of it was real.

Then suddenly a loud shout from outside filled the air.

Something sailed through a window, shattering it, and in the moment of surprised stillness that followed, a violin began playing.

Within seconds the air was filled with the wild and incredibly beautiful sound of violin music and Madelyne's heart leapt.

Her gypsy lover had come to save her.

* * * * *

Viktor's heart wasn't leaping.

It was thudding with fury as he peered through the opposite window to the one Gyorgy had smashed with unerring accuracy.

He'd had one glimpse of what was going on inside and realized that he'd been just in time. One minute more…

He shook his head to clear the anger and watched as Eventyde flung Madelyne away from him with a snarl and Hucknall wrenched himself away from the whore, gathering his breeches up and retying them as best he could.

Eventyde's footman burst in, followed by two more servants—rough-looking men whose fists were at the ready.

Viktor grunted. Bully boys. Master and servant were one of a kind it seemed.

All the men crowded to the window, leaving the whore in a crumpled heap and Madelyne—Madelyne was stealthily making her way away from them.

And him. Fuck.

Cautiously, he tapped once on the windowpane, and thank God above, she heard him.

Her face lit up as she saw him peering at her, and he motioned with his head to the door.

She nodded and quietly snuffed out several candles, letting the darkness help conceal her flight.

Viktor's attention turned again to Eventyde and Hucknall who were yelling furiously out of the windows at the cavorting minstrels at the front of the house.

Lukasz was yelling back, laughing and playing wild melodies in counterpoint with Matyas.

Viktor bit back a grin as he picked up a few choice Hungarian expressions. They were telling Eventyde exactly what they thought of him, his behavior, and his ancestors, and making a few highly improbable suggestions as to what he could do with various parts of his anatomy.

"*Az anyad!*"

The expletive echoed through the melody as Gyorgy slid on damp grass and his bow twanged awkwardly.

Viktor chuckled as the other men laughed and played on. Fabyan's tambourine clattered loudly, and taken together the ruckus was quite amazing.

Since there were only four gypsies playing.

* * * * *

Heart in her mouth, Madelyne slipped quietly from the room under cover of the raucous chaos that had erupted outside. Obeying some instinct, she held herself close to the shadows in the hallways and crept silently to the small door through which she'd entered the Dower House earlier that evening.

As soon as she'd opened it a pair of strong arms grabbed her and hauled her roughly against a firm chest.

His chest.

She'd know that chest anywhere.

They were already moving, finding soft turf and dark areas to hide their passage when Viktor's whisper stirred her hair.

"Are you all right, Madelyne? Did they...did he..."

She turned into his body and shook her head. "No, they didn't. Thank God there wasn't time. But if you hadn't come when you did—"She felt the small tremor of fury that swept him.

"You're safe now. Trust me."

And she did. She'd known him for an instant in time, shared a little passion with him, and hadn't even thought to ask his last name. But she knew she trusted him with her life, her heart and whatever else he wanted. There was a security in his arms that she'd never found anywhere else.

It was an unusual feeling, and one that Madelyne would have liked time to explore, but their rapid progress into the darkness of the night made such things difficult if not impossible.

Being barefoot didn't help matters, and she bit back a curse as she stumbled over a root. Viktor swept her up against him, lifting her off her feet.

"Not much further, love, just hang on."

"I'm all right, Viktor. Just stubbed my toe. Put me down, we're too slow this way. He'll catch us."

Laughing a little, Viktor did as she told him. "That's my girl. Come on...not far now. Step carefully."

Holding tight to her hand, Viktor pulled her onwards through the trees and over the grasses, damp now with the dew of the cool night air. She felt brambles rip her gown, and her hair was flying in a tangled mess, but she didn't care. Her heartbeat pounded out a joyous rhythm…free…free…*free.*

Within moments they reached a small clearing, only to find a caravan sitting darkly off to one side.

Viktor paused, holding her tight and cocking his head as if listening.

"Pyotr?"

"Here, Viktor."

Madelyne gasped as a man eased from the shadows. She'd not heard a sound but suddenly he was there.

As tall as Viktor, this man possessed a lush moustache and a quick grin, flashing white teeth at her as he smiled. "Good evening, Miss Eventyde. It's a pleasure to meet you."

"Uh…" Madelyne was at a loss for words. His voice was lightly accented and charming, and she wished for more light so that she could get a good look at his face, but it was not to be.

"All is ready?" Viktor's quick words took her mind back to their immediate problems.

"All is ready. Did you even doubt us?"

"Not for a second, my friend. But time grows short." Viktor led Madelyne to the caravan as Pyotr followed.

"I have the horses tethered a little way away. I'll be off with them in moments. We'll lay a trail that will take our pursuers on a wild goose chase, and they'll be far away from here before you know it." Pyotr was already buttoning his coat.

"Godspeed, Viktor. And you too, Miss Eventyde. We'll meet in London, my friends. Until then…"

The man called Pyotr casually saluted them and vanished once more into the darkness. Within moments the silence was broken by the jingling of harnesses and the sound of horses crashing through the undergrowth, heading away from the clearing, the caravan and Madelyne.

She turned her eyes to Viktor, letting them ask the questions trembling on her lips.

He dropped his own to hers and pressed a quick kiss on her upturned mouth. "Welcome to my home, Madelyne, love. Come inside quickly now…"

Very confined, grimaced Viktor to himself, as he found his cock hardening against the soft mounds of flesh pressing against him.

It was going to be a *very* long wait.

He left the seat upright, knowing it would have to come down at some point, but not quite ready to seal them in.

"Did you mean that?" Madelyne's voice was little more than a whisper but she shifted slightly against him as she spoke.

"Mean what, love?" *Jesus,* he was hard.

"What you said about…about me being a gypsy wife?"

Viktor grinned, albeit somewhat painfully. "Yes. It was my rather uncouth way of asking you to marry me. I should have gone down on one knee of course, and done the thing properly—"

"Yes."

Viktor blinked. "Beg your pardon?"

"I said yes. I'd very much like to marry you. To be a gypsy wife. Thank you very much for honoring me with your proposal."

It was a formal little response, simple and to the point, and it took all the breath from Viktor's lungs. The little twitch of her bottom helped.

"God, Madelyne, I want to kiss you so bad I'm aching with it," groaned Viktor. "I've never had very good timing, but you'd think I'd be able to find a better place to propose marriage."

Madelyne's husky chuckle charmed Viktor and hummed through him to his crotch. "Viktor, I don't care about stuff like that. I want to kiss you too. I want to do other things as well…" There was that damned wriggle of her bottom again. Dear God, she was going to be the death of him if she kept that up. "And we'll have time for all of them if this plan of yours works."

Carefully he eased an arm around her and pulled her even tighter against his body. So what if he self-combusted? They'd survive.

"It'll work, darling. It'll definitely work. As soon as your father realizes you're missing, he'll start searching. He'll find this caravan, but not us. This hiding place was designed for just such an eventuality. And sooner or later he'll discover the tracks of two horses which Pyotr is diligently making right at this moment, leading far away from here. Once they pick up that trail, we'll head off in the opposite direction."

"He's not going to like it, you know," she said thoughtfully.

Viktor huffed in disgust. "He gave up any rights to like *anything* when he mistreated you."

His hand slid upwards and found a warm breast. The nipple was hard beneath his fingers and Madelyne's breath hitched in her throat.

"Viktor?"

"What, love?"

"Can I ask you a question?"

"Anything at all, sweetheart. Anything at all."

Madelyne paused, shifting her head slightly against the old quilt that cushioned them. "Tonight, I saw that woman...she was doing things that surprised me."

Viktor felt the heat of her blush as it warmed the breast in his hand.

"And Hucknall was doing things to her, too." She pushed her buttocks hard against his arousal.

"Things that...that involved her mouth and another part of her. Things that surprised and horrified me as I watched, but now they make me wonder..."

Viktor cursed himself. Of course she could ask him anything, but did she have to ask him about *that*, right *now*?

"Would you...could we...umm..."

His voice strangled in his throat and for a moment he was afraid nothing but a squeak would come out. He coughed quietly. "We can do anything and everything you want, love. But not right at this moment."

"Well, I realize *that*, silly," she giggled. "But since you're holding me *here*..." She pushed her breast into his hand and made him groan. "I thought I might be able to at least return the favor." She paused. "And share the pleasure..."

Her voice was seductive and soft, and she freed one hand from his arms. Gently she reached down and slid her nightgown up high, baring her backside and pressing it hard into his...hard parts.

He gulped.

Viktor couldn't ever remember being this aroused. They were waiting for a man who would probably kill them both, they were tucked into a secret hiding place in his caravan that barely left them room to breathe, and his Madelyne wanted to play.

Well, fuck. So did he.

He could smell her body, her heat as she lay next to him, spooned against him so close that their bodies practically melted into each other. Awkwardly he struggled with his laces, appreciating her attempts to give him some room to maneuver his cock, which at this point probably required a hiding place all to itself.

God only knew if there'd be room for the three of them.

He slid a little lower and with a groan freed himself, hammering Madelyne's spine with his erection as it sprang loose from his breeches.

She hummed with pleasure. "Aaah, better, Viktor. I like that."

Damn. She had to learn how to tease *now*?

He wiggled and fidgeted until he was able to slide himself between her legs. It was heaven and hell combined.

He wanted to be inside her, but a portion of him was listening for sounds outside the caravan.

That portion was going to be seriously distracted if he did what he wanted and just turned her so that he could plunge deep into her. He simply couldn't afford the distraction right now.

Especially since his sharp ears had picked up *something*...

"They're coming."

* * * * *

Madelyne tensed at the soft whisper and realized that Viktor was lowering the lid of the seat over their heads. Now they were completely encased in darkness, with little room to move and little more to breathe.

As silence fell, Madelyne realized there was a small carving near her head, which allowed a breeze to penetrate from the outside. It was quite tiny, would have been practically unnoticeable if she hadn't had her face within an inch of it, and yet guaranteed that they'd have enough air.

That is, if Viktor didn't steal it all away with the hot cock that he'd nestled between her thighs and against her most sensitive flesh.

Her mind swirled, not with thoughts of the horrors she'd experienced this night, but with thoughts of what she'd like to do to Viktor. And that very nice body of his.

Her mouth watered at the thought of kissing his cock. Perhaps licking and sucking it like that other woman had done to Hucknall.

There was no shudder of disgust, only one of eagerness. There wasn't a part of Viktor she didn't want to taste. Not a part she didn't want to caress, to learn, to touch and tease, and then do it again. A lot.

She was turning into a wanton and loving every minute of it.

As voices neared the caravan, Madelyne ruefully admitted that she could probably have picked a better time to discover her sensual desires.

She forced her instincts down from the boil to a simmer and held her breath as her father's voice boomed out.

"Check that thing, Perkins. Filthy gypsies."

"No lights, Alfred…"

That was Hucknall. He'd taken part in the hunt too. Why was Madelyne not surprised? It would be the sort of thing that appealed to a man like him. Hunt down a woman and take her any way he saw fit, like an animal, only with less concern.

Once again, Madelyne offered up a prayer of thanks to whichever guardian angel had sent Viktor into her life and across her path when she needed him the most.

Footsteps sounded in the caravan and rattles and bangs accompanied the progress of whoever "Perkins" was as he searched the little home. It was small enough that within moments, the footsteps faded.

"Nothing, my Lord. Empty. The lamps are cold. If anyone's been here it was hours ago."

"Fuck…"

Her father's voice curdled Madelyne's gut. She hated that man with a passion. What could make a parent behave like that?

She vowed that she'd care for her and Viktor's children a damn sight better than she'd been cared for.

"My Lord…" A new voice called through the stillness of the night. "There's one horse in that clearing. Looks like he's been there all night. But we've got a trail…two horses, moving fast, heading south…"

Harnesses jangled, hooves thumped on the forest floor and leather creaked as the men remounted.

"We've got 'em, Hucknall. I'll see that dirty gypsy strung up to the nearest tree before sunrise and you can have the girl to play with all you want."

"Now you're talking…" Hucknall's coarse laugh followed her father's pronouncement, and Madelyne curled her lip.

Wrong, Father. You're so wrong.

The sound of their pursuers faded into the night, and Madelyne's tension eased.

"Don't move," breathed Viktor.

She turned her head a little, not understanding.

"Old army trick. Leave one man behind to surprise those who may have been hiding."

Madelyne nodded slightly, understanding his point.

They waited, Viktor's cock throbbing with his heartbeat between Madelyne's legs. She knew she was moist now, and probably soaking it, but she didn't care. He still had one hand clasped firmly around her breast, and he could probably feel her heart pounding too.

The whimsical thought occurred to her that she'd like to sleep like this. Naked and warm and held by the man she loved. It was safe and comforting and arousing all at the same time.

Moments passed, stretching into long minutes as they waited in their hiding place.

Madelyne's sense of danger eased, only to be replaced by a growing and fierce arousal. Her mound twitched against Viktor's cock, and she caught his sigh of pleasure.

Cautiously she lifted her knee a little, keeping as silent as she could, but opening her body to his.

His hand jerked on her breast, clasping it tightly and finding the nipple with eager fingers.

She bit her lip against the moan that was choking her.

The head of his cock was so hot, scalding her flesh as it wept over him. He moved slightly, just rubbing himself through her moisture.

She devoutly hoped the coast was clear, because if Viktor kept doing what he was doing she was going to reveal their location to half the county with one loud and long scream of pleasure. Any minute now…

Chapter 7

The heated and squirming armful of woman plastered against him was driving Viktor out of his mind.

It had been silent outside for quite some time, and although his senses advised caution, his cock was screaming for something else altogether.

With painfully precise moves, he lifted the seat above them and let the cool air swirl over their bodies.

Their half-naked bodies.

He listened to the sounds of the forest at night. All was as it should be. The little army of thugs had gone.

"Is it safe?" Madelyne breathed the words quietly, her voice raspy.

"From them? Yes. From me...?"

It took less than the blink of an eye for Viktor to whisk them both out of their cocoon and lower the lid back down. The bed was in place, and Madelyne stripped of her nightgown and flat on top of it before the echo of his words had died away.

He tossed his own clothing away. "I can't wait, love," he groaned.

"Come to me, then," she urged. "I want you too."

She splayed her thighs wide and Viktor's cock sank into her with the unerring accuracy of a homing pigeon to its roost.

Slick, hot and welcoming, her cunt seized him and pulled him deep within her, molding itself to him and holding him where he had longed to be.

Her hands found his back, sliding up to his shoulders and then stopping short.

Viktor froze.

Her fingers had found the wrinkled and puckered skin between his shoulder blades.

He should have told her. But there'd been no time. He should have prepared her for the ugliness she'd find, the scars that marked his stay in a French prison.

So many memories flashed through his mind as he lay buried inside her, waiting, scared, wondering if and how she'd withdraw from him once she knew how badly he'd been scarred.

Other women had cried out in horror, unable to look at the two deep marks that had nearly taken his life. Would Madelyne be the same? Sympathetic but sickened by the injuries?

Their loving had happened so fast, and so completely that he hadn't had the chance to explain...to talk with her about what had happened to him. To prepare her in some small way. He'd gone ahead and asked her to marry him. *Fuck.* He simply couldn't lose her now.

He must have withdrawn slightly without realizing it, because to his surprise, Madelyne's thighs clamped around him and her legs locked his in place.

"Viktor." It was a soft word, but there was a command beneath it. "Love me, Viktor. Now. Please..."

Her hands moved again to his shoulders and his cock shuddered as she shifted her hips beneath him, drawing him deeper.

He was lost.

Lost so far inside Madelyne that he didn't know where he ended and she began. All he knew was that she was his, her body was his, and he'd find a way to make her heart and the rest of her his as well.

He drew back and plunged again, as she gasped beneath him. Her cunt trembled around his cock, and her breathing was ragged in the silence of the oncoming dawn.

His strokes grew firmer, his balls tightened and sweat broke out all over his body, doing nothing to cool the fire that burned in his soul.

Madelyne cried out as he thrust hard and fast, letting his cock find its way to the entrance of her womb. There was no question of him withdrawing this time. He would brand her, plant his seed deep within her, and claim her as his for once and for all.

"Viktor...now..."

Now it was.

With a hoarse shout, Viktor exploded. Barely aware of her cunt clamping down on him, he let his release pound over him, pressing himself against her heat and erupting in a mighty stream of hot come, filling her, giving her all that he had. And all that he was.

She urged him on with her own climax, inner muscles rubbing, drawing more from him than he had ever given before.

Little sobs of pleasure broke from her throat as they rode the fire together, only to subside to whimpers as she shared the joy of this moment with him.

Stunned and exhausted, Viktor collapsed on her, drained of all his strength, his tensions and his fears.

She loved him.

They lay still for a little while as the first light of dawn began to illuminate the small caravan. He rolled to one side and let his cock slide free of her body, biting back his urge to stay inside her forever.

He found soft lips brushing his face and his neck, and hands running over his sweat-slicked chest.

"I love you so much, Viktor. So much." Madelyne's tongue found a bead of sweat on his collarbone and licked it. "I love all of you, your body, your music, but most of all..." She laid her hand over his still-pounding heart. "I love what's in here."

Viktor sighed in contentment. "I love you too, Madelyne," he whispered.

She snuggled close. "So tell me about those scars."

✽ ✽ ✽ ✽ ✽

Madelyne struggled into the costume that Viktor had given her, tightening the cords that closed the loose blouse and shaking the brightly colored skirts around her calves. She hadn't asked where they'd come from, why a man should have an assortment of women's clothing in his caravan, or if anyone had worn them before her.

Even the red leather boots matched the embroidery, a little loose on her small feet, but they'd serve the purpose.

Viktor was harnessing the horse to the caravan traces, and they were about to leave this damned forest. Forever, Madelyne hoped.

The sunlight streaming in through the small windows had nudged them from each other's arms before she'd had chance to learn Viktor's secrets, but she fully intended to hear the whole story once they were on the road.

"How does it fit?" Viktor peeked in through the door.

"You tell me. Have I got it right?" She pirouetted, letting the full skirts swirl around the tops of her boots.

Viktor grinned. "You are beautiful in anything. Or nothing. But I don't think I've ever seen anyone look less like a gypsy."

Madelyne pouted. "Well, for heaven's sake. I've got the clothes on."

"It's all that golden hair, love. And those dark blue eyes of yours. We gypsies have angels too, and I'm guessing that they look just like that. But you're going to stick out like a sore thumb unless we do something about it...hold on a moment..."

He rummaged in the clothing trunk and produced a white scarf, edged with gold flowers. "Here. Stuff your hair up underneath this and tie it tight. For today, at least, we want to attract as little attention as possible. By tomorrow, we'll be far enough away for you to relax a little."

"And will you relax a little?"

"Me? I'm relaxed."

Madelyne snorted as she tied the scarf tight and tucked a few errant curls out of the way. "You've been fidgeting around this morning like a nervous filly. I want to leave too. I'm ready. What are we waiting for?"

Viktor's eyes burned. "Not a damn thing. I can't wait to get going, head north, and settle this business."

Madelyne followed Viktor from the caravan into the dawn and clambered up beside him on the front seat.

"North?" She asked the question as he clicked up the horse and the caravan rolled off over the bumps and onto the narrow lane that bordered the forest.

"North." Viktor glanced at her. "I intend to marry you at the earliest possible moment, and I have a couple of friends a few days' journey from here who will be happy to help. Once you're mine, nobody can touch you, Madelyne."

She allowed a wicked grin to curve her lips. "Except you."

He narrowed his eyes. "Except me."

She sighed and rested her back against the hard wooden slats. "Sounds very nice to me."

"Me too."

The lane widened and the fields rolled past as the sun rose into a clear blue sky. Madelyne kept her eyes downcast for the first few miles, hoping that a gypsy caravan and its occupants would not occasion much comment from the field workers or farmers that they passed along the way.

Viktor's attention was focused, alert, and she could almost feel the tension in his spine as they made their journey through the countryside towards their goal of freedom.

And each other.

"You know, Viktor..." Madelyne broke the silence. "I'm probably going to be an awful wife."

A surprised chuckle erupted from Viktor's throat. "What on earth makes you say that?"

"Well I don't know the first thing about gypsy life. I've never cooked over an open fire, I can't play any kind of instrument, and there's so much I have to learn about you, and this caravan and...oh...*everything*..."

Viktor grinned. "Um, darling, I have a confession to make."

Madelyne frowned at him. "Oh God. Don't tell me you have another wife somewhere."

"No. Good God, *no*. I've never been married, never even thought about it until I met you, and certainly have never asked another woman to share my life. You're the first. The *only*..."

Madelyne knew she was smirking, and couldn't help it. She was almost drunk with the combined joys of love and freedom, and right this moment if Viktor had told her he had a dozen other wives she probably could have forgiven him.

Well, perhaps not *that*. But her heart sang as the horse's hooves pounded along, and whatever Viktor wanted to share with her, it couldn't possibly destroy her happiness.

"So you were going to confess something?"

"Um. Well, it has to do with who I am."

Madelyne blinked. "You're Viktor."

"Yes, I am." He paused. "But you never asked me my last name, and to be honest I was so busy loving you that I forgot to tell you."

"All right. So tell me now."

Viktor cleared his throat. "Well, actually, I'm Viktor Istvan Karoly."

"Karoly...hmmm. That's a nice name." Madelyne rolled it around in her mind. "Mrs. Viktor Karoly. Madelyne Karoly. Yes." She turned to him. "I like it."

"Uh...you won't be able to use it in exactly that way, love."

Madelyne frowned. "I don't understand."

"Well...you'll be correctly known as Countess Karoly."

Her vision swam for a few moments as the world turned upside down and then righted itself again. "You're a *Count*?"

"Yes."

"A real, title-holding *Count*?"

"Yes."

"A member of the aristocracy-type *Count*?"

"Yes. Sorry."

"Good God."

Viktor grinned at her. "Does it matter?"

Madelyne gasped for air. "I...uh...no. I suppose not. But a *Count*?"

"Um, you've said that several times now. Could we perhaps move on?"

"Well certainly." She sat upright. "Perhaps we should move on to exactly how a *Count* comes to be masquerading as a gypsy and running away with a very lowly and socially unacceptable woman."

Viktor slowed the horse to a walk. "I've never *masqueraded* as a gypsy, Madelyne. I *am* a gypsy. First and foremost. And I'm not running away from anything, I'm running towards my future. With the woman I love. Who happens to be beautiful, elegant, sadly mistreated, and the person I intend to spend the rest of my life worshipping."

Madelyne thought about that. "Worshipping?"

"Absolutely."

"All the time?"

"As often as possible."

"Oh." A grin passed across her face. "Does this worshipping involve us, together…um…naked?"

"Oh yes. Without question." A matching grin lightened Viktor's face and he urged the horse onwards.

"Very well then. I can adjust to that. Even Countesses need worshipping, I suppose."

"They most definitely do."

Madelyne snuggled close and rested her head on Viktor's shoulder. "I'll just have to get used to the idea, then. But Viktor…" She paused.

"Yes, love?"

"Tell me about it? Tell me how it all came to be? How did you all come to be together, and…I need to know about those scars…"

Viktor sighed. "It's a long story, Madelyne. It began years ago when Europe was upside down, armies were fighting, men were dying at the whim of generals who thought nothing of sacrificing valuable lives for a few yards of land…"

She slipped her hand onto his knee.

"Go on…"

"There were a few young men, love. All trying to live, to survive the devastation of war. They came together one night at a small inn tucked away in a quiet hillside village…"

* * * * *

As Viktor began telling his story to Madelyne on the road leading north, Pyotr was pulling up his exhausted horses and watching the early sun dapple the leaves of several willows that dangled low beside a stream.

He'd ridden hard, and loved every minute of it.

The challenge of finding his way over and around obstacles, laying down wild and improbable trails, and crisscrossing his path several times to confuse his pursuers had fired his senses and spurred him on. He was many miles from Eventyde now, and knew that the men who followed him would either have given up or were hopelessly lost. He was good at what he did.

He'd had enough practice in France.

His mind darted briefly to a similar nighttime ride, when he'd laid another false trail. That one had resulted in the rescue of an entire family from the approaching armies that would have left no survivors.

He grinned. A job well done, indeed.

His horse's flanks were heaving, and even the second horse was sweating at the end of the rein he'd tied to his saddle.

It must be close to eight o'clock now, and Pyotr figured he could certainly let his mounts drink and rest for a bit. He eased the thirsty beasts to the edge of the river and lifted his leg over the saddle, sliding to the ground with a sigh of relief.

As he did so, a branch above him groaned, cracked and fell.

Right on him.

He narrowly avoided the solid lump of willow, but not the body that followed it.

The horses neighed and shook their heads, jangling their tack as Pyotr tumbled onto the bank. He rolled quickly and found himself on top of a slight form, staring down into a pair of very surprised green eyes.

They blinked at him.

Short tufts of red hair stuck up around a milky white face, which was scattered with freckles. There was one particular freckle...a star-shaped freckle...

The green eyes widened and the full lips beneath sucked in air.

He knew those eyes. He *knew* that freckle...

"Good God. *Freddie*?"

The mouth worked and a choking gasp broke free.

"*Peter*?"

Chapter 8
Pyotr's Passionate Problem

The Honorable Frederica Howell struggled to free herself from the heavy body squashing her into the riverbank and tugged her breeches back into some kind of order.

Inwardly, she was cursing, using every lurid word she'd ever heard and inventing a few more.

Of *all* the people in *all* the world, she had to go and fall on *him*.

Peter Maloney. Or Lord Chalmers now, she supposed.

He stared at her, still sitting in a heap on the moss with mouth agape, looking every bit as delicious as he had the last time she'd seen him.

It must have been at least six years ago.

Of course, he'd not had that full moustache then, and his hair had been shorter, perhaps a little darker. But now he looked like the answer to every maiden's dream.

She used the pretense of straightening her shirt to study him from under her eyelashes.

His shoulders were broad, his body lean, and his eyes still that whiskey brown that sometimes turned to amber in the sunlight. He'd aged, as had she, but time had been kind to him, turning him from the young man she'd tumbled madly in love with to a grown man she could…she could what?

He stood, brushing off his breeches, and still staring at her. A frown gathered between his brows.

"Is this some prank of yours, Freddie? What the devil do you think you're doing dressed like that? It's *extremely* improper. And what on earth happened to your hair? It looks like it's been attacked by a rabid badger." His voice was disapproving, as was his expression.

Freddie's temper flared hotly.

"You impertinent lout. How *dare* you frown at me like that? And where the hell have you been for six years?"

She closed the distance between them and poked him in the chest. Hard. "It's none of your business where I've been, what I've done, or whether badgers attacked me or not. You stupid…*man*."

Peter stood his ground. "Look, we've got to be more than forty miles or so from Lyndham. And you drop out of the sky on top of me dressed like a…like a…what the hell are you supposed to be, anyway?"

"I'm not supposed to *be* anything. And you're supposed to be out of the country. Permanently. Why don't you just keep on going until you reach the ocean, find a boat, and sail off to wherever you were?"

She turned her back to him and looked around for the floppy felt hat that had fallen from her head while she was falling on Peter.

"Does your mother know you're here…dressed like *that*?"

Freddie stilled.

The water rippled past them and the horses nickered softly as they grazed on the grass growing nearby. "My mother's dead."

The words tumbled out into the silence between them, and she heard Peter's steps as he neared her.

She pulled away. If he touched her now…

"Your father?"

She nodded. "Him too." She moved again, keeping a distance between them.

"Freddie, I'm sorry. What happened?"

Oh *now* he was all sincere and sympathetic. Freddie tried to lash up her temper again. "What does it matter to *you*? In case you've forgotten, you're in exile, Peter. You could probably be arrested just for standing here. So why don't you move on before I summon the constable and make sure that happens."

"It matters, sweetheart."

Damn. He was too close. She could smell the mixture of horse and man, and it was lethal.

She sighed. "Look, I haven't got time to go into any of this right now. It was a surprise to see you again. Glad you're well. Don't let me keep you from wherever it is you're off to. Enjoy the rest of your life."

She crammed the disreputable hat on her head and turned towards the path only to be brought up short by a firm hand at her elbow.

"I don't think so. Not until I find out why my childhood friend is dressed like an urchin and lurking up a tree."

* * * * *

Peter swung Freddie around to face him and barely restrained a gasp at the mixture of pain and fury blazing from her eyes.

"Freddie...*Freddie*, tell me. What the hell's going on?"

He kept his hand firmly around her arm, feeling the bones beneath his grip. Damnation, she was too thin. Too pale. Something was seriously amiss.

She lowered her lashes, veiling those expressive green eyes.

He wanted to shake her. "Don't hide from me. You can't hide from me. I will know the truth, Freddie. Come on, sit down here and tell me. I can't believe you won't take ten minutes to just sit and catch up on old times."

She glanced around and again Peter felt the tension in her, the urge to flee. He'd seen it and felt it often enough in his travels through battle-scarred villages to recognize it for what it was. A lethal blend of adrenaline and fear. Mixed in with a healthy dose of defiance. Probably more than a healthy dose in Freddie's case, since he knew her temper of old.

"Please?" He let his grip soften and his hand stroke her arm soothingly.

She shivered a little and nodded briefly. "Ten minutes."

"Good girl."

He urged her to a nearby log and sat her down, taking a seat next to her and reaching for her hand. He was a little surprised to find that she allowed it, and even more surprised to feel the rough calluses and hard spots that had no business marring such delicate skin.

"Start at the beginning, sweetheart. Your parents...what happened?"

Freddie sighed, then straightened her spine and stared across the river. Peter had the distinct impression that she was looking at her past, not the scenery.

"It was the winter after you left. There was some kind of illness in the village. My mother insisted on helping where she could. She came home unwell and was gone within the week. My father was distraught, and no more than a month later he was gone too."

The words were short, bald, and unemotional, but Peter knew what pain they must have been hiding. He squeezed her hand in sympathy.

"I'm so sorry, love. It must have been a terrible time for you."

She made a sound between a snort and a sob. "Yes."

"Go on. What happened then? Did your cousin send for you?"

Peter remembered the older man, Geoffrey something-or-other. He'd have been the logical person to take care of Freddie.

"Yes."

Damn. She wasn't telling him *anything*. "And?"

"And he arrived at the Chase, moved in with his family, and I became..."

"Became what?"

"Their maid. Their children's tutor. Their housekeeper. The sort of general person who does everything and gets nothing in return."

Peter bit his lip. It wasn't an unusual story, but he knew Freddie. It must have been incredibly hard on her. To see her home taken over by another, and to relinquish her position as daughter of the house to another. To have to suppress her natural instinct to lead, to organize, to charm and laugh with those around her.

"That was not good, was it?"

She snorted. "You could say that."

"So what happened next?" He was going to have to drag each and every detail out of her, but he intended to hear the whole.

"My cousin's daughter found herself a suitor."

"That's good." *Come on, Freddie. Tell me, for God's sake.*

"Unfortunately, this man discovered that he had more of a partiality for redheads than blondes. I was 'dismissed'."

"*Dismissed*? It was your *home*, Freddie. They couldn't dismiss you like some wayward servant, could they?"

"They could and they did. I was sent to 'help' a friend of my cousin's. He had a young child, his wife had died, and he was older. I was sent to Fallow Grange as governess and housekeeper."

"Oh God. How awful."

Freddie pulled a little away from Peter. "Yes, it was. But at least I was away from the Chase. That lasted for about a year, and in all fairness, it wasn't too bad. I grew to like both Johnny and his father. At least they were kind, and I was treated better by them than I had been by my cousin."

"So then…?"

"Then? Johnny left for Eton. It was considered time. My cousin didn't want me home. I had nowhere to go, no money to support myself, since the Chase was now my cousin's, and I had no inheritance of my own until I came of age."

"So what did you do?"

Freddie stared down at her ragged breeches. "I accepted an offer from Charles Fallow to become his mistress."

Peter's breath left his lungs and it took him a moment or two to suck air back in again.

"You WHAT?"

His shout disturbed the birds in the willow trees along the bank and they flew up with a squawking clatter that echoed the emotions screaming in his brain.

Freddie squared her shoulders and turned, looking him straight in the eye without a blink.

"I became Charles Fallow's mistress. It was my choice. I had few other options. I could have applied for another governess position somewhere, but I had no experience or credentials, and let's face it, redheaded twenty-year old girls aren't likely to be hired willingly by any woman with a lick of sense. I could have been a servant perhaps? Or hired out to a dairy farm? Do you have any idea how many people are trying to find work doing just that? The war was ending. Soldiers were coming home. I'd have been extremely fortunate to find a job as a scullery maid."

She looked away again. "I am who I am, Peter. I made the choice to live in a house where there was a wooden floor not a dirt one. Where

I could at least sleep in a real bed and eat regular meals. Where life was something like what I'd known before. Giving Charles my body was a small price to pay."

Peter reached for her shoulders and pulled her around roughly to face him. "Tell me he didn't force you." He couldn't keep the harshness from his voice.

"He didn't force me." Freddie met his gaze. "He was...kind. I grew to like his affections, I suppose. It was pleasant being touched...held...like *that*."

Peter swallowed past the knot of anger in his throat and dissected her words. Of course it had been pleasant. The man had given her warmth and security. What more could a bruised and lonely girl ask for?

"Did he love you? Did you love him?"

Freddie snorted in derision. "Love is not something that either of us considered. A useless and often dangerous pastime, Peter. Don't tell me you've turned into a romantic over these past years."

"So why didn't he marry you?" Peter was not about to be swayed by any attempt to turn the conversation from Freddie and her troubles.

"Peter, *darling*," she drawled. "One doesn't marry one's mistress. Surely I don't have to tell you that."

He could hear a world of hurt beneath her words, blasé though she'd pretended to be.

"Sadly, one does marry eligible widows, especially when they're possessed of a nice annual income. And that's what Charles eventually did. Leaving me, of course, out in the cold again."

A tight and brittle laugh slipped from her lips. "So I decided to take my future into my own hands. I cut my hair, stole the stable boy's clothes and I've worked for my food and my lodging ever since. As a boy. Although recently..."

"Recently?"

"I'm not a very good farm-hand, it seems."

"You've been working in the *fields*?" Peter's mind spun once more at the vision of the Freddie he'd know all his life laboring in a farmer's field.

"It was simple stuff once I got the hang of it. Unfortunately, last night one of the other workers got the idea that I wasn't quite as 'manly' as I seemed. I had to get out, and fast."

She knotted her fingers unconsciously on her lap. "So there you have it. I'm running away, like some stupid chit in a Fanny Burney novel, and trying to work out where I'm going to go next."

She glared at him as he covered her restless hands with one of his. "And don't think you're going to talk me out of it."

"I don't see anything to talk you *out* of." He knew his words were stern, but he also knew she didn't need or want sympathetic noises right now. "However, give me a little time here and I'll think of something to talk you *into*."

He glanced absently at her, running all the possibilities, intricacies and considerations of her situation through his mind at lightning speed. "Where exactly are we?"

His question must have surprised her since she jerked her head up at his words. "Um...we're about twenty miles east of Little Steering. Harlow would be north of here and..."

Peter nodded. He'd already developed a reasonably accurate map of the area in his head. "Excellent."

"Excellent?"

He grinned. "Yes, excellent. We're probably little more than a two-day ride from Aunt Margaret's. I'll take you there."

"You will *not*."

Peter's eyes narrowed. "Oh yes I will. If I have to tie you up and sling you over my saddle."

An odd expression flashed through her eyes, gone in an instant. "Peter, be serious. Look at who I am. What I've been. What I've done. You can't take me to Lady Margaret. She's one of the highest sticklers for propriety..."

"Who used to be an actress before she married my uncle."

"You're joking."

"Nope."

Freddie digested this information. "But you can't be seen to be in the country. Had you forgotten you're supposed to be in exile?" She let a little look of triumph curve her lips.

Peter shook his head. "My exile ended when my father died, Freddie. You know that. It was his word alone that got me sent abroad. I've been quite content to let Mark have Chalmers, I don't want it or the burdens that go with it. I don't want to be Lord Chalmers—bluntly even the name turns my stomach. In fact, I…"

"You what?"

Peter grinned. "Well, if you want to hear my story, you'll just have to agree to go with me to Aunt Margaret's."

Freddie grimaced. "Does Mark know you're in England?"

Peter thought of his staid brother and his placid sister-in-law and squelched a grin. They would not have appreciated six wild gypsy musicians erupting into their lives.

"No, dear, I haven't told him."

"But you'll tell me what you've been doing?"

"Some of it. But only if you agree to hop on that very convenient second horse of mine and head out towards Aunt Margaret's. With me."

Chapter 9

Freddie absent-mindedly watched the sun as it dipped behind a few clouds gathering in the skies above her. Her arse was sore and stiff, and she couldn't remember the last time she'd ridden for so long. It showed too.

Peter was slightly ahead of her, relaxed in his saddle, and riding as if he'd been born to it. Well, stupid, he *had*.

They'd left the riverbank and headed into the morning, Peter smiling and chatting about nothing in particular, and she...what was she?

She was confused.

She wanted to rest her head on his shoulder and let her troubles vanish for a while. She wanted to find that happiness she'd known as a child, chasing around after Peter, and sometimes Mark, as they'd created all kinds of adventures for themselves. She wanted to tell him that he'd stolen something very special from her when he'd come to say goodbye on that fateful night so long ago.

When he'd left and dropped a light kiss on her lips. Not her cheek or her forehead, but her lips. She'd been so young, so angry at him for leaving, for being so stupid as to kill a man in a duel and get himself sent out of the country.

And so damned in love with him she couldn't stand herself. And now?

One glance from his gorgeous eyes and she could feel herself tumbling headfirst off the edge of a precipice all over again.

Dammit. She wouldn't let her heart get involved and shattered once more. She would not love him. She would *not* love *anybody*.

But she ached. She knew what lovemaking entailed now, and what pleasures it could offer.

She licked her lips. The thought of Peter, naked and aroused and leaning over her was one hell of an image. And he had yet to tell her what he'd been doing with his life. She'd bared her soul, told him every darn thing, and he'd been tight-lipped as a clam.

Well, that was going to change. As soon as she got off this damned horse and stretched out the muscles that were kinking at the base of her spine.

Freddie's thoughts scampered around like bewildered rabbits. To have sunk so low and yet to be so free. It was an odd combination of horror and joy.

Shamed before the country society she'd grown up in, and yet freed of the restrictions she'd chafed against for so long.

Able to travel anywhere she wished on a whim, without the confining presence of groom or relative, and yet unable to go anywhere at all, since she was now pretty much "nothing" in the eyes of the world.

She chuckled to herself. Life was full of contradictions.

Peter was certainly one of them.

He turned slightly and flashed a grin back at her, keeping the pace steady and the horses comfortable. It was a good way to travel over long distances—tiring neither mount nor rider, but inexorably heading for one's goal.

His smile warmed her heart. And other places.

She licked her lips once more, almost unconsciously this time. She wanted him.

And why, came the thought, why couldn't she *have* him?

Why not indulge her wanton instincts, just this once, for *her* pleasure, on *her* terms? Why shouldn't they enjoy each other? It was a sure fact that Peter could handle himself. The man oozed sensuality and had the body to back it up.

She found herself glancing down at his breeches where they molded around his buttocks on the saddle. He was solid, muscular, and a very good-looking man.

If he didn't mind his women a bit on the skinny side, and with hair that had been—what had he said? "Badgerized" or something—that was it…then they could pass the time quite pleasantly. Before she left him.

And that was going to be long before they reached his Aunt Margaret's, no matter what *Peter's* intentions were.

Freddie considered the question. Doubtless Peter would still regard her as a child. And even if he didn't, there would be the whole business of "childhood-friend" to overcome.

Yes, there was no doubt in her mind now. If Freddie wanted him, she was going to have to seduce him.

Something low in her body leaped at the thought and she shifted once more in the saddle, just as a fat drop of rain pelted her on the nose.

A curse from ahead told her that Peter had felt it too.

"Freddie...blasted rain. Over there. Don't dawdle or we'll be soaked." Peter pointed to a patch of trees that rose from the fields surrounding them. He spurred his horse to a canter and Freddie followed, ducking her head against the raindrops spattering down with increasing force.

Together they rushed for the sparse shelter offered by the trees and slid damply off their horses, breathless and panting.

And laughing.

* * * * *

Hearing Freddie laugh was music to Peter's ears.

He'd struggled to come to terms with what she'd endured over the past six years, and cursed himself for the moment of insanity that had sent him careening off to Europe without a care in the world for anyone but himself. Their long ride together had given him a chance to do some serious thinking. Not only about Freddie and the devilish predicament she was in, but about himself and his life too.

He was smart enough to know that he and his five friends had been useful. That what they'd done had saved lives and made a difference, in a small way. It had helped him get past the fact that he'd killed a man.

A man who surely deserved it, but a man, nevertheless. Peter's life since then had been turned towards righting that wrong. Making amends. Becoming Pyotr the gypsy violinist, and Pyotr the stealthy agent of a small band of men who simply wanted to help their fellows.

Leaving Peter Maloney, the Chalmers name and all that went with it, far behind.

But now, thanks to Freddie, it would seem that it had all caught up with him again.

She laughed once more as the rain dripped through the trees onto her nose, and held her arms out letting the spatters soak through her shirt.

Peter gulped as his smile faded, to be replaced by the heat of…something else.

She was Freddie, for God's sake. The child he'd played with. The little girl with braids and short skirts.

He blinked as the rain dampened worn cotton and revealed a pair of incredibly beautiful breasts. Dark areolas circled tight budded nipples, thrusting through the thin fabric. Dammit, she might as well be naked. She sure as hell wasn't a child anymore.

She raised her hands to that dreadful mass of shorn locks and her breasts pushed even more against the wet cloth.

Peter's cock didn't give a damn who she was. It responded with a surge of lust that rocked him to his toes.

Shit. Not now. Not *Freddie*.

Her laugh was deep and full-throated and shot through Peter's body, heightening his arousal. He must have been too long without a woman. There could be no other excuse for his response to her.

He turned away and busied himself with the horses, hoping like hell that she hadn't seen his very obviously hard cock leaping against his breeches.

"Peter—isn't this *fun*?"

He snorted. "Your definition of 'fun' and mine differ somewhat, Freddie. I don't see getting soaked, having no shelter and…" He rummaged in the small saddle bag, "…two pieces of day-old bread and a little cheese, as 'fun'."

"When did you get to be such an old stick-in-the-mud?"

"When I discovered how much I hate mud." *And when I got a look at your breasts.*

Freddie laughed again. "Well, you don't know what you're missing. It's…liberating, Peter. It's just rain. It'll dry off. Enjoy it."

He turned, only to find his words of rebuke dying on his lips.

She had her back to him and was taking her damned shirt *off*.

Skin like cream, dotted with a few freckles across her shoulders, emerged as she slid the wet shirt down her spine. Her lovely smooth spine that just begged to be licked from neck to...

"Freddie. Stop that this instant."

She tossed a look over her shoulders that burned him. Green eyes full of mischief glittered and her mouth pouted adorably.

No. *Not* adorably. Those were Freddie's lips. They were not kissable or adorable, nor were they meant to open and slide down the length of his cock.

Oh *fuck*. He was in trouble now.

"Spoil sport. It's my way of taking a bath. Do you know how hard it is to keep clean when you're working in the fields?"

The shirt slipped from her hands to the ground at her feet and she moved her hands in front of her. Terrified that her breeches were about to join the shirt, Peter leaped forward.

"Freddie, enough..." He reached unthinkingly for her shoulders and gripped them firmly.

Which was a *big* mistake.

Velvet smooth skin met his touch, warm and slippery from the rain. And she didn't help by leaning back against him.

"What's the matter, Peter? It's only me."

Peter swallowed as an armful of desirable woman pressed her back into him. And parts of him that were even harder than the muscles of his chest.

Her bottom wriggled slightly, settling his cock in a perfect spot...

He made another mistake by looking down.

Over her shoulder he could see those gorgeous naked breasts. Full and round, they glistened as the rain dropped on them, little droplets gathering on each nipple and slipping slowly from the hard peaks.

His mouth opened, but whether from a desire to berate her for her behavior or suckle away those raindrops he had no idea.

She shivered a little. "Isn't this nice? But a bit chilly...Peter, warm me up..."

She grabbed his hands from her shoulders and pulled them around her waist, snuggling herself even closer into his body.

Peter fought a fierce internal battle with himself. He had a wet armful of beautiful woman, naked from the waist up, and rubbing herself against him with all the skill of the most wanton and passionate creature he'd ever encountered.

She was giving off signals that would have been clear to a blind man in the middle of the night.

When she slid her hands over his and moved them upwards to cup her breasts, fireworks exploded in Peter's brain. And his cock nearly exploded in his breeches.

"Oh, that's much better," she sighed.

It was on the tip of Peter's tongue to ask "For whom?" It wasn't better for him. It was twenty times *worse*.

In spite of the fact that his hands had automatically turned to accept the warm weight of her breasts and they were now lying pillowed in his grasp, Peter bit down hard on the tide of lust that was swamping him.

"Freddie." He cleared his throat of whatever it was that made him squeak and tried again. "Freddie. It's a good thing you picked me to try these wiles on. Someone else might have taken advantage of this situation."

Christ. Now he sounded like an eighty-year-old dowager.

"How?" Freddie's voice was slightly husky too. Must be pollen or something.

"How what?"

"How would they have taken advantage of me, Peter?" She drew in a breath and her breasts swelled in his palms. "Would they have done...this...perhaps?"

She pushed his hands up a little further, making sure that her nipples were now pressing into his skin. "I don't think I would have minded that so much. It feels...ooh...*lovely*."

Peter's conscience threatened to choke him. Of course it didn't really matter, since his cock would strangle him long before he ceased breathing.

"Or perhaps..." She turned in his arms, slowly letting his hands drag over her nakedness. "Perhaps they would have done this..."

Pushing her breasts hard against his chest, she slithered her hands to his neck and drew his head towards hers. Her green eyes flickered as she dropped her gaze to his lips and parted her own.

Peter groaned and surrendered.

His hands slid behind her, feeling her heat through the dampness left by the rain. She was all silk and cream and slender as a reed, but strong enough to hold his head captive as their lips met.

He couldn't help the reflex action that brought his cupped palm up to her hair as he angled her for the kiss.

He couldn't help the little groan of pleasure as he felt her softness welcoming him, or her tongue slide across his in a swiftly seductive lure.

He couldn't help crushing her tight to his body as mouths opened, breaths mingled and tongues dueled, fired on by some tumultuous desire that apparently was consuming both of them.

He couldn't help but realize he was totally and completely *mad*.

His need was overwhelming, hammering at his brain from his cock and his balls, and demanding that he lay Freddie down in the wet grass, strip those disgusting breeches off her and plunge deep into her heat. He could do it, too. He knew she'd let him. Knew she wanted it. And him.

Her little whimpers of pleasure were telling him so in no uncertain terms. And his little groans of matching pleasure were telling him that he was in the right place at the right time and he should just go right ahead and follow his natural impulses.

He should take her, love her senseless, let her rest and then do it all over again. She'd demand everything he could give her and then some. He knew his Freddie.

His *Freddie*...

Like a shower of cold water, the realization that this was Freddie cascaded through Peter's mind and snapped it back into place, letting rational thought take over.

He eased back from the embrace, missing her heat the instant they parted, but determined, for *once* in his life, to do the right thing.

Fuuuuck.

Chapter 10

All of Freddie's plans and schemes had shattered as soon as Peter's lips touched hers. His warmth, his taste, the feel of him had blown away any conscious thought and replaced it with a desire that threatened to knock her clean off her feet.

She ached. She could feel her cunt crying out tears of hot desire and her nipples hurt from wanting his mouth to claim them for himself.

And he was pulling away from her.

Fighting the urge to scream with frustration, she drew on her inner strength and raised an eyebrow at him. It took every ounce of courage she had to face him, all but naked, and not do anything more than raise that one eyebrow.

"Is there a problem?" Miracle of miracles. Her voice still worked, too.

Peter cleared his throat. Aha. She *had* reached him. And pretty thoroughly, if that very nice bulge that threatened to burst open his breeches was any indicator.

"Yes. There's a *big* problem."

Her eyes dropped to his crotch. "So I see."

Incredibly, Peter blushed. "And you saying things like *that* is part of it." He turned away to the horses again. If he fussed over them any more they'd probably kick him.

"So I'm not allowed to say things like that? To comment on…*that*?" She made sure she drawled out the word so that he'd be in no doubt of her meaning.

Peter whirled back to face her, temper lighting his eyes and his moustache twitching. "No you're bloody well *not*."

Freddie felt her eyes narrow as her own temper rose. She put her hands on her hips, heedless of her nakedness. "Well, isn't that just like a man? You expect to kiss me, do whatever you want, let your…your lust free, but I'm not supposed to be able to do the same."

"I didn't kiss you. You kissed me."

"Last time I looked, it took two, Peter, and that's a pretty weak answer."

Peter stalked to her and picked up her shirt from the ground. "Put this on. I don't care if it's wet—maybe it'll cool down that heat that seems to have boiled up inside you."

"Me? Inside *me*? I'm not the one standing around with a cock hard enough to shoe that damned horse you keep fiddling with."

Peter's jaw clenched as he thrust the shirt into her breasts. "Put. This. On." He spun on his heel, grabbed the reins and mounted, grunting a little as his crotch met the saddle.

Good.

She hoped his cock would break off.

Struggling with the damp fabric that made her shiver, Freddie pulled herself up into her own saddle. The rain had eased and Peter urged his horse out from under the trees and back out across the fields.

She had little choice but to follow him, although the urge to gallop as fast as she could in the opposite direction was very strong.

For several miles, neither spoke, but eventually Peter reined in, pausing to look around and gather his bearings. Absently he passed her a piece of bread as she pulled her horse alongside his.

"Here. Eat something. You're too thin."

Freddie looked at the bread. Right. This would certainly help her fill out. Opening her mouth to respond, she noticed the muscle twitching in his cheek, and thought better of it.

For once, her brain told her, it might be best to keep silent.

It would seem that Peter had worked himself into a fine temper. Freddie snickered under her breath. *Serves him right.*

"If I recall this area correctly, there's a small village less than a couple of miles from here. We'll put up there for the night."

"Yes, sir." She snapped a sharp and irreverent salute.

It was met with a frosty glance from dark eyes. "You will do as I say, Freddie. Somehow I've got to put this situation to rights. And it will go a lot smoother without you fighting my authority every step of the way."

Thoughts of caution disappeared into the wind. "*Authority?*" The word was close to a shriek. "You've got absolutely no authority over me whatsoever. How dare you even *think* about assuming such a position?"

She shut mental eyes against the quick image of some of the positions she'd like him to assume.

"Do you think I'm too thin?" The question popped out of her mouth before she could stop it.

Peter heaved a deep sigh. "Freddie. I need to talk to you like a...like a brother..." There was an odd sort of choke to the last word. "You can't go on like this. Wandering around the countryside, working in the fields, acting like a...like a..."

"Like a what, Peter? Like a woman who knows what she wants?" Freddie stared out at the fields, not wanting to meet his eyes anymore, afraid of what she might see in them.

"Yes, like that too." His words were short.

"I am not afraid to be who I am." Freddie raised her chin. "I cannot be who I was raised to be, so I will be who I choose. I like my freedom, Peter. I'm not bound by any of those silly conventions. I can go where I please, do what I want, and as long as I can get a bit of food in exchange for work now and again, I'm content."

Peter turned and stared at her, an odd expression in his eyes. "And what happens when winter comes, Freddie? When it's so cold your teeth are chattering, you've got an empty belly because the crops are gone, there's no work to be had, and nowhere to sleep but some rickety cow byre?"

She swallowed, held captive by those dark eyes boring into her.

"Will you relish your freedom when you wake shivering with fever? Or try and sustain yourself with that 'freedom' when you're forced to dig up whatever leftover vegetables you can find from some half-frozen field in order to hang on to life? Is that freedom, Freddie? Is that what you want?"

His voice was harsh and cold. "Do you know what it's like to freeze to death, Freddie? Your body will curl up into itself, trying to hold on to what little heat it has. But with no food and hardly any shelter, it'll be fighting a losing battle. You'll get tired. You'll want to sleep and your eyes will grow heavy. Then you won't really feel cold anymore. You won't know that your skin is freezing and you're turning blue. Nobody will know, until the spring thaw reveals what's left of you."

Freddie stared at him. "You've seen it." She'd never been more certain of anything in her life. Peter spoke with a heat that came from some private hell. One she couldn't begin to guess at.

He looked away. "Yes."

"Peter...I...I..."

He waved his hand in dismissal. "Let's find ourselves someplace for the night."

Just like that, the discussion was over.

Freddie tried to lash her temper back up to its fiery peak, but failed, since all she could see was the agony in Peter's eyes as he took her to task. Where had he been? What had he seen that had left such an indelible mark on him?

Truly, he was not the Peter she remembered from her youth. He was...he was something else now. A man. And one she was learning more about every minute. He was still dictatorial, and still had a distressing tendency to want to boss her about, but there was more to him. A depth—a pain perhaps. Something.

And she fully intended to find out what that something was.

She resolutely hardened her heart against the notion that he was even more attractive now than he had been six years ago. She refused to accept the notion that her desire for him was anything more than just that...desire. Lust.

A plain and simple need to sate the urgings of her young and healthy body.

Men did it all the time. Why couldn't she? There was absolutely no question of any deeper emotions involved.

There *couldn't* be.

* * * * *

Peter let his horse plod down the well-traveled lane to the lights that were beginning to appear in the village ahead. Dusk was falling, the air was cool now, and his thoughts were somber.

He hadn't meant to lash out at Freddie. In fact, he wasn't quite sure where his attack had come from.

No. That was a lie.

He knew exactly where it had come from. It had come from the small family he'd found at the foot of a hill one spring as he and his fellows had traveled south near the Rhone river. The beauty of the French Alps had lured them into a nearby pass and the melting snow had revealed the terror of the winter just past.

It was clear that Nature had taken its toll on the woman and the two small bodies she'd held so close. Rotting timbers lay strewn around them, a visual memorial to the small barn in which they'd sought shelter. It hadn't been enough, and Peter blinked away hot tears as he remembered the silence that had fallen on their merry group. They'd buried the family together, in death as in life.

So many dead. No food, little shelter—all seized by Napoleon's troops as they made their way through their own country to conquer new lands, and wreak more havoc. For what?

That incident had left a mark on him, changed him in some indefinable way, and made him more convinced than ever that what they were doing was right. Men who were little more than lads had been conscripted into the army, leaving wives and children alone, defenseless, and at the mercy of whatever miseries befell them. If there was any way to get these innocents away from the approaching troops and their almost certain death, Peter and his friends had taken it.

They'd spirited whole families deep into the forests, dressed young men as old women, lied, cheated, and stolen what they'd needed to in an effort to protect those who could not protect themselves.

Their music had kept them sane, and had lightened a few hearts along the way, letting their listeners forget their worries and their fears for an hour or so. It had also helped Peter forget too.

Perhaps he'd forgotten too much. Perhaps that was why seeing Freddie, the last person who should be wandering through the English countryside trying to survive, had brought the memories back.

Dear God in heaven. *What* was he going to do with her?

A loud sneeze from behind him made him frown. That was all he needed. For her to catch some ague or other. It would serve her right, of course, for standing damn near naked in a rainstorm.

He blinked back the image of her body slicked by raindrops and her breasts, so perfect and full and ready for his hands...his mouth...God *damn*. He'd carry that picture in his brain until the day he died, most probably.

His cock stirred in agreement. He snarled a curse at it under his breath.

Of *course* it wanted Freddie. She'd grown from a pretty young girl into a stunningly attractive woman, if one disregarded the hair. And he had no trouble disregarding the hair. The rest of her was more than appealing—it was downright mouthwatering. It was just his damn brain that was having trouble reconciling the new Freddie with the old Freddie.

And to think she'd been someone's mistress...

His teeth clenched together sharply at the idea of some other man's hands on that body. He realized if that man had popped up in front of him, Peter would have run him through without a qualm.

"Peter?"

He almost jumped at Freddie's voice, so mired in his thoughts was he at that moment. "What?"

"There's a small inn ahead, I think. Were you intending to stay there for the night?"

She was right. Lights shone from a few tiny windows, but there was definitely a sign in front.

Peter sighed. "Yes."

They dismounted and Freddie came to the horses' heads to take the reins.

"What do you think you're doing?" He knew he was sharp with her, but his usual charm seemed to have completely deserted him. He had a headache too.

"I'm taking the horses to the barn. You can get a room. I'll sleep in the stable."

"You will not."

Freddie's sigh mirrored his. "Look, Peter," she said carefully. "I'm dressed as a boy. It's easiest if I pretend to be your servant or your groom or something. The fewer questions asked, the quicker we'll be on our way. You're the one who's moaning about the proprieties here, and it would not be proper for a gentleman to request a room for a lowly groom."

Peter snorted. "Take the horses to the barn then, if you must. But you will return. You will sleep inside tonight, in a real bed, and have some real food. If you don't come back, I shall be forced to come and fetch you. And I shall not be pleased."

Freddie bit her lip, and Peter could almost see the wheels turning in her mind.

"Forget it, Freddie. You aren't slipping away from me that easily. Wherever you go, I shall find you. You cannot hide from me now any more than you could when you were little. You're stuck with me, and I'm stuck with you. Might as well get that straight between us right this minute."

He frowned as another wave of pain seared through his skull. "Now get on with it. My head aches damnably, I'm hungry, I'm getting cold standing out here arguing with you and my patience is very nearly at an end."

Freddie nodded, and Peter heaved a sigh of relief.

Finally, something was going right.

*   *   *   *   *

Freddie tossed and turned, unable to sleep. She wasn't sure if it was the unaccustomed luxury of a real bed, or the sounds from the room next door that were keeping her awake, but whatever it was, it was a bloody nuisance.

True to his word, Peter had procured them lodgings, demanding a room for his "boy", which had turned out to be little more than a closet leading to Peter's bedroom. It was fine with Freddie. The small pallet was covered with a soft mattress and a real pillow cushioned her head.

It was a rare pleasure to be able to snuggle beneath a clean blanket and sleep only in one of Peter's shirts he'd tossed at her from his bag.

"Here. Take this. You can't possibly spend the night in those filthy rags."

He'd been abrupt, and Freddie could see something going on behind his harsh expression. His face was flushed, he'd eaten little of the meal brought by the innkeeper, and all indications pointed to either a headache or something worse.

She'd slipped into the garment, sniffing the scent of man and horse and—him. It was heady and seductive, and she'd stifled the urge to rub the darned thing all over her body.

A groan came from the large bedroom, and Freddie sat upright. Something was definitely wrong. She slid silently from her bed and peeked around the door that separated their rooms.

The firelight showed her a distressing sight.

Peter was tossing and turning as much as she had earlier, but he'd pushed the blankets back and was moaning in his sleep. The night was cool. He should have been chilled, not warm.

Quietly, she crossed the room and with that maternal gesture that had comforted children since the beginning of time rested her hand softly on his forehead.

He was burning up.

Freddie clenched her teeth. He had a fever, and a high one at that. She hurriedly pulled the covers back up over him, ignoring his nakedness, his wonderful body, and all the things she found so appealing about him.

Her concern was for the shudders that were starting to tremble through him.

She rushed into her room, pulled on her breeches and shoes and headed downstairs to the kitchen area of the inn.

The first crows of the cockerel outside told her it was still early, but she hoped someone might be stirring. She needed help and she needed it fast.

"Hello, lass."

A large woman was smiling at her from behind the kitchen table, arms heavily floured from the bread she was kneading.

"Um…good morning."

Freddie was caught off guard. This woman had immediately pegged her sex, but seemed undisturbed by the disguise.

"Ye're up early? Bread won't be ready for a bit yet…"

Freddie swallowed. "It's not breakfast I need. My…my…husband. He's sick."

The lie slipped out so naturally that the woman thought nothing of it, but focused instead on her last words.

"Sick, is he? Caught in that rain yesterday, I'll warrant." She frowned. "Yer husband. I'll be guessing there's a good reason for all this…this…" She gestured with one floury hand at Freddie's clothing. "But that can wait. Best we get him well first. Running a fever, is he?"

Freddie nodded, knowing that her eyes reflected her worry.

"Never fear, lass. Got just the thing here."

She walked to her cupboard and rummaged inside, bringing out a small vial of liquid. "Willow bark. We'll make up some tea with it, keep him drinking it, along with a lot of water, and he'll be back on his feet and in yer bed in next to no time."

Freddie sighed with relief. "You think so?"

"Never failed me yet. Unless he's sick with summat other than a simple fever. He got any coughs or ailments ye haven't told me about?"

"Um…no. He's very strong usually."

A little smile flickered around the older woman's lips. "I'll bet he is too. With a pretty young wife like yerself."

Freddie blushed. She couldn't help the heat she felt spreading over her skin from forehead to knees.

"Here ye are, love. Now just get him to drink this. If ye need help, pop down and holler for Betsy." The woman passed her a teapot and a cup. "That'd be me, of course. My husband is already out caring for the stock, but I'll let him know what's happening."

"Thank you so much, Betsy," said Freddie gratefully. "I suppose we'll be here a little longer than we originally told your husband. I hope it's not going to be a problem…"

"No, lovey. Don't worry yer little head about that. 'Tis mostly quiet in these parts. Not as if we've got quality lined up to reserve rooms."

"They don't know what they're missing then," grinned Freddie. "Thanks again. I'll take this up to Peter."

Taking it up to Peter was one thing. Getting him to *drink* it was another.

With the typical fretfulness of someone who was sick, hated being sick, and wanted simply to be left alone to die in peace, Peter was turning into the proverbial pain in the arse.

"You shouldn't be in here, Freddie." He grumped at her after she'd managed to rouse him a little.

"I know. Drink this."

"What is it? I don't want anything to drink. It's too hot in here. Open a window or something, will you? Get these damn blankets off me."

She ignored his complaints, tucked the blankets around his chest and poured the willow bark tea. "You're sick, Peter. You have a fever, and we've got to get it down and get you well."

"I'm not sick. I never get sick."

That statement was in direct contrast to his over-bright eyes, flushed face, and the occasional shiver that wracked him.

"Well, if you're not sick, then you won't mind having a sip or two of this tea, will you?" Freddie's voice oozed patience and sympathy, but beneath it was a will of steel.

"Don't want it."

She sighed. Something about men and illness just didn't go well together. They suddenly reverted to the age of twelve.

"Please, Peter," she crooned. "For me?"

She raised the cup to his lips, holding his dark eyes with her gaze and putting every ounce of pleading she could manage into her tone.

"Freddie, when did you turn into such a beauty?"

The hand holding the cup shook a little, but she continued to press the hot tea towards him, breathing easier as he finally took a sip.

"Urgh. That's awful stuff."

"I know. But it will make you well."

Another shiver rattled his teeth against the china. "Damn. It's cold, Freddie. Why don't you come and keep me warm?"

His eyes were brilliant, but a flush of red tinged them, and Freddie knew his fever was truly on him. "I will, darling. As soon as you drink your tea."

Obediently, Peter swallowed some more, his gaze never leaving her face. "That's a promise, Freddie."

She nodded, feeling a little smile cross her lips. He wanted her. He might be delirious, sick, and stuck in bed, but he wanted her. "I always keep my promises, Peter."

"Yes, you do. Always did. Not like some people…"

He had finished the tea without realizing it, and Freddie heaved a sigh of relief as she put the cup back down beside the bed.

His eyes were closed now, and his teeth clenched against the chills shaking his body. "Fuck…it's so damn cold…" His eyes opened a little and he focused blearily on Freddie. "You didn't hear me say that."

She grinned and brushed the hair away from his face. "I've heard the word before. Even used it a time or two myself. Just rest, now, Peter."

"You said you'd keep me warm," he shivered.

"And I will." She stoked up the low fire, putting a couple more logs on and feeling the heat steal into the room. Grabbing the blankets off her bed she added them to the ones already covering Peter and cocooned him from head to toe.

"Not enough..." he hissed.

Freddie bit her lip. He was really shaking now, in the grip of the fever. How long would it take that willow bark tea to work?

Quietly, she crossed the room and snapped the bolt home, locking them into their own little world. She knew he needed as much warmth as she could give him. And she wanted to give him all she had.

Slipping out of her clothes, she eased herself beneath the blankets and closed the distance between their bodies, suppressing a hiss of pleasure as their flesh met. "Rest, Peter," she soothed.

Surprisingly, he did.

He nestled against her, pulling her tight to him and throwing one heavy thigh across her legs. "So warm, Freddie. So soft," he murmured tiredly.

His head was a heavy weight on her breast, and his hot skin burned hers as they touched...naked and together in a lump underneath the blankets.

She cuddled him close, for once letting her heart dictate her actions as he fell asleep. It had been too long since she'd held someone, or been held—body to body, skin to skin.

And it had never been quite like *this*.

It had never been *Peter*.

Chapter 11

Peter surfaced into consciousness like a man swimming through soup.

He was lightheaded, disoriented, rather sweaty, and had no clue where he was. The room surrounding him was dark, lit only by the flickering flames of a crackling fire, he was buried under a mound of blankets, and a plate of half-eaten food lay next to the bed.

A sound from beneath the covers beside him shocked him into full awareness.

Short red curls tumbled over the pillow, and he suddenly realized a soft body was pressed tight against his.

He bit back a groan.

Oh God. *Freddie*. What had he *done*?

The memories came flooding back. He'd been so cold, she'd made him drink something disgusting several times, and he'd slept. Through the whole day by the looks of it. Bloody hell. He'd been sick and he was *never* sick. Years of scouting the European countryside in all kinds of weather and nary a sneeze.

A day with Freddie had put him flat on his back.

At least she was still here. She hadn't run from him to make her own way once more. Just the thought of that happening sent a chill down his spine that had nothing to do with any sickness.

Another pressing need made itself known. His bladder was bursting.

Cautiously he eased himself from the bed, tucking the blankets back around the sleeping woman. The air was cool against his skin but not uncomfortably so, and he quickly slipped into his clothes. He had to find the privy. He'd not take the risk of waking her by using the chamber pot, and he'd probably flood the damn thing anyway.

Silently he made his way from the room.

"Ah, good to see yer up and around, lad." A motherly woman was smiling at him. "Feeling a mite more like yerself then, are ye?"

"Uh...do I know you?"

"Well, ye should, since I helped that little wife of yers get that fever down...right nasty it was too. But my good old willow bark tea helped, and those cooling sponge baths just about did the trick by the looks of ye."

Peter blinked.

"Ye'll be after the privy, I'm guessing." She nodded over her shoulder. "'Tis right down yon path. Ye can't miss it."

For the first time in a long time, Peter was speechless. He'd apparently acquired a wife, and a nurse, and was being told to use the privy. He gave up.

"Thank you. Er...don't go away. I'll be right back and I want to talk to you."

Oh God, do I want to talk to you. About my wife!

The woman grinned and returned to her chores, welcoming him back with the same sunny smile when he returned feeling a little more clear-headed, a lot more comfortable, and with some very pressing questions that needed answers.

"That's better, lad. Ye look more yerself."

Hah. He'd never felt less like himself in his life.

"About my *wife*..."

"Sweet thing she is, too. Ye're lucky to have a lass like that one. Stayed by yer side and did everything needful, she did."

"She did?"

"Aye. For the last three days she's been tending to ye. With my help of course."

"*Three days?*"

The woman raised an eyebrow at him. "Ye've been bloody sick, lad, if ye'll pardon my plain speaking. Whatever ye and yon wife have been up to is none of my business, fer sure, but if ye'll take a motherly word of advice, ye'll that girl home where she belongs and get some babies on her. Settle her down. She's tuckered to the bone, what with nursing ye and worrying about ye." She put a few scones on a plate and added them to the tray she'd been busy preparing.

"Now, if ye've the strength, take this back up and get her to eat summat."

Peter found the tray thrust into his hands. "Er...yes. Yes of course."

"Good lad."

He supposed he was dismissed.

Carefully balancing the tray, Peter climbed the stairs to his room, struggling with the developments that had apparently taken place over the three days he'd lost. Viktor would probably be in London by now, and the others on their way.

They wouldn't worry about him overmuch, since they'd always allowed plenty of flexibility when it came to schedules. He still had time to deal with the issue of Freddie.

His *wife*.

His hand shook a little as he tried to put the tray down quietly next to where she still slept. Those two words had rocked him, but what had been even more stunning had been the heat that had swept him at the thought of Freddie in his bed. Permanently.

He stared down at her as the first rays of the morning sun lightened the room.

So small, so fragile, and yet possessed of such a strong will that she'd have made Bonaparte's forces quake. She'd been a young society miss, a governess, a man's mistress and a field hand. And she wasn't even...what...twenty-two?

She'd lived several lifetimes in so few years. And she was so lovely.

She stirred in her sleep and reached out towards the emptiness where he'd lain, sighing as her hand met only cool sheets.

Her shoulder peeked from the covers, its milky whiteness luring his body and her warm and loving soul luring his heart.

What a wife she'd make. A partner. A friend. A woman whose strength was unmatched by any Peter had run across in his whole life. She knew his secrets and didn't care. He knew hers and cared more than he wanted to admit. Even to himself.

Without a second thought, Peter shucked his clothing and lifted the blankets, sliding in beside her and pulling her heat against him.

He knew what he wanted now. He knew what would make his life complete.

He wanted Freddie.

She stirred again and hugged him close, half asleep but still checking up on him.

He grinned and dropped a light kiss on her nose. "Hello sleepyhead."

Her green eyes flickered wide. "*Peter*. You're awake..."

"Most definitely."

Her hand automatically reached up to his forehead, checking his fever.

"I'm fine, Freddie. The fever's gone. Thanks to you and a very nice lady whose name I completely forgot to ask."

She giggled. "That would be Betsy."

He reached for the hand as she would have pulled away from his face, cradling it in his palm. "Such a small hand." He dropped moist kisses on her fingers. "And yet such a caring one."

"Peter?"

He let his mouth wander down to her wrist, licking a little and tasting her. "So sweet."

"Peter, I...what...what are you doing?"

"Saying 'thank you'." He paused and met her puzzled gaze. "...To my *wife*."

A red blush spread over her face and down her neck. "I...you...we..."

Peter grinned again and continued his progress, managing to free her from the covers and find a very nice spot on her shoulder. "Mmmm?"

"I...oh..."

He nipped and licked the small bite.

"Peter..."

The word was more of a sigh, and Peter took it as implicit permission to continue doing what he was doing. Not that he could have stopped. One taste of her skin and he was on fire.

He traced his way up her neck to her lips, pausing before he lowered his head. "It's time to claim my husbandly rights, Freddie..."

She opened her eyes and stared at him, and he saw desire banked within their green depths.

She sighed and slid her arms around his neck. "Long *past* time, Peter."

* * * * *

For Freddie, it was like waking from a dream and finding herself in a fantasy. Peter's dark eyes were blazing down at her and his hard length was pressed against her as he raised himself over her body.

She wanted him so much she ached with it.

For three days she'd cared for him, made him drink, bathed the sweat of his fever from his skin and tried to ignore the magnificent masculinity beneath her hands. All that time she'd suppressed the feelings inside her, refusing to allow her touch to linger where it shouldn't, even though his hard muscles beckoned and his eyes had followed her every move.

She knew he was ill. And she wouldn't take advantage of that fact. It was likely he'd not remember any of it.

But now he was lucid. Awake and, to judge by the solid length pressing her thigh, aroused.

How could she turn him down?

She'd quickly grown accustomed to sleeping next to him, warming him, guarding him, and finding her own pleasure in the body curled around hers. The comfort of sharing a bed with Peter was one thing. The heat that flared in her belly when she stared at him was another.

And that heat was mirrored in his eyes as he lowered his lips to hers.

"Are you sure, Freddie?"

The question was a breath against her lips. Her voice was frozen in her throat, blocked by a lump that refused to move. So she let her body answer for her.

Her back arched, her breasts thrust against him, and her legs parted, opening wide to make a space between them for him. If he didn't understand what she was telling him, he wasn't half the man she thought he was.

He didn't disappoint her.

His mouth descended on hers, and although she could sense his wish to be gentle, it took only one touch for a fire to explode between them.

His hands were everywhere at once, caressing her, finding her nipples and teasing them into screaming hardness, and then slipping lower to find the secrets of her pleasure.

His tongue fought hers, plunging in and out of her mouth as his hips pressed against her, thrusting his cock against her mound.

She moaned, opening her legs even further, needing to be filled with that hardness.

"Now, Peter, please now...don't wait..."

His fingers sought her clit, bringing her to the edge of her orgasm with just a light flicker. She gasped and bowed beneath him, rubbing as much of herself as she could against him.

"Jesus, Freddie..." choked Peter.

She reached around him and found his buttocks, digging her fingernails into the firm flesh and trying to get him where she needed him.

She was hot, wet, and so ready that if he didn't fuck her right this minute she was going to explode in his arms.

He eased a hand between them, grasped his cock and slid it around her pussy, through the moisture that welled from her cunt.

"Peter..."

He thrust into her.

Heaven. It was sheer heaven.

He was big, stretching her, making her feel full and complete and mad for him to move.

She locked her ankles behind his waist and pulled him deeper still, wanting every single thing he had and more.

He was pounding her soul.

She came with a scream, letting her body have its way and release all the pent-up pleasure it possessed. Her cunt clamped down on his cock and shook her with the ferocity of its spasms. Peter never stopped moving, riding with her as she erupted into her peak and tumbled into insanity.

She sank down into the bed and opened her eyes to see Peter pulling his cock from her. He was still hard, reddened and swollen, and glistening from the juices that were dripping from her in a sensual flood.

"You didn't..."

He glanced at her tightly. "I won't risk getting you with child, Freddie..."

He reached for himself, but she stayed his hand. "Wait. There's another way."

Heedless of what he would think of her, and focused solely on bringing him the release he'd given her, Freddie rolled over and raised herself onto her hands and knees.

"I...*Freddie*?" Peter's voice was a croak as she spread herself for him, letting her hands pull her buttocks apart.

"Take me here, Peter. Go ahead. I...I don't mind. In fact, I find it...pleasurable."

Peter swallowed as he stared at the beautiful arse waiting for him.

Her swollen cunt was glistening with moisture and he couldn't resist the urge to run his fingers over the hot flesh and smear her juices around the tight little ring of her anal muscles.

She shivered and moaned in pleasure.

Jesus God. She did like it.

And so did he. But he'd never imagined this particular activity with a woman like Freddie. "I don't know..."

"Please...oh please..." she whispered, wiggling her bottom even more.

Peter's cock swelled painfully. It was either touch himself and come on her back in two seconds flat or...take what she was offering.

"Are you sure?" He seemed to be asking that a lot. He wondered who he was actually asking...himself or Freddie.

"Yes...God, yes...*please*."

Carefully, Peter eased his cock into the cleft between her buttocks, letting a hiss seep between his clenched teeth as he stroked more of her moisture around the little rose that lured him.

He pressed against her and felt her muscles relax, opening for his penetration. She was hot and tight, and he kept his movements gentle, just easing the tip of his cock within.

"More."

He slid his hand beneath her and found her clit, caressing it gently, and letting a new arousal build slowly inside her. He could sense her body responding and she opened even more, encouraging him to move deeper into her darkness.

Like a perfectly-fitted boot she hugged him tight, his slick cock sliding further and further and her moans of pleasure reassuring him. His balls touched her, hot honey pouring from her and soaking him.

He withdrew and slipped in again, timing his movements with little flickers of his fingers against her clit.

She sobbed. "Oh *God*..."

She was taking him. *All* of him. Encouraging him with her groans and sighs and telling him with her body of the pleasure he was giving her.

And the pleasure she was giving him was...breathtaking.

Her spine arched in a smooth curve away from him and he ran a hand over her silky buttock, bringing a whimper to her lips.

"Freddie," he breathed. "Freddie."

It was all he could manage. His wits were gone, his thoughts ablaze with the sight of her body and his cock ready to admit that it had never been like this before—with anyone. *Ever.*

Daringly, obeying some half-imagined whim, Peter dropped a light spank on the curve of her bottom.

She moaned and thrust back against him. "Yesss..."

His brain fizzled and popped as he did it again, harder this time, making the little slap ring through the room.

"Again...more..."

Hips moving rapidly, Peter spanked her once more, putting some force behind it and realizing the sound of flesh meeting flesh was as exciting to her as it was to him.

"*Freddie...*" He tensed, toes curling, feeling his balls tightening into rocks as they touched her and the heat of his slaps spreading through her pussy and her arse into his cock.

He rained slaps on her buttocks and cried out as he thrust one last time.

"Now..." she screamed.

Now.

Peter exploded. Great shudders racked his body, his spine shot tingles from his feet to his ears and he emptied himself into Freddie. Hot jets of come spurted in an endless geyser, filling her, overflowing her tight passage and bathing him in his own flames.

It was impossibly incredible, and for a moment Peter's world vanished as he crashed his way through the most momentous orgasm of his life.

Vaguely aware of her body pulsing around his, he held her tight, sobbing breaths of air into his starving lungs. Lights flashed behind his eyelids, he was hoarse from his roar of completion, and his thighs were threatening to turn to jelly within seconds of his release.

Dear God in heaven. *Freddie.*

Chapter 12

Freddie kept her face buried in the pillow.

Perhaps if she stayed there long enough, Peter would go away and give her room to breathe, to think, and to deal with the incredible emotions she'd just experienced. Of course, the fact that she was just too limp to move had something to do with it as well.

She felt the bed dip beside her and the covers brush her skin as he settled them both, his breathing as exhausted as hers. A soft kiss touched her shoulder.

"Hello."

Oh lovely. Now he was going to be sweet. She'd just become the most wanton trollop this side of the nearest brothel and he was going to be sweet.

She didn't want *sweet*.

She wanted him to yell at her for being such a hussy, to rant that no young woman should have offered to take him in such a way, and scream that she was no better than a whore. She wanted *him* to say the things she was screaming silently at herself.

"Freddie, won't you look at me, love?"

"Mmmpff." Freddie shook her head in the depths of the pillow and struggled to breathe through the feathers.

"Hmm." Peter's voice was thoughtful. He ran his hand gently over her damp skin. "That's a shame. I wanted to see your face, all flushed from our loving."

Freddie squirmed. *Flushed* just about covered it. When she thought of what they'd just done, what she'd enjoyed so much, she *flushed* from head to toe.

"And I really wanted to see the look in your eyes when I kiss the sweat away from your neck...and your shoulders...and..." His hand strayed down beneath the covers to caress her buttocks. "Did I hurt you, sweetheart?"

"Mmmpff." Freddie shook her head again. Oh God. Why didn't he just go away and let her die of shame?

His chuckle sounded much too close to her ear, and she squeezed her eyelids tightly together as he rolled her onto her back. She refused to face him. Or herself.

"Freddie, love...look at me."

No. Absolutely not.

"Why won't you look at me, sweetheart? You can't possibly be embarrassed."

Freddie cracked one eye and raised the lid slightly, squinting at Peter in the semi-darkness. "Why can't I?"

She heard his chuckle and clamped her eyelids back together.

"Two people who did what we just did shouldn't be embarrassed about anything."

Freddie clenched her jaw. "I'm embarrassed about *what* we just did, you idiot."

"Ah."

Peter's hand continued stroking her skin, soothing, smoothing, making her want to purr beneath his touch. She wished he'd stop it, because she was having great difficulty concentrating on the assortment of worries that had slipped into her sex-dazed brain.

"So you didn't like what we just did?"

"I didn't say that." Freddie bit her lip. "I didn't say that at all."

"Good." He leaned over and kissed the curve of one breast, and she dared lift her eyelids a fraction as his moustache grazed her softness. God, he was beautiful.

"Because *I* liked it a lot. I liked it..." His lips dotted little pecks over her nipples. "I liked it more than I've liked anything in a long time." He paused, lightly licking one firm bud. "More than I've liked anything...*ever*."

Freddie opened both eyes, entranced at the sight of his tousled head on her chest. "Really?"

He turned his head and smiled at her. "Really."

"And you don't think I'm some sort of ...whore...or something?"

Peter frowned. "Good God, no. Of course not."

"But, I mean...I...we...the way I..."

"Freddie." Peter's voice was as firm as the lips surrounding her nipple. He sucked a little and then pulled back. "We made love, sweetheart. It gave us both a great deal of pleasure. Whatever two people choose to do together, as long as it's by mutual consent, is never wrong."

Freddie's brow wrinkled as she considered his words.

"Oh."

"Did you enjoy our loving, Freddie?" His question was softly breathed over the moist trail left by his tongue.

"Yes, thank you Peter. It was…quite wonderful."

Peter grinned. "So polite. But yes, it was wonderful. And you know something, Freddie?"

"What?"

"We're going to do it again, you and I."

"Right *now*?" Freddie wondered if she had the strength to raise her eyebrows, let alone get energetic with him all over again.

Peter's laugh rang out and he moved his head away from her breasts, tugging her hard against him as he cuddled them both into a warm heap. "No, sweetheart. Not right at this moment. We're both tired. But we have our lives ahead of us, darling. Lives that we're going to spend together."

Peter's warmth settled into Freddie's bones and relaxed her muscles. His presence surrounded her with comfort and a degree of safety she'd missed for too long. Sleepily she tried to focus on his words. "Indeed?"

"Indeed. Sleep now, love. *My* love. We'll plan our future when we're both fresh."

Funny thing. Freddie could have sworn Peter said "our" future. That would be so nice, she thought, slipping into sleep. *"Our" future.* Hers and Peter's.

So nice…

* * * * *

Peter's mind whirled like a smoothly-oiled machine, considering, discarding and then deciding on the best course of action.

He was, in effect, charting the course for the rest of his life. His future. The one that had just materialized in front of him and revolved around the woman beside him.

First and foremost he had to get her to agree to marry him. He wasn't quite sure how he was going to do it, since Freddie could be prickly at times, and her experiences of life hadn't exactly taught her to trust. Or to love.

It was up to him to teach her that.

His cock stirred at the memory of exactly how a lot of those lessons were going to go. Yes, this was one time when the pupil and the teacher would both end up learning things. Peter had no doubt that he'd always find something new and entrancing about Freddie, whether it be her honest sensuality, her willingness to play, or her independent spirit that had been forged in the hardest way he could imagine.

He eagerly looked forward to a lifetime of exploring her contradictions, her humor and her strengths. Along with a lifetime of loving her, caring for her, protecting her and having children with her.

Thoughts of family jarred him from his rosy-hued dreams and reminded him he had his own family to settle with.

The past must be laid to rest—and soon.

Peter weighed his options. His mind clicked into that regimented and compartmentalized way of thinking that had served him so well during his adventures in Europe.

Firstly he must marry Freddie. Aunt Margaret would see to all that.

Secondly, he should make sure that she understood what lay ahead for them. He saw no real alternative to reclaiming his name and his title. Messengers would have to be sent to Mark alerting him that Peter was home.

The transition might be awkward, but with Peter's father's death, no threats of prosecution hung over his head to mar his homecoming.

Peter clenched his teeth. Freddie knew he'd killed a man in a duel. She knew that Peter's father had thrown him out of the country and threatened to have him tried for murder if he set a foot back in England.

But had she known why the duel had occurred? He hoped not. The screams of the country girl that man had been abusing still haunted his nightmares. The look on his own father's face as Peter had tried to explain the circumstances also reappeared in his dreams on a regular basis.

Peter's father had firmly believed in "*droit du seigneur*". A titled nobleman was permitted to take his pleasures where and when he willed it, regardless of the woman involved. He'd been livid with Peter for interfering, and even more furious when Peter had rid the earth of the monster he'd challenged.

To Lord Chalmers, the actions of his eldest son had been tantamount to treason. A completely outrageous attack on the beliefs that had provided the foundation of his life. Ignoring the pleas of his family, and behaving in the way he felt best represented his notions of the aristocracy to which he belonged, Lord Chalmers dismissed his oldest son. From his presence, from his estate, from his very country.

Peter had transgressed against the establishment. Such a sin was, in his father's eyes, unpardonable.

And Peter's father had gone to his death believing it.

Even when other charges against Peter's victim had been revealed, along with a lengthy and unpleasant history of abuse, there was no surcease in the anger of Lord Chalmers for his son.

The authorities had forgiven and forgotten. Lord Chalmers never would.

And *that*, thought Peter, was fine with him. He'd had close on six years of adventures with the finest men he could have ever hoped to meet.

Which put him in mind of another thing to do...notify Viktor and the others.

Making mental lists, assigning priorities and writing messages in his mind, Peter closed his eyes and snuggled his head over Freddie's, letting her short hair tickle his chin. A passing thought that he rather liked her hair this way made him smile.

Another thought that he'd have the rest of their lives to find out other ways he liked her hair made him hold her close, and as he drifted into sleep he realized that *this* was the only way he ever wanted to sleep from now on.

Holding Freddie.

* * * * *

Waking next to Peter, cuddled tightly against his heat, was a moment of joy for Freddie, but within seconds the realization that their situation was totally and completely impossible hit her like a brick.

There was simply no way she could allow herself the luxury of even considering marriage to him. She was little better than a strumpet, had been another man's mistress, and he was...well, she wasn't quite sure what he was, but she knew he deserved better than someone like her.

Cautiously she peeled herself from his skin and slid from the bed, making as little noise as possible as she slipped into her old clothes. The sky was grey and cloudy, but some inner clock told her dawn was past. Peter slept on, no fever chills shaking his body, or restless tossing disturbing his slumber.

Cursing the occasional creak of the old wooden floor, Freddie muffled the click of the door bolt with her hand and eased from the room, sighing as she left her heart behind her. God, it hurt.

She bit her lip as she made her way downstairs, fighting back tears for what might have been. But by the time she'd reached the last step, her control had returned, and she dashed away the lingering moisture from her lashes.

It was the hardest thing she'd ever done, but it was for the best. She'd survive. She'd done pretty well up to now, and at least she had wonderful memories to warm the chilly and lonely nights ahead.

Thumps from the kitchen told her Betsy had already started her day. Bread had to be made, and other chores completed, and a woman's work was truly never done. Quietly, Freddie opened the kitchen door.

"Good morning, Betsy."

The older woman looked up quickly. "Yer lad all right today, then?"

Freddie couldn't help a slight blush. He was so much better than *all right*. Especially last night.

"Never mind, lass. I know that look." Betsy chuckled over her dough.

"Betsy, I...I'm going to be leaving..."

That statement earned her a sharp look from beneath the greying eyebrows. "Ye are, are ye?"

Freddie nodded.

"Yer sure that's what ye want to do?"

The question made Freddie blink. "I...I have no other choice, Betsy."

The older woman sighed and reached for the ever-present teapot. "Have a cuppa, lass, there's time before dawn. Ye can't lope off without summat in yer stomach."

Freddie slid onto the well-worn bench and watched as Betsy lopped a chunk of yesterday's bread onto a platter and surrounded it with cheese and some of her pickles. A huge dollop of butter joined the bread and the whole thing was shoved under Freddie's nose with the strict command "Eat."

She swallowed. How the hell could she eat when a lump the size of Devonshire House was lodged in her throat? She could barely swallow. Tentatively, she broke off a piece of cheese.

"Go ahead. It won't poison ye. And while ye eat, I'll tell ye a thing or two." Betsy poured the tea. "Seeing as ye've no Mam to tell you what's what, I'm thinking a word from me won't go amiss."

She sat herself down and glared at Freddie, who realized nothing short of the end of the world would stop Betsy from having her say. Freddie obediently munched on the cheese.

"Now. Ye've a fine lad upstairs. Yer mad for him, and he can't take them lovely eyes of his off ye. Ye've been trying to spin me a tale about yer being wed, but a body with a lick of sense can see yer not. Does he not want to marry ye, lass?"

To Freddie's horror, a huge tear dropped down her face and trembled on the tip of her nose. She brushed it away. "Oh no, Betsy. Quite the opposite. He *does* want to marry me. I just...*can't*, that's all. I can't."

Betsy frowned. "Seems like he's doing the right thing by ye. Ye've got that well-plowed look about ye this mornin', if ye'll pardon an old woman's bluntness."

Another tear threatened to join the first. Damn, this had to stop. She'd be flooding her teacup if she kept this up. "Look, Betsy, you're right about many things. But I know that marrying Peter would be the worst thing I could possibly do to him. I'm not the woman he should be thinking about making his wife."

Betsy's eyebrows rose. "And why would that be? He's got it bad for ye, love."

"I know." Freddie's answer was scarcely more than a breath as she recalled the look in Peter's eyes last night.

"And ye've got yerself a bad case of heartache this mornin', if I'm not mistaken..."

Freddie nodded.

"Do ye love him, girl?"

"Too much, Betsy. I didn't want to love him. I knew him when we were young, and I suppose I got one of those awful young girl crushes on him. But now, I've learned..."

"What, lovey? What have ye learned?"

Freddie choked down a sip of tea, struggling to find the words to explain not only to Betsy, but to herself as well. "Loving someone is the hardest thing in the world, Betsy. It only leads to pain when it all goes wrong. People...leave you. They die. They leave a hole in your heart that can never be filled. I can't see that it's worth it. It leads to disappointment, disillusionment and heartache. Look at me now. I should never have let things go as far as they have."

She shook her head to clear her thoughts.

Betsy's rough hand reached across the table and brushed a tear from Freddie's cheek, threatening to completely overset her.

"Lass, loving someone is about taking a chance. Finding enough courage to dare to feel that way, no matter what lies ahead. It's about knowing that the joys of loving will always be with ye even if yer alone. It's about being brave enough to say, well, mebbe I'll not have him forever, but I'll settle for the time we have."

Freddie sniffled. "But...but...I don't know...what if..."

"Lovey, life is full of 'what if's'. It'd be a sad world if we never said 'bugger *what if*', I'm goin' to do it anyway. 'Tis a special man ye've found fer yerself. Yer sharing one of life's greatest adventures. Think twice before you turn yer back on it, is all I'm askin' here."

Betsy swigged back the rest of her tea and rose, leaving Freddie staring at her half-eaten food and wondering why a simple country woman had made more sense in five minutes than all the governesses and tutors she'd had her entire life.

But Betsy's advice notwithstanding, the barriers that existed between her and Peter were still too large for them to overcome. She still had to leave.

* * * * *

Peter stood silently in the hallway of the old inn, shamelessly eavesdropping on the conversation between the two women in the kitchen.

He'd awoken the minute Freddie had slipped from his arms, but curious to find out what she'd been up to at that hour of the morning, had feigned sleep and watched. It had taken only a few moments to realize that she planned on leaving him.

He called down blessings on Betsy's head for delaying Freddie's departure. It had given him time to dress, creep down the stairs with his boots in his hand, and hear Freddie say she loved him.

He knew in his heart that she did—no woman could have given herself the way Freddie had last night unless her heart was involved, but it still sent a shot of joy through him to hear her admit it.

He moved away from the door and silently pulled on his boots. Freddie would head for the stables and he planned on being there first. She was *his*. And it was time he made her aware of that fact in no uncertain terms. No stupid conventions or societal restrictions were going to keep them apart.

He didn't have long to wait.

Hidden in the grey shadows of the barn he heard her approach the horses, talking softly to them, and opening the stall door to the one she'd ridden behind him just a few short days before.

He held a length of leather rein idly in his hand and looked at the woman who was his future.

She was beautiful.

The daylight pulled the fire from her hair, and sparkled from the tears that still moistened her eyes. Her nose was a bit red, her clothing disreputable, she was sniffling, and Peter knew he didn't want to spend another day of his life without her.

She struggled to reach the saddle straps. It was time.

"Need a hand?"

Freddie jumped a foot into the air. "Peter? What the devil are you doing here?"

Peter grinned. For a smart woman she could be remarkably stupid on occasion. "Apparently you're planning on a morning ride. I knew you'd like some company."

Freddie frowned. "No thank you."

"Really?"

"Yes. Really. Peter...no games. You know I have to leave."

"Well in that case you probably need some help with the tack." He moved towards her, rein in his hands, and she stepped back expecting him to lift the saddle from the rail of the stall.

She was not expecting him to grab her wrists and loop the leather around them in one swift move. She gasped.

"Now, Freddie. I think it's time you and I had a little chat."

Peter pulled her away from the horse and into the shadows at the rear of the barn. He could hear her swallow noisily in the silence, the nickering of the horses and the sounds of the hens outside a soft accompaniment to their movements.

Her bonds were secure, and although she tugged, she could not free herself and was helpless to do anything but follow where he was taking her. She stumbled behind him and he slowed, but refused to let go of her bound wrists.

"Peter...what are you doing? Peter...damn you, let me go." Her voice was harsh, no begging or pleading, just a firm demand for her freedom. The one thing he had no intention of ever giving her.

He reached the back wall and with a quick twist he turned her, raised her arms above her head and hooked the leather over a protruding nail.

She was secured tight, back against the rough planks, almost on tiptoe and ready to spit fire at him.

"This is...this is outrageous. Untie me this instant."

Her green eyes flashed temper, her words came out on a hiss, and her breasts rose and fell as she struggled to contain her anger.

"No."

Her mouth snapped shut and she blinked.

"I'm not untying you until we've had a small chat about things like our future together, and how it is that you're leaving me even though you're in love with me."

Freddie's eyes narrowed. "I don't know where you got that idea from, but you're quite wrong."

Peter leaned down and avoided a kick, tugging her worn leather shoes from her feet.

"Oh really?" He drawled the word as he slipped the other shoe off. Such delicate toes, and he could see them twitch as she fought her bonds.

"Yes really."

He heard her gasp as she squirmed away from his searching hands. He'd freed her breeches and her wriggles sent them into a pile around her feet.

He stepped back and looked at her, a writhing mass of temper and passion, naked legs gleaming. Her shirt barely hid her nipples and he smiled as they grew hard beneath his gaze.

"Freddie? You're a terrible liar."

Chapter 13

What the blazes was he doing?

Freddie's mind spun out of control leaving her in her shirt and her temper as Peter slid her garments away from her. The...*bastard*. How dare he expose her like this? It wasn't her body she was worried about, either. It was her heart.

She narrowed her eyes, trying to read his expression. His face gave nothing away but his eyes were heated as they traveled up her naked limbs and over her breasts to her face.

Freddie raised her chin. "This is futile, Peter. Face reality. I'm just about as close to a whore as a woman can get without actually being one. I've worked as a field hand. I've been another man's mistress. I've shared your bed, also without benefit of marriage. I'm completely unsuitable as any man's wife. You know it, and I know it. Now let me go, damn you..."

She tugged again on her arms, vainly trying to free herself.

Peter sighed and stripped off his own clothes. Freddie's eyes widened as he revealed himself, cock erect and reddened, and casually tossed his breeches onto the growing pile of garments at his side.

"Peter?"

"It seems that you and I need to reach an understanding, Freddie." He stepped close to her, and his heat flowed across the space between them.

His hands slid under her shirt and cupped her breasts.

"You love me."

She shook her head in denial, but words of contradiction caught in her throat as his fingers found her nipples and toyed with them. Damnation. Her body was betraying her as hot moisture gathered between her thighs.

"Yes you do. You may be saying 'no' with your lips..." He brushed his own against hers, holding her chin with one hand when she tried to duck aside. "But your body and your heart know the truth."

He grabbed her shirt and ripped it apart, glancing down at her breasts and then crushing them with his flesh. She was neatly sandwiched between the hard wall of the barn and the even harder wall of Peter's chest.

"We fit, Freddie. Our bodies, our souls. You are *mine.*"

His cock rammed into her soft belly, searing it with heat and desire.

"Peter," she moaned.

His hands slid behind her, cupping her buttocks and raising her so that he could rub himself across her mound and find her clit.

"Open your legs."

She shook her head and pinched her eyes tight shut. She wouldn't—she *couldn't*—let this happen. She had to fight it, and him.

But he refused to allow her to avoid him.

He licked her lips and without conscious thought she parted them. He was inside before she could breathe.

They were sealed together, fused by some mutual desire that went beyond the physical into realms of need that stunned Freddie to her toes.

She struggled against her bonds, longing to hold him even closer, to touch him and pull him inside her heart. But he ignored her silent pleas.

He rubbed his chest roughly against her nipples, bringing a growl of pleasure and arousal to her throat. His fingers clamped onto her buttocks, pulling them slightly apart and adding to the tension that was making her shudder.

"Open your legs." It was a command she could no longer refuse, since she was fast losing control over her mind and surrendering to Peter's seduction.

As soon as she slid her thighs apart, Peter was there. Lifting her even more, his hips pushed into her warmth and his cock sought entrance.

Without even thinking twice, Freddie raised her leg, twining it around the back of his and opening herself to him. She wanted him, desired him, loved him and needed him inside her so badly she would surely die if it didn't happen within the next two seconds.

The rough wood at her back chafed at the shirt that still covered her, but all she could feel was her hot honey flowing, her cunt aching and empty and her body screaming for its mate.

"Jesus God," she sobbed, as Peter's cock brushed her clit.

"Look at me Freddie. I want to see your eyes as I take you."

Peter's voice was rough, his hands hard on her soft flesh. Reluctantly, she obeyed him.

In the soft morning light, his eyes blazed at her. Passion, heat, desire…all mingled in the whiskey-brown depths that met her gaze.

He took her weight fully with his hands and raised her even more.

The expression in his eyes changed as his cock slid into her welcoming cunt. The passion mixed with warmth, the heat flared and the desire bloomed into something…something *more*.

At that moment she knew the truth.

He loved her!

* * * * *

Peter slipped into Freddie's body and knew he was home. This was where his cock and his heart belonged. There would be no more gallivanting across continents, no more quick seductions, and no more lighthearted conquests.

This woman encompassed his cock with a grip of iron, and she probably didn't realize she was encompassing his heart as well.

He began to move. "Yesss, Freddie," he groaned.

She sobbed out his name on a breath and let him hold her as she slid her other leg around his back. Having her at his mercy like this was intensely arousing, and Peter knew he couldn't hold back for long, not while she clamped down on his cock with a cunt that blazed hotter than the sun.

He did his best to cushion her from the wall, but his hips pressed hard against her as his rhythm increased and his arousal grew intense, almost to the point of pain.

He slammed into her, trying to drive his soul into her. To make her understand what they had together. And how he would never want anyone else. Ever.

Their gasps mingled as he took her, harshly, roughly and with every ounce of desire he'd ever possessed.

His skin abraded hers, her nipples dug into his chest, and he did his best to make sure he hit her clit with every single thrust of his hips. He wanted her to come with him, but damned if he could hold back.

His technique was raw, and he felt more naked and vulnerable than he'd ever been with a woman in his life. The sounds of their loving echoed through the quiet barn, and the scent of Freddie's body mingled with those of fresh hay and horses.

Peter's heart soared as his spine tightened and his balls knotted at the entrance to Freddie's body.

She was sobbing in time with his thrusting, locking her ankles behind his back and pulling him so far inside her cunt that he wondered if he'd drown inside her. He didn't mind. He wanted to.

Her thighs began to tremble and her breath to come in whimpers. Fuck it, she was as close as he was to that special moment.

Peter let go. He rammed his cock deeply into her, deeper than he'd ever gone before, and heard her cry of joy as her spasms began.

She came apart around him and he felt himself erupt into her sweet body. Again and again he thrust, spurting deep inside her, drawn on by the inner massage her cunt was giving his cock.

She trembled and cried out his name, a sweet sound of longing and passion, and together they rode out the orgasm they shared like a tandem team of high-stepping horses. Each move was timed to give the other maximum pleasure, and Peter found himself sobbing for air as his balls emptied, his skin turned to fire and lights danced in front of his eyes.

He blinked, trying to watch Freddie as she came. The green eyes were glazed and unfocused and she shuddered and shivered in his arms.

Finally, their bodies eased.

Peter let her legs slide down his thighs, holding her tight to him still, and willing his cock to stay inside her. He didn't want to leave her. Ever.

He rested his forehead against hers.

"I love you, Freddie."

She closed her eyes and fought for breath. "I love you too."

✻ ✻ ✻ ✻ ✻

Five days later, London

The dark head looked up at the butler's entrance.

"Your pardon, my Lord."

Viktor put down his pen and leaned back in his chair. "What is it, Matthews?"

"You have guests, my Lord."

"At this hour?" Viktor raised an eyebrow. It was past midnight, and the quiet Mayfair neighborhood wouldn't see the influx of carriages returning from the evening's entertainment until several hours later.

Viktor and Madelyne had chosen to remain at home this evening. The Count and Countess Karoly had taken the Ton by storm, but were not eager to parade themselves before prying eyes, much preferring their privacy instead.

Viktor knew they were but a nine-day wonder, and hoped the nine days would be up *very* soon.

"Lord and Lady Chalmers to see you, my Lord."

Viktor frowned. He couldn't place the name at all.

Suddenly, an unmistakable sound filled the house. Wild violin music echoed over the marble foyer and filtered into Viktor's study.

"Damn. *Pyotr...*"

Viktor nearly tipped over his chair in his rush to get to the door.

"Pyotr...*Pyotr...*"

There in the hallway with a wicked grin on his face, was Pyotr, a violin in his hand and a woman by his side. "May we come in, Viktor?"

Viktor strode to Pyotr and enfolded him in a strong embrace. "*Szervusz*, Pyotr. As if you need ask, my friend."

With a huge grin, Viktor led Pyotr into the study, noting that the woman followed. There was certainly a story here.

112

"You are well?"

Pyotr smiled back. "I am indeed. And you?"

A knock on the door drew their attention.

"I heard the music. I couldn't resist." A blonde head with an impish grin peeked around at them.

"Madelyne, *kedves*, come in...come...it's Pyotr and...?" Viktor raised a polite eyebrow at Peter's companion.

Peter cleared his throat and colored slightly. "Well, actually..." He leaned over and grasped the woman's hand. "This is my wife."

Viktor's grin grew even larger and he threw an arm around Madelyne's shoulders. "Well now, it would seem we've been of like minds, friend Pyotr. This is *my* wife."

There was a moment of silence followed by the rich laughter of the two men.

It took no time at all for formalities to be discarded, and for all four to find themselves seated around the fire exchanging stories.

Freddie and Madelyne had found kindred spirits, and were soon chatting away as if they'd known each other all their lives.

Viktor leaned back with a contented grin and glanced over at Pyotr.

"So, Pyotr. Or I should say, *Peter*. Will you now shed your music for your duties?"

Peter grimaced. "I have no choice, unfortunately. I must claim the title, but I have no wish to remove Mark and his family from the country. I'm of a mind to take the Chalmers town house. My wife and I..."

Viktor stifled a smile at the pride in those words. The delightful redhead had certainly captured Peter's heart.

"My wife and I have a few ideas for some things we'd like to do."

Viktor raised an eyebrow in question.

"There's a need for places where those who seek refuge can be safe."

Freddie broke off her conversation with Madelyne to slip her hand into Peter's. "I want to make a sanctuary, Viktor. Somewhere where anyone, but women especially, can find food and shelter while they sort out their lives."

Peter nodded. "Here in London, there is a great need for it too. Can you imagine how many women find themselves at a loss, released from their positions and penniless? There are few alternatives but to take to the streets in order to survive. That is *wrong*, Viktor."

Madelyne nodded her agreement. "Truly, such a place would have helped me. There were many times I would have fled my father's brutality, but having no money and nowhere to go prevented me. As he well knew."

Her mouth curved in distaste at the memory, but softened as Viktor dropped a kiss on her hand.

"It's not unlike what we did on the Continent, Viktor. Helping those too poor or too fragile to help themselves."

"And we have so much..." said Freddie quietly. "We're the lucky ones."

There was a moment of silence as the truth of Freddie's words sank home to everyone seated by the warmth of the fire.

"Speaking of lucky ones," said Peter, "Do you have any idea where the others are?"

Viktor shook his head. "Not a clue. I heard from Fabyan...he is in London. I do expect him soon. But as for Gyorgy, Lukasz and Matyas..." He shrugged.

"They'll turn up. They always do." Peter laughed.

"Without a doubt." Viktor paused and stared absently at the ring on his wife's hand. "I could certainly use them, however. There is a visit I plan on paying shortly."

Peter's eyes narrowed. "I recognize that tone."

"I have a personal debt to settle."

"Viktor, no..." Madelyne paled.

"Your father needs to be taught a lesson or two, love. And Francis Hucknall is a piece of filth that should be sluiced from London's streets."

"I'm with you, Viktor." Peter's tone was firm.

"And I." Freddie's chin rose slightly. "I dislike vermin."

Madelyne couldn't help laughing. "Well, damnation. If you three think we can do it, I don't mind saying I'd like to settle a few old scores myself."

"Oh we can do it, love," smiled Viktor. "Our years in France taught us exactly how to plot out various schemes and work together to achieve a common goal. Back then it might have been life and death…"

His voice dropped slightly and Madelyne's hand squeezed his. He knew she was remembering his tale of imprisonment and torture. Sometimes he wondered if he should have told her, but some secrets were better shared. She'd kissed his scars and proceeded to fuck him into limp and sated bliss. Yes, sharing had certainly eased his pain. And a few other things too.

"Now we have only our own goals to worry about."

"And quite a relief that is too. I'm not sure if we could actually spirit a dozen people around London as easily as we did the French countryside." Peter's words sparked some memories and he and Viktor kept the women laughing for the next few hours as their stories of life in Napoleonic France grew more and more unlikely.

"Enough, you two," scolded Madelyne at last. "You are stretching the truth to a point where I can hear it screaming for mercy."

"They are shameless frauds, Madelyne," chuckled Freddie.

"We'll remember more tomorrow." Peter waggled his eyebrows at his wife.

They stood, and as a discussion was held on the subject of rooms and schedules, Peter neared Viktor and spoke quietly.

"I'll stand by you in this business with Eventyde, you know that. Any ideas on how to handle it?"

Viktor leaned closer to Peter and nodded at their wives. "Preferably without those two if we can manage it. I have some thoughts…it may take a few days or so to pull it all together."

Peter nodded, eyes on the women. "Agreed. And by God, having Gyorgy along would be a help as well. I wonder what *he's* up to?"

* * * * *

What Gyorgy was actually *up* to at the moment his friends in London were pondering his whereabouts, was his armpits. In bathwater. It had not originally reached so high around his body, but the addition of the luscious wench who had so readily clambered in to wash his back had inevitably resulted in a rising of the water level, and now there was quite a bit of oversplash.

"Ooh, Georgie. Such a lovely cock you've got, love."

Gyorgy winced. Jenny was certainly enthusiastic, but clearly her hearing wasn't all it could be. He'd pronounced his name quite clearly, several times, but to no avail. He was "Georgie".

He really disliked that.

For a second or two he wondered what the hell he'd been thinking, inviting her into the tub. Then she slithered her breasts and the rest of her around him and without further ado sank down onto his cock.

Aaah. Yes. *That's* what he'd been thinking.

Jenny moved and rubbed her ample body against his, squishing herself closer and riding him. Heedless of the sudsy tide swamping the sides of the tub, Gyorgy thrust upwards and accepted the nipple that was flying around his face.

He sucked hard and heard her gasp, enjoying her pleasure with her. He slid his hands behind her and helped her rise and fall on his cock, the water adding to their sensations.

Her breasts were pendulous and full, and her arse overflowed his grasp.

This was just how he liked his bedmates. Buxom, enthusiastic and hot. Jenny fulfilled all three requirements, and within moments she was shuddering around him and screaming out her orgasm.

"*Geeeoooorrrggiiieeeeee...*"

This time, Gyorgy's expression was one of pleasure. What the fuck did it matter what she called him? As long as he could empty his balls into a willing cunt, had money to burn, and no obligations, his life was good.

Gyorgy spent himself with a sigh of relief, feeling Jenny milk his seed with her body.

Yes, the simple life was good. Very good indeed.

Chapter 14
Gyorgy's Games

The small country fair was in full swing by the time Gyorgy wandered into the town square. Tables were groaning under the force of the local produce, pies and other delicacies were disappearing at a rapid rate, and children were running everywhere shrieking with laughter.

Gyorgy spared a moment to just enjoy the sight. Such happiness, such pleasure...no fear or terror lurking just beyond the next hill. He blinked as he realized that it had been a while since he'd actually felt this relaxed.

The time he'd spent in France with his fellows had scarred him. Not physically, like some of the others, but mentally. He'd become used to keeping his sixth sense alert for the presence of danger, to calculating the most effective escape route should one be needed within seconds, and to observe the eyes of everyone around him.

It was all in the eyes, he'd discovered. A slight shift, a dilation of the pupils...there was something in a person's eyes that would give their thoughts away. To him, at least. It had helped him avoid disaster several times in the past.

But now, refreshed by a good night's sleep, *and* the previous evening's activities with his buxom bedmate, Gyorgy was content.

He was in England, where life was relatively tranquil. Where the people managed to eat and live and love without the horrors of war hanging over their heads. There were troubles, of course, but death and savagery seemed a long way away from this rural tableau.

He was making his leisurely way to London, where he knew he'd find his friends. There was no hurry. As if by mutual consent, they'd split up—each wandering where the wind blew them as they journeyed towards some inner peace. The green and pleasant countryside eased their troubled minds and the occasional nightmares that had accompanied them. Even while enthralling London society with their music, the tension had still possessed them, almost as if by being together they were still functioning as a unit.

Now—alone—it was time to let go.

Gyorgy breathed in the soft air, redolent with the scents of the fair, and turned as a loud cheer bellowed from a crowd at one end of the square. He strolled over, ignoring the sizeable number of female heads that turned and watched as he passed.

An impromptu archery contest had been set up on the village green. Gyorgy's interest was sparked. Although no marksman with a bow, he had other talents. And a nearby table held a number of interesting looking items.

He stood quietly and watched as a local lad with a sharp eye notched his arrow into his bowstring, took aim, and plugged the bull's-eye with quite amazing accuracy. Gyorgy joined in the applause with enthusiasm, laughing at the boy's embarrassment as his mother hugged him with pride.

A couple of older men approached the table and picked up the dueling pistols, which lay ready. With much chaffing and teasing, they challenged each other, loaded the pieces and waited for the targets to be set up. Bets were placed, noisily and often quite rudely, to the amusement of the crowd.

The pistols were old and had clearly seen better days, but Gyorgy was pleased to see that both men were accurate marksmen, taking their time with their aim and enjoying the cries from the ladies as their guns exploded loudly into the sunshine.

Here were two men who probably could provide plenty of meat for the winters ahead. *Fuck*. He was still having thoughts like that, even surrounded by merrymakers in rural England.

A soft murmur in the crowd caught his sharp ears. Nothing more than the swish of skirts—perhaps a greeting or two—but it was enough.

Senses on alert, Gyorgy turned.

A woman was approaching the crowd, which respectfully gave way before her. She was not tall, but carried herself like a queen, elegantly and proudly, with a slight smile curving her beautiful lips.

Her gown was simple, blue silk possibly, trimmed with a little lace. It wasn't ostentatious, but she wore it like it was a robe of ermine.

Gyorgy couldn't see her eyes since they were shaded by the brim of her large straw bonnet. He leaned to a man by his side. "Excuse me, friend. Can you tell me…who is *she*?"

The man glanced over. "Ah. She's come then. Didn't know if she would."

The man's words made Gyorgy's mind veer off into surprising paths. *I could make her come.* He blinked, astonished at the bolt of lust spreading even now from his crotch through his body.

He hadn't even gotten a good look at her face.

"That's the Dowager Duchess."

"Doesn't look like any Dowager I've ever seen," said Gyorgy quietly.

"Oh she's…" The man paused and took a closer look at Gyorgy. Reassured by his gentle smile, he continued. "She's the widow of the old Duke. *Real* old he were when he married her. They say she broke hearts right and left in Lunnon after the old coot kicked the bucket. Had to come down here after some scandal or other. Dunno what. Never did hear much more 'bout it. They called her the 'Meddy-something-or-t'other'."

"Medici?"

"Nah. One of them goddess folks. The one with snaky hair or summat."

"Medusa?" Gyorgy raised an eyebrow.

"Yep. That's it. You got it. Smart lad." The old man grinned and treated Gyorgy to a flash of the one remaining tooth in his gums. "Don't care what they called her. Down here she's been right nice to us all, helping them as needs it, quietly going 'bout her business. We takes folks as we find 'em round these parts."

Gyorgy thought about this as the woman moved through the crowd, nodding and exchanging a few words here and there. A tilt of her head brought the sunshine onto her face and Gyorgy's breath caught in his throat.

This was why they called her "Medusa".

Limpid blue eyes swept his. Not a lick of any other color marred their depths. The purest blue he could ever remember seeing. Eyes so clear they could have been painted on a china doll. Her pupils were dark, but they only served to heighten the impact of the delicate tint to her irises. Her gaze passed on, veiled once more by her eyelashes and the shadows of her bonnet.

They were completely expressionless.

For once, Gyorgy found himself at a loss. His much-vaunted sixth sense was useless. He couldn't read this woman. Couldn't tell from that one glance if she was friend or foe. She could have been either. Or more.

She could have fucked him to the edge of madness or stuck a knife in his throat. He had a feeling her eyes would not have changed whichever course of action she followed.

Gyorgy was intrigued.

"She likes them contests." The old man nudged Gyorgy with a sharp elbow. "Last year we had a couple of gents fencing with swords. Real good at it they were. She gave a prize to the winner."

"Really." He kept his eyes on the Dowager Duchess.

"Yup. An' the year before that it was wrestling. *That* was summat to see, lad." He grinned. "Them lads stripped to their breeches, gruntin' and sweatin'—seemed to like it a lot, she did."

"Hmmm." Gyorgy glanced at the table. "And this year?"

"Dunno yet. Although by the looks of it..."

Both men stared at the long whips coiled neatly and resting alone now on the scarred wood.

A wicked little grin curved Gyorgy's lips. Perhaps it was time for him to play a game. And perhaps win himself a prize.

✳ ✳ ✳ ✳ ✳

The object was simple. Strike as close to the target with the end of the whip as possible.

The target, in this case, had been fixed to a bale of hay, at a distance paced out by the knowledgeable and cheered by the onlookers. A brightly colored ribbon now fluttered a little in the summer breeze, and several men were waiting to try their luck.

One was a farmer, two were coachmen, one a local lad who claimed to be able to take a fly off the ear of a pig without a second thought, and at the end of the line—Gyorgy.

The Dowager had taken up a position off to one side, flanked by her servant and maid. She'd refused the offer of a chair with a smile, and simply stood enjoying the day with the rest of the crowd.

But she was definitely not one of the crowd. Not to Gyorgy anyway. He found himself aware of her every move. Without staring at her, he could detect the smallest flutter of her gown or gesture of her hand. As if some small window in his mind had opened and a portion of his brain was leaning out. Watching her.

The contestants slowly dwindled down, doing their best to flick the long leather thong at the ribbon. The farmer came close, but did no better than a puff of hay. One of the coachmen achieved a respectable crack before aiming, to the delight of the crowd, but could come no closer than the first entrant.

The second coachman was more accurate, making the ribbon shake and shudder as he caught one flying tail.

The local lad was also very close, bringing a gasp and a shout of encouragement to the lips of his supporters.

Then it was Gyorgy's turn.

He picked up the whip and turned it in his hand, feeling for its balance and weight. The braided leather was smooth beneath his fingers and the tail bore marks of years of use. It was a fine whip and would serve his purpose well. Not as well as his own would have done, but no matter.

He smiled as the judge butchered his name. "Mr. Georgie Varguss." His Vargas ancestors were probably rolling in their graves.

With a slight movement he flicked the whip and tested it, allowing the tip to crack softly. It was a trick he'd perfected as a boy...letting those watching know he was familiar with the instrument, and yet revealing nothing of his skill.

The crowd had fallen quiet, struck perhaps by the tall stranger in their midst, handling the whip so comfortably.

Gyorgy focused on the ribbon, knowing all the while that a pair of blue eyes were now focused on him.

One side of his mouth curved up as he drew his arm back, and with a deft move swept it unerringly towards its target.

The ribbon fluttered free and fell to the ground.

There was dead silence for a second, and then a lusty cheer broke free.

"Did you see that?"

"Gor blimey, the man's good with that thing..."

"Well, I never..."

The judge slapped Gyorgy on the back with a hand the size of a ham and nearly knocked him over. "Well done, lad, well done." He turned to the crowd. "We have our winner," he shouted.

Applause followed his words and Gyorgy was surrounded by smiling faces, complimenting him on his skill.

He demurred. "A simple trick, no more. Your lads were equally skilled."

"A trick, sir?"

The voice was cool, the tone polite. She stood a short distance away, a little smile playing around her lips. "'Twould seem you excel at such tricks."

Gyorgy bowed. "Gyorgy Vargas at your service, Ma'am."

She nodded in acknowledgement. "I would like to see some more of your...tricks."

I'd love to show you. But you'll have to strip off that gown.

Hushing his inner thoughts, Gyorgy raised an eyebrow at her. "What would you have me do, Ma'am?"

She allowed her smile to widen. "Perhaps..."

She strolled towards the hay bale under the watchful gaze of the crowd, and pulled a small handkerchief from her sleeve. She waved it to one side of her body.

"Perhaps you could hit this, sir?"

The crowd gasped. "My Lady, you should not..." said one woman.

"Oh, I think Mr. Vargas can accomplish such a simple...trick?"

Gyorgy rose to the challenge. Other parts of Gyorgy threatened to rise as well at the sight of her standing with an arm outstretched and breasts thrusting against the blue silk gown.

He quenched the inner demons and nodded. "Please extend your arm, Ma'am, and remain still."

Without a second glance, she did as she was bid.

Even the birds held their breath, and not a sound came from the assembled villagers.

Gyorgy sighted on the fluttering cloth and flicked his whip. With a small crack it connected with her handkerchief and tugged it free of her hand. With a touch of showmanship, Gyorgy allowed the thong to circle upwards after his stroke, releasing the lace and dropping it into his outstretched hand..

He caught it, and casually strolled towards her. "Your handkerchief, Ma'am."

The crowd roared.

For a split second, Gyorgy saw something flicker behind those tranquil blue eyes. And it shot right to his groin.

Then the expression was gone, and the polite smile had taken its place. "My congratulations, sir. You are indeed most skilled."

And you may think you have ice blood in your veins, but I know better.

Without thinking, Gyorgy looped the whip and tucked it into his pocket. It was an action so natural to him that it passed unnoticed.

"I am the Dowager Duchess Kirkwood, as you may have been informed. Should you ever be passing, you may be assured of a welcome at my home." She nodded at a house barely visible over the treetops. "I thank you for an interesting afternoon's entertainment."

Within seconds she was gone, surrounded by villagers, children and her servants. Gyorgy was the immediate recipient of a great many compliments, slaps on the back and laughter.

The chaos and confusion separated them, and Gyorgy bit down hard on the urge to go after the Dowager.

There was unfinished business between them. He'd never been so sure of anything in his life.

Chapter 15

The shadows were lengthening as the fair wound to a close, and the country folk began the tedious process of clearing away the remaining mess.

Gyorgy had watched the Duchess throughout the afternoon, but had been unable to get near enough to exchange any conversation with her, and now his teeth were aching with the need to pursue this intriguing woman.

He'd carefully observed her release her servants to enjoy themselves at the fair, he'd seen her retie a bow in a small girl's hair, and he'd enjoyed a quiet laugh as she'd sampled the local cider and found it a little harsh for her tastes.

It was plain to see that she'd found a home in the hearts of these simple country folk, and Gyorgy wondered yet again what had driven such a beauty away from the gaieties of London and into this rural tranquility. She was a puzzle, a conundrum, and one that was slowly driving him insane.

Gyorgy was suffering from a major case of lust. It wasn't the first time, and he doubted it would be the last. But something about this smoothly unattainable woman had lodged itself into his balls and was irritating them. Of *course* he wanted her. He wouldn't be any kind of a man at all if he didn't.

But it went deeper than a need to sink into her cunt and explode there. He wanted to make *her* explode.

To bring an assortment of expressions to those eyes of hers. To light a few fires inside her and make her scream and writhe as he plunged deep within her body. To make her *feel*.

As the fair ended, he got his chance.

Quietly and unobtrusively, the Dowager Duchess left the field, heading for the trees and a small path that presumably led to her home.

Glancing around him, Gyorgy saw the villagers busy with their chores, and in an instant he'd followed her, silently letting the shadows hide his passage.

The path led into the forest, past a tumble of undergrowth, the occasional stalk of foxglove and a mass of ferns. It was quiet after the noise of the afternoon, and the flattened grass beneath his feet hushed Gyorgy's steps.

It was no hardship for him to pursue her, since he'd been trailing far more dangerous people through forests similar to this one for years. Blending in with his surroundings was second nature to him.

But this time, his prey was of a different nature, and he saw no need to conceal himself.

It seemed that she too had her own set of senses on alert. She stopped in a small clearing, and turned slowly.

Gyorgy stood still. There was no point in trying to hide. He wasn't there to hurt her or frighten her.

"You are following me." It was a statement only. There was no fear or interrogation in her voice, no query as to why. A simple arrangement of words served up like a meal on a cold white plate.

"I wished to ensure you reach your home in safety."

She stared at him, unblinking for a moment. "There is no danger to me here. I appreciate your thoughtfulness, but it is unnecessary."

"And I disagree." Gyorgy watched her, still unable to read her eyes, and cursing inwardly.

She merely nodded. A tip of her bonnet. Then she turned away.

"One moment, Madam." Gyorgy's voice rang out and she halted at the tone of command.

He'd reached for the whip without thinking about it, and it rested in his hand like a long lost friend. "We have not quite finished our demonstration of my...tricks."

The Duchess remained motionless. "I believe the exhibition is at an end, Sir." Her back was to him, and her voice calm.

"Not...quite...yet..." Gyorgy flicked his whip

With delicate and yet perfect accuracy, Gyorgy sliced through the laces at the top of her gown.

It sagged a little, and yet she did not move. "Another of your tricks, Sir?"

The whip flicked again, severing the middle laces. The gown was now perilously near to falling off her shoulders.

"I have more. Would you care to see them?"

Slowly, very slowly, the Duchess turned to face him. She allowed one hand to steady her gown, which clung loosely to the curves of her breasts. Gyorgy walked towards her, coiling the whip back on itself and tucking it away.

Her face was shadowed now as the light faded, and again Gyorgy felt he caught a glimpse of something…something heated in her gaze.

"Who *are* you?" The question fell from her lips with more than a casual sound.

"Gyorgy Vargas. Gypsy violinist. Traveler."

"And skilled with a whip."

"Among other things."

"I have heard of six Gypsies taking London by storm." She tilted her head to one side. "You?"

"And my friends, yes. We have temporarily separated, to meet again soon in London."

"So you are simply journeying through the countryside? For amusement?" One eyebrow rose delicately.

"For peace, Ma'am. To find a measure of relaxation impossible elsewhere. To see a land prosper for once. To see children that do not starve, and families that thrive without the shadow of war over their homes."

She nodded. "I understand."

Oddly, Gyorgy believed she did.

"And do women figure into your adventures, Sir?"

"Undoubtedly."

She raised her chin and met his eyes squarely. "Then I have a proposition for you, Mr. Gyorgy Vargas, Gypsy musician."

Even holding her dress to her breasts, she was every inch the queen. Gyorgy drew in a breath. "I am yours to command."

"One night."

Gyorgy blinked. "I beg your pardon?"

* * * * *

She fought an inner battle with herself and lost.

"My name is Marie-Claire Devereaux, Dowager Duchess of Kirkwood. I am twenty-five years old. I have lived a strange life which has brought me here..." She waved her hand idly at the forest that surrounded them.

"For the past couple of years, I have been without...male companionship. In truth I have desired none."

His eyes had darkened at her words, and he'd neared her. *Not too close. Not yet.*

"And now?" The words were a caress in themselves, and Marie-Claire fought yet another battle against the sensation.

"Now I see before me a man who might fulfill my...needs. A man with whom I believe I could find some pleasure."

He raised his hand and gently eased her gown back up to her shoulders. "Only for one night?"

"Only for one night." On this she would be adamant.

"And your needs?"

Her teeth bit down on the soft skin inside her mouth. Now was the moment that would reveal if he was truly the man she thought she'd seen.

"You may—bring your whip."

He didn't betray surprise by so much as the flicker of an eyelash. "Very well. Anything else?"

Damn, he was as cool and collected as she herself. Truly this man was a good choice. "I have everything else we may need."

The forest was quiet, and for a moment Marie-Claire thought she could hear the pounding of his heart.

She did hear the rustle of his clothing as he offered her his arm. "One night, Madam. One night of pleasure—my whip—and me."

"You may call me Marie-Claire." She placed her fingertips onto the sleeve of his jacket and allowed him to escort her up the darkening path to her home.

The silence that fell between them lasted until he followed her over the threshold of Kirkwood House.

"Welcome to my home, Mr. Vargas. I shall have a meal prepared for us."

He smiled. Dear God, such a smile. "I doubt that the hunger I feel will be assuaged by food...Marie-Claire..." He leaned towards her as he spoke her name softly, and she breathed in, scenting woodsmoke, leather and a musky hint of man. "And my name is Gyorgy."

She licked her lips, noting how his eyes followed the movement of her tongue. She swallowed down the flood of desire that cascaded over her. "In that case, I have some brandy in my suite. If you would follow me?"

The staircase was elegant, the house quiet, and her servants unobtrusive. All this was as she liked it, and yet tonight she was aware of none of it. Her senses were focused on the man slightly behind her.

They'd been focused on him from the moment she'd seen him.

A head taller than the villagers, he'd stood out from the crowd, his black hair shining, his near-black eyes alight with laughter, and his body lithe and well-muscled. He was clearly a stranger, and yet had managed to blend in with his fellows, not an easy task with village folk.

And when he'd picked up that whip...Marie-Claire had felt a shiver all the way down to her toes. Her instincts had screamed at her that here was a man who could chip away some of the ice that had formed around her soul. A man who might be able to ease her body and warm her heart.

For once, here might be a man who could understand the relationship between pleasure and pain.

She was about to find out.

✳ ✳ ✳ ✳ ✳

While Marie-Claire excused herself and slipped into her bedroom, Gyorgy poured brandy into two crystal snifters and strolled around the adjoining sitting room.

A large vase of flowers stood in the empty fireplace, and long windows had been opened to admit the summer breezes. It was a charming room, with all the right pieces of furniture. A small table and two chairs next to the hearth, an elegant writing desk, and a long chaise for when Milady required a rest.

And yet—it was amazingly impersonal. The few paintings on the walls were of landscapes, there were no miniatures or family portraits. No pile of unanswered letters rested untidily on the desk and no books lay half-read next to the couch.

All the hallmarks of an elegant lady's rooms were present, but there was nothing of the lady herself. Perhaps she saved those things for the privacy of her bedroom. Gyorgy couldn't wait to find out.

A slight sound behind him made him turn.

She stood quietly, dressed now in a simple white robe. She'd loosened her hair, and it fell in soft waves of warm brown across her shoulders and over her breasts. It made her look more vulnerable and younger, until he looked into her eyes.

Those blue depths studied him, assessing him perhaps, and still not betraying a single flicker of her true thoughts.

"Does the brandy meet with your approval?" Her voice was gentle and correct, but for the first time Gyorgy detected a slight touch of an accent.

"Indeed. A very fine vintage. I poured you a little..." He extended his arm and offered her the second glass.

She accepted it and their hands brushed lightly, surprising Gyorgy as warm fingers touched his flesh. For some reason he'd expected her to be chilled.

"May we sit for a moment and enjoy our brandy?" He needed to pull himself together. To sound out this intriguing woman. To arouse her, perhaps, push her a little. To see exactly where this night would lead. Besides her bed, of course. Gyorgy knew without a doubt they'd end up in there.

"Of course." Marie-Claire moved to the couch. She seemed a little taken aback when Gyorgy took one of the chairs instead of sitting beside her.

Good. It was beginning.

"I detect a slight accent, Marie-Claire. Along with your name, I might deduce you are originally from France?"

She dropped her gaze to her glass. "You would be correct in that deduction. I was born in France."

"Ah." Gyorgy did some rapid mental calculations. Given her age, that would have put her in the middle of some pretty nasty goings-on. "You were fortunate to escape."

Her eyes flashed to his. "I was indeed."

"How old were you?" *Damn.* She was giving him nothing. Just polite responses.

"A child. Just a child." She sipped the brandy. "I was lucky that relatives here in England were willing to take me in."

"Yes. That was lucky." He too sipped politely. "And so you married?"

"If you can call it that."

Aha. A flicker of some emotion had crossed her serene face. It was gone in an instant, but Gyorgy had caught it. "It was not a happy union?"

She raised one eyebrow as if to rebuke his personal question.

"Forgive my prying, Marie-Claire. But if we are to enjoy our night together, it will help me to know the extent of your...experience. Your likes, your dislikes...something of your past perhaps."

She exhaled slowly, a little less than a sigh, but more than a breath. "Very well." She placed her glass down on a small table and folded her hands together. "I was married at seventeen to the Duke of Kirkwood. He was sixty-seven. It was, I need not add, an arranged match with the sole aim of producing a direct heir. In that, it failed. Within the year he'd passed away from a lingering illness. Since then, I have been relegated to the position of Dowager Duchess, I have been granted possession of Kirkwood House by the present Duke, and I have taken several lovers."

Gyorgy blinked. "And yet you remain here without a man?"

"It is my choice." She allowed a small smile to curve her lips. "The lovers I took were, by and large, uninteresting. They satisfied my curiosity, but little else. Only one...fired my enthusiasm for his company."

Gyorgy allowed his expression to ask the question. This was an oddly civilized conversation to be having about a very uncivilized topic.

"He was shot and killed in a duel over my favors. Ironically I would not have accepted the other man as a lover, but he seemed to think otherwise. From that point on, it seemed better to remove myself from London. It was a decision I have not regretted."

"And yet you have invited me here for tonight..."

"Yes. I have. A whim, perhaps? A chance notion that you might be interested?"

"I wouldn't be here if I wasn't." Gyorgy fought to keep the growl out of his voice. To sit across from this incredible woman and discuss her sexual history was both bizarre and arousing.

She reached for her brandy glass once more, and sniffed the fragrance, allowing her small smile to creep back across her lips. "Good."

"And your likes and dislikes, Marie-Claire. Tell me. Tell me how that one lover of yours 'fired your enthusiasm'..."

It was her turn to blink, and Gyorgy watched the skin of her throat move as she swallowed her brandy. Blue eyes rose to meet his, calm as ever.

"I find I respond well to a man who takes what he wants."

Gyorgy's cock stirred at the images her words produced in his mind.

"I respond to a man who is unafraid to make a woman obey his bidding. A man who demands that a woman feel..." She hesitated.

"Feel what, Marie-Claire?"

For a moment, a look of uncertainty crossed her face. "Feel..."

Gyorgy sensed she was seeking the right words.

"Feel her emotions *intensely*."

Gyorgy leaned back. "So...let me see if I have this right." His fingers played with the bowl of the crystal snifter in his hands.

"It would be acceptable for me to demand that you submit to my instructions?"

She nodded.

"And you would find pleasure in, say, my hands on your body?"

She nodded again.

"And if I were to insist on using my mouth on your body?"

She swallowed and nodded once more.

Gyorgy put down his glass and rose, strolling casually to the windows. It was time to start his games. His cock hardened, but for now he ignored it.

"I find that such pleasures can often be heightened when one party is restrained, Marie-Claire." He turned to see her profile. "Might that be to your liking?"

Perhaps it was the candlelight, but he could have sworn a slight flush rose in her cheeks at his words.

That little dip of her head came again.

Gyorgy strolled on, stopping behind her. "And if such pleasures were combined with a mild punishment…might *that* be to your liking?"

He could see her nipples harden beneath her robe. She didn't need to nod for him to know she was getting aroused by his words.

He delicately ran one finger along her shoulder and eased her hair from the silk. "Were I to bare your doubtless beautiful buttocks, Marie-Claire, and perhaps administer a spanking…warm them to a pink glow beneath the palms of my hands…would that be to your liking?"

A very slight tremor disturbed her breathing. "Yesss…"

"Or perhaps flick them, and other pink and glowing parts of your body…" He let his hand slide down over her robe to rest on the soft swell of her breast. "Just a touch with my whip…would that be to your liking?"

"I might…find that pleasurable." Her voice was lower now, and a slight trace of hoarseness lay beneath it.

"Shall we try, Marie-Claire? Shall we see if we can find some games that will be *mutually* pleasurable?"

She stood.

Gyorgy waited, heart thumping, as she glided around the couch and moved to face him. She was so close he could smell the light fragrance surrounding her, yet her eyes told him there was still a barrier between them.

"I would like to play such games with you, Gyorgy."

Gyorgy made himself a promise at that moment. He was going to arouse this woman to fever pitch. He was going to make her writhe and squirm as she welcomed each and every thing he planned on doing to her. He was going to make her scream with pleasure. He was going to watch her eyes as they finally told him of her ecstasy.

And above all, he was going to make her *feel*.

Chapter 16

This man surprises me.

The thought flashed across Marie-Claire's mind like summer lightning as he dipped his head and brushed the lightest of kisses across her lips.

No thrusting tongue or hands pulling her tight against him...just a light caress. It made her thirst for more.

But he moved back. "Shall we adjourn to your bedchamber? Or would you rather play here?"

She suppressed a little shiver of excitement. "Perhaps my chamber would be more suited to our needs." He'd never know how she trembled inside, or how her pussy was already moistening from his words. No one needed to know that, but her.

She led him into the semi-darkness of her room.

Several candles were lit, sending drifting shadows across the walls and the large bed in the center. She had set out a selection of lengths of silk across the spread, and she watched as he took it all in with one comprehensive glance.

"Shall I..." Her hands went to the tie on her robe.

"No."

Again, he surprised her. She waited, tamping down her roiling emotions as he strolled around, slipping off his jacket as he went and folding it neatly onto a chair. His loose cravat came next, and the whip was placed on the spread next to the silks.

He was telling her he'd seen them. *He understood.*

Silently he picked up two of the pieces of fabric and moved to the foot of the bed. He beckoned her. A simple gesture, just a crook of the finger, and she was almost unbearably aroused.

Obediently she moved at his command, standing with her back to the bed, facing him.

She swallowed down her excitement as he began to attach the silk to her wrists. Within moments, each was secured to one of the posts at the foot of her bed. She was spread-eagled before him.

"Good." He nodded complacently. Then, once again, he did something unexpected. He knelt to each of her ankles and secured them too.

Now she was totally at his mercy. Splayed before him like a slave awaiting punishment. It was not uncomfortable—he'd left enough play in the fabric for her to stand without straining, but she was quite helpless.

What now?

Nothing, apparently. Gyorgy strolled around the room, moving a candle, touching a painting, sniffing at her perfume on her dressing table. Marie-Claire could feel her heart pounding beneath the white silk as she closed her eyes and listened to him move.

To be caught like this, trapped, awaiting his pleasure, was arousing her to fever pitch. The cool air swirled beneath her skirts and clashed with the moisture smearing her thighs.

Gyorgy returned to stand before her and she opened her eyes.

"I like your choice of fragrance." An innocuous statement, but accompanied by his hands unfastening the ties on his shirt. Buttons were loosened, and he tugged it free of his breeches.

"Thank you." How she got the words out she had no idea. Every drop of her saliva had dried up at the sight of his chest. Muscles rippled as he slipped the garment off his shoulders. Dusky whorls of hair brushed the upper chest, narrowing into a line that delved down towards...

She raised her eyes back to his, knowing he was watching her. "I approve."

He hadn't asked for her approval, but she caught the amusement in his gaze. "I'm glad."

"You are in excellent shape for someone idling their way across the countryside."

He turned away from her and dropped his shirt onto his jacket. "I have not always 'idled', as you put it. I spent some time in France recently."

"Ah." A few pieces clicked into place in Marie-Claire's mind. "You and your fellow Gypsies were traveling in dangerous places, Gyorgy."

"We were indeed, Marie-Claire." His lips firmed, punctuating his words. He would say no more on that topic, she was sure.

He strolled over to the bed and picked up his whip. She swallowed, trying to catch her breath.

A few flicks produced a soft crack of the thong, and he returned to stand in front of her. "Are you particularly attached to this garment?"

Incapable of forming the words, she simply shook her head.

"Good."

He dexterously flicked his wrist and sliced neatly through the tie at her waist, allowing the two halves to fall free and bare her body to his gaze.

Try as she might, she couldn't help it. She moaned.

✱ ✱ ✱ ✱ ✱

Finally.

It had taken but a flick of his whip and he had a reaction out of her. A slight sound, no more, but it went straight to Gyorgy's cock. Refusing to bend to its need, he left his breeches fastened for the time being. Soon, though...

Her body was gleaming in the candlelight, all sleek curves and shadows, with the darkness between her thighs beckoning him like a Siren.

The robe had caught on her breasts. That would never do.

Carefully, Gyorgy lashed again. This time, the tip of the whip sliced the silk neatly, dropping it off one breast. Her nipple was a hard bud, casting shadows over the soft swell of her flesh.

He could smell her now, her musky woman-scent blending with the floral perfume she wore. She was certainly responding to his unorthodox method of stripping her. And *fuck*, so was he.

Another flick, another tattered piece of silk drooped lower. One more, and she was as near naked as she could be.

The remains of the robe draped from her wrists and arms, and it took a few simple lashes to pull them away from her body. The fabric was lightweight and embraced the tip of the whip, eagerly leaving the warmth of Marie-Claire's flesh for the sting of his thong.

Like her.

It was time to find out if she really did want to play.

Her eyes remained fixed on his, clear blue still, but with pupils that were dilating. He still couldn't sense her mood, or the level of her pleasure, but her body was telling him that she was enjoying this experience.

Drops of moisture glistened between her thighs and her breasts looked fuller and heavy, their tips puckered tightly.

They drew his attention.

Very carefully, with all the skill he possessed, Gyorgy flicked his whip once more. The merest kiss of leather on that rosy little peak.

Marie-Claire gasped. "Oh *God*..."

His cock jumped painfully against his breeches. Her groan had damn near finished him. Without a second thought he stripped himself bare, and once again laid a delicate touch on the other breast.

This time, she flinched a little and sucked in a quick breath.

He knew he wasn't hurting her. His skill was too good for that. But she'd be stinging a little, the blood rushing to her nipple, heightening its sensitivity. His cock could practically feel the heat as it rolled off her body in waves.

He let a flurry of small lashes caress her breasts, which glowed pink from his attentions.

She sobbed out another cry, and her head dropped back.

Enough for the moment.

Gyorgy neared her and lowered his head. He swept his tongue around her rock hard nipples.

"Gyorgy..."

The word was a plea, a sigh...a moan of delight.

The skin was hot beneath his touch, her pulse throbbing in her neck and her chest rising and falling with her rapid breathing.

He slid one hand down over her body and let his fingers cup her pussy. She was so wet. So hot. Running with boiling juices, just from the kiss of his whip.

He stroked her, soothed her, and caressed her down from the heights a little as his tongue eased the sting of the whip from her breasts.

She shuddered at his attentions, sighing once again.

His fingernails grazed her clit, and she cried out in pleasure. He withdrew, making her bite back a sob.

"Not yet, my lovely. Not yet."

Ignoring his cock, which throbbed as eagerly as the heartbeat beneath his lips, Gyorgy nibbled the soft underside of her breasts. She was becoming more and more responsive now, each of his actions eliciting a movement, a moan, a sigh from her.

"Marie-Claire. Open your eyes. Look at me, Marie-Claire." He thrust one finger deep into her cunt as he rasped out the words.

Jumping a little at his intrusion, she jerked her head upright and opened her eyes.

Yes. *Now.*

Now the clear blue eyes were starting to burn. Now the pupils were inky black pools in the center of a stormy lake. Now Gyorgy could see the beginnings of her pleasure.

It was working. She was starting to feel.

He let his hand work her for a while, in concert with his lips on her breasts, arousing her a little, and maintaining his attentions to her body, while his mind raced with possibilities.

He fought an inner battle, since there was nothing he wanted more right at this moment than to grab her buttocks, raise her up and plunge deep into her hot moisture. But he'd made himself a promise. He was going to make her feel. More than she was feeling right now. More than she'd ever felt before.

A little prickle up his spine told Gyorgy that he might, in fact, feel it right along with her.

He gentled his movements and withdrew his hand. "So good, Marie-Claire."

Her eyes focused on him as he raised his hand to his mouth and slowly licked the taste of her from his fingers.

She seemed spellbound by his tongue, following its every move as he traced the length of his fingers, swiping at the gleaming trails of honey her body had left behind.

"You taste so good."

She gulped, a rough movement at odds with her normal elegant demeanor.

Gyorgy smiled.

* * * * *

"Fuck me, Gyorgy."

The words were wrung out of her as he pulled back from her body. She couldn't hold them inside. She was boiling, blood thrumming in her ears, breasts hot as cauldrons and cunt crying out with need.

Watching him lick her taste from his fingers had been the most erotic moment she could ever remember and she wanted him...deep inside her...right this minute.

"Soon, my sweet. But not yet."

"Damn you..." It was a curse and a sob, yet inside her something was melting. She could wait. She could wait for whatever moment it was he chose to take her. To end this ache in her pussy.

She drew herself up a little, ignoring the beating of her pulse that threatened to deafen her. She squelched down the fires that burned inside her.

She could wait. Or could she?

His smile nearly undid her resolution.

She realized he was naked. Splendidly naked. His cock thrust away from its nest of dark hair, a sliver of light marking the moisture that had gathered on its head. At least she wasn't the only one aroused by their games.

Where was he going? What was he doing?

She watched as he picked up a candle and brought it close to where she was tethered. He moved out of her line of sight, and spent long moments away from her, doing God-knew-what. Then he returned, her writing quill in his hand.

Her mind scrambled to make sense of his actions.

It damn near collapsed with shock when it did.

With careful movements, Gyorgy dipped the end of the quill into the melted wax that had gathered around the candle flame. He gently allowed a drop or two to fall on his arm.

He raised his eyes to Marie-Claire and her breath stopped.

He wasn't...he wouldn't...oh God. He was. He would.

Dark as night, yet lit by some burning emotion, Gyorgy's gaze lowered to her body as he dipped the quill once again and softly touched it against her breastbone.

The heat of the wax seared her skin, but cooled rapidly, taking away the sting of his touch.

He traced a line with the warm wax down between her breasts to her navel. Each move, each dip of fresh wax, sensitized her already-screaming skin. As it hardened, it tugged on her flesh, adding to her excitement.

He drew lines around her navel, then traced a path with the quill to her hipbones and let the wax fall into the hollows he found there. Never burning her skin, nor allowing a drop to go anywhere but where he intended.

His control was unbelievable, and the sensations he was creating were driving her slowly insane. She was almost afraid of where he'd go next. Her breasts were tingling still from the touch of his whip, and Gyorgy must have sensed that, since he left them alone.

He discovered new areas to play with. Places like her inner thighs. Dodging her own moisture, the quill found areas that aroused her and left her breathless as he painted them with the wax.

Eventually, he seemed satisfied, and stepped back to survey his handiwork. "Very nice, my sweet."

His voice was harsh, and betrayed his own emotions. He was as excited by this game as she was.

Marie-Claire involuntarily struggled against her bonds. The wax had hardened on her skin, tightening and arousing her, and she wanted to be able to touch him now... to learn his body, to take that cock deep inside her, and to scream out her desire.

She was one fiery mass of need.

She surrendered. "*Gyorgy...no more.*"

Slowly she allowed her eyes to meet his. There were no barriers, no safeguards, nothing to prevent her from letting her emotions reveal themselves.

She wanted him. And she wanted him now.

"Ah, Marie-Claire. *At last.*"

She frowned a little, tugging on her wrists. "At last what?"

"At last you're showing yourself. The real Marie-Claire."

"I don't...I don't understand..." It was the truth. She understood little or nothing of what he was saying. She was driven by a deep and overwhelming need, the likes of which she could not ever recall experiencing before.

"I knew you were in there." He released her bonds and pushed her back onto the bed, arranging her to his liking. She was limp in his hands, moving where he willed her. "I knew that eventually the woman you are would let herself go."

"So here I am. Gyorgy, for God's sake...just do it."

Shamelessly, she parted her thighs, the invitation obvious.

That erotic grin curved his lips once more. "You can go higher, love. Just wait..."

She bit her lip against a scream of frustration. "Damn you."

"Patience, sweet."

Chapter 17

I could use some of that myself.

Gyorgy's cock was harder than marble, almost painful now, and purpling as it sought the release it so desperately craved. But he was a man with a mission and bedamned to him if he sacrificed his goals just to satisfy his needs.

He watched her eyes as he neared her, and showed her the letter opener he'd retrieved from her desk. Sharp and glittering in the candlelight, it made her freeze into immobility as he clambered up onto the bed next to her.

Slowly and carefully, Gyorgy lowered the blade to her body. And scraped away the hardened wax.

"Don't move, Marie-Claire," he warned.

She showed no signs of moving any time soon. Her concentration was focused on his hand and the knife as he scoured down her body, gently lifting away the blobs and rivulets that marked her.

Only her heart, pounding beneath his touch, told him of just how aroused she was.

When he reached her inner thighs, he was met with the overwhelming scent of her juices, and he smeared them onto her skin as he removed the last of the wax.

With a small sigh she shifted slightly, and Gyorgy tossed the knife away, not caring where it fell.

He leaned forward into her and buried his face in her pussy.

Her cry was sharp and immediate, and her hips squirmed, thrusting against him and demanding he satisfy her.

He sought her hardened clit with his tongue, pushing and pressing and learning every nook that hid her secrets. Her moisture overflowed, soaking his face, and her flesh burned him, on fire and hotter than the wax he'd dribbled on her.

She struggled a little, but Gyorgy refused to let her move away from his mouth. This would be her first orgasm of the night and he wanted to taste it. To give it to her, and her alone. To let her travel the road to oblivion by herself, accompanied only by his lips, his tongue, and his hands as they clenched hard into the softness of her buttocks.

He kept up his touches, poking and prodding her farther along the way.

It wasn't a long trip.

Within moments, her breath shortened, and he felt the muscles in her body contract. A sob broke from her throat and she trembled...on the edge of that magnificent fall.

He flicked her clit, running his tongue around it and sucking hard.

She fell.

Her thighs clamped around his head and her cunt shuddered and shook as she exploded against his mouth. He thrust his tongue deep into her, letting her muscles suck it and tug on it, loving every twitch and rolling caress.

She screamed, her voice cracking as her body rode out her climax, fingers scrabbling unconsciously on the linens, and lost in the vortex he'd created within her.

It was incredible, and Gyorgy hung on to his own emotions by the skin of his teeth.

For long moments he stayed against her, letting the tremors ease and waiting...waiting for the right time.

He felt the first easing of her thighs around his neck.

Now.

He raised himself up on his arms and positioned his cock at her entrance, bathing it in the wet flames that flooded her.

With one thrust he claimed her, and with the next brought her back up to her peak, stroking firmly now, ever deeper, making her shudder anew and taking the breath from her lungs.

She was so hot around his cock, slick with her own juices and trembling as his hips met her pussy, pounding her now, urging her even higher.

Her legs rose, ankles locking behind him, holding him near. As if he could have left her. There wasn't a thing in the world that could have stopped Gyorgy at that moment. He'd aroused Marie-Claire to undreamed-of heights, and in the process he'd found himself drowning in her passions.

Her eyes opened, and their gazes met and held.

Blue eyes, burning now with a desire that seared his soul, stared at him…speaking to him eloquently of her need, her desperation, and her pain. And telling him how what he was doing to her was fulfilling her.

Tears trembled at the corners, and he knew she'd see an answer to her questions in his own gaze.

Gyorgy had *never* felt anything like this.

Both were too far gone to last very long. With a final thrust, Gyorgy lost himself in Marie-Claire, his cock plundering her right up to her womb. His spine tingled with heat, his balls tightened to rock-hardness, and his breath left his lungs.

She was right there with him. Watching him, blue eyes wide and glittering as she felt him begin his own ride into madness.

She moved her hips, rubbing her clit against his body.

And screamed again.

This time, they journeyed together, Gyorgy groaning and spurting his seed deep inside Marie-Claire, who milked every drop, holding him tight against her as she came again.

For long moments they stayed thus, caught in a timeless embrace, locked together as one, sharing the most intimate of experiences.

Then, with a sigh, they parted.

Gyorgy's softened cock slid from her body, and he rolled to her side, gathering her close. Words seemed irrelevant, and truthfully, Gyorgy couldn't think of a single thing to say.

Marie-Claire yawned and snuggled into his chest. "Thank you."

Within moments, she slept.

* * * * *

Gyorgy awoke to the sounds of birds and the sunlight dappling his pillow. He stretched, languorous and content, enjoying the caress of the fine linens against his naked skin.

And his early morning erection. He yawned and smiled, and reached for Marie-Claire. Only to find the bed empty.

Cool sheets met his seeking hand, and he realized she'd been gone for some time. A servant tapped on the door, and with a curt command, Gyorgy bade him enter.

"Where is your mistress?"

"Good morning, sir. The Duchess sends her regrets that she will be unable to breakfast with you. A meal has been prepared should you desire to fortify yourself for your journey."

Gyorgy, who seldom ate early in the day, brushed the man's words aside. "Where is she?"

Heedless of his nakedness he jumped from the bed. The servant took a step backwards. "You'll find tea and some scones on the tray, sir. I believe the Duchess left a note. Other than that, I cannot answer as to Her Grace's whereabouts."

The man seemed unsettled by Gyorgy's appearance and his eyes skittered everywhere but on Gyorgy. "A bath has been prepared for you and your clothing awaits." The hint was clear.

Gyorgy dismissed him. "This will do. Thank you."

His eyes were fixed on the elegant tray and the folded paper propped against the silver teapot. He ignored the tea, the sound of the door closing behind the servant, and just about everything except that paper.

The one that bore his name in elegant flowing script—Gyorgy Vargas.

He couldn't help but notice the slight chill that crept down his spine as he picked it up, and he knew it had nothing to do with the fact he was naked. Absently grabbing a blanket, Gyorgy wrapped it around his waist and sat in one of the elegant chairs.

He stared at the note. He stared at his hand, amazed that there was a slight tremble to it. He swallowed roughly and broke the seal.

"Dear Gyorgy,

It is almost impossible for me to find the words to thank you for last night…"

The chill down Gyorgy's spine turned into a fully-fledged shiver. He took a deep breath and poured himself a cup of tea after all. He had a feeling he was going to need it. A foreboding of bad news was creeping up on him.

"…So I will not try. I will only tell you that playing your games brought more into my heart and my life than I ever could have imagined possible, and for that I shall always be eternally grateful.

I asked only one night of you, Gyorgy, and you fulfilled each and every one of my desires, and so much more. But our night has ended, as all such nights must. I shall be forever happy that our paths crossed, and forever sad that they must part again.

But part they must. You have a journey to complete and a life of your own to live. Your friends await you in London, and I have a feeling that you will soon find new challenges to meet. My life is here. It can be no other way. I can never return to London, nor do I wish to. And I would never ask that you make a choice that might eventually lead to your despair. I could not do that to someone for whom I have come to care so much in so short a time.

Forgive me. Forgive me for not being brave enough to stand before you and tell you this in person. Forgive me for leaving you as you slept. Forgive me for not pressing my lips to yours in farewell.

And forgive me for being a coward. For a coward I am. This is why I had to leave you, and why you must leave me. I fear the power your touch could have over me. It would be all too easy to lose myself in you.

If you can find it in your heart to understand my cowardice, then let me know by bidding farewell to my home. Go, Gyorgy. Do not try to find me, since I will be long gone by the time you read this letter. My servants will see that you are well equipped to continue your journey back to London. I wish you well in all things, and safe passage to wherever life takes you.

I hope you will remember our night together as I will…with joy.

Ever yours,

Marie-Claire"

Gyorgy stared at the signature, unable to comprehend for a moment or two that she'd actually gone.

A fierce longing erupted into his throat, burning him and making him want to crumple the paper into a ball and scream out his anger and pain.

How could she leave him?

Did she not realize that last night had taken his world, shaken it, turned it upside down and realigned his entire life?

Slowly, it dawned on him. No. She *didn't* know that, because he hadn't told her. He'd let his body and his desires speak for him, and assumed that her responses indicated that she understood. But he'd never said the words. Never said out loud that their loving had been special. A one-of-a-kind experience that had marked his soul.

"*Az anyad!*" The curse broke from him in one explosive breath.

He stood and threw the blanket down, striding into the next room where his bath awaited. It was time to plan. To think clearly about what his next step should be. To ask himself some questions and to answer them with an honesty he wasn't sure if he could manage.

And, maybe, it was time to leave. For now.

* * * * *

Less than two hours later, a man appeared on the front steps of Kirkwood House and mounted the horse that awaited him.

With a nod to the stable boy holding the reins, the man rode smartly down the formal drive and into the lane beyond, picking up speed as the road opened up and beckoned travelers towards London.

He never looked back.

And never saw an elegant face watching from a far wing of the house—never saw the soft draperies fall back into place as she released them.

And never saw the pain in a pair of cool blue eyes as tears fell from them to the sill on which Marie-Claire Devereaux, Dowager Duchess of Kirkwood, rested as she watched him leave her life forever—taking her heart with him.

No, the man never saw any of those things. In truth, he barely saw where he was going, which was very unusual for a man like Gyorgy Vargas.

His mind was still circling his problems, exploring options, seeking solutions. He knew he had to honor Marie-Claire's request and leave. He'd honored her request for one night. Neither of them had talked about more.

But it was likely that neither of them had realized what that night would mean to them.

Gyorgy's spirits rose a little as he re-read her letter in his mind. Those were not the words of a woman unaffected by passion. They were not the words of casual thanks and dismissal he'd feared. They were the words of a woman who hated to say goodbye.

And why did she hate to say goodbye?

Probably for the same reason he did. Something had been born last night. Something had begun between him and this mysterious blue-eyed Medusa. Instead of turning him to stone, she'd melted him. She'd touched places no other woman had even come close to.

She'd challenged him and driven him to new heights of pleasure, but it had been so much more. Her eyes had told him, as loud as if she'd spoken the words. Gyorgy knew, without a shadow of a doubt, that Marie-Claire had found pleasure last night in his arms. A pleasure that had swept away her past, taken her into realms she'd not even guessed at, and started an emotional avalanche that had frightened her even as it was sweeping her off into her orgasm.

He had to overcome that fear. Along with some of his own. His fears that an unimportant Hungarian landowner would have nothing to offer a Dowager Duchess. His fears that his past as a rebel, a Gypsy, a musician and erstwhile soldier-of-fortune would not recommend him to one as gently bred as Marie-Claire.

Yes, there was a journey ahead of him, but this one wasn't counted in miles or in the hoof beats of his horse. It was counted in the beats of his heart.

The heart he'd left with Marie-Claire.

And damned if he wouldn't be back to claim it. But this time, he'd not come empty handed. This time he'd have information, facts, knowledge about her that he so desperately needed. And he could only get that knowledge in London.

Gyorgy touched his spurs to his horse.

He had a mission.

Chapter 18
London

Count Viktor Karoly stretched out his legs in front of his fire and sighed with contentment. Across the hearth, Lord Peter Chalmers did much the same thing.

The two men grinned at each other.

"I love them dearly, but...damn. Sometimes a man needs to just...relax a little." Peter's smile was rueful, and Viktor's matched it. He passed the cigar box over to Peter.

"I know what you mean. Madelyne and Freddie together...they're a force to be reckoned with. What do you think of this place Freddie's found?"

Peter pulled at his cigar and watched the fragrant smoke coil upwards into the darkness of Viktor's study. "I like it. The building is sound, the work is coming along well, and you wouldn't believe the response she's received from women wanting to work there."

Viktor tilted his head in inquiry.

"Well, free room and board is a huge lure, of course, but when they found out that it was to be a sanctuary of sorts, they started to put their hearts into it too. Wonderful thing to see." Peter leaned back in the large leather chair. "Freddie has more workers than she needs right now, and the first signs that word is spreading are starting to show. Two women appeared today asking for help."

Viktor stared into the flames. "It's really appalling, isn't it? That a woman has nowhere to go to escape from abuse or other horrors." He shook his head. "Thank God we're helping, if only in a small way."

"It's what we do, Viktor." Peter's voice was quiet as he too watched the fire. "It's what we've done for how many years now?"

Viktor chuckled. "I've lost count. I remember the day Fabyan got us all drunk and made us take a vow to help those in need."

Peter smiled. "I remember that too. And he did it without saying a word. Damn, I miss him. Any word from him?"

"No. Not since he left a message that he was visiting friends. Nothing from Gyorgy, or Lukasz and Matyas either. Still..." Viktor drew on his cigar. "They know where to find us."

Peter nodded. "So where do we stand with the Eventyde thing?"

"Ah yes." Viktor's voice took on an overtone of menace. "And his cohort, the unspeakable Francis Hucknall."

"I'd rather not speak of him, if you don't mind. Sours my port."

Viktor snorted. "Agreed. We'll deal with him separately I think. But as for Eventyde...I have managed to find out a few things."

Peter raised his eyebrows and glanced around making sure the door to Viktor's study was closed tight. Neither man wanted anything of this conversation to reach the ears of their wives.

"Anything useful?" Peter leaned forward.

Viktor nodded. "Oh yes. And interesting too. Our *friend* Eventyde is stretched very thin financially. His investments are scattered throughout a variety of interests, and several have not done well recently, now that the war is over."

Peter's lips curled into a sneer. "One of those, was he?"

"Definitely. If there was a profit to be made, regardless of the cost, Eventyde would jump at the chance. However, now he's suffering some losses. And also, I hear, looking for newer opportunities. He's sold out of several companies, and has sunk a good portion of his remaining money into one venture. A shipping company."

Peter thought about this. "I'll wager Hucknall was going to come up with some financial support in exchange for Madelyne."

A swift flicker of fury licked at Viktor's eyes as he met those of his friend. "No doubt."

"But..." Peter continued his line of thought. "If he's putting most of his ready assets into one company..."

"And that company should fail..."

"Doesn't even have to fail," said Peter. "Just a hint of impropriety. Enough to send the value tumbling and wipe out Eventyde. He'd be finished. Financially *and* socially."

"Good." Viktor's face was a mask.

"We don't often set out to destroy someone," mused Peter. "But in this case, I can't imagine doing anything else. And right after him...Hucknall."

Viktor sighed. "It's wrong to be so vengeful, I know. But these men are a blight. A vicious and destructive force that cannot be allowed to ruin more lives than they have already." He sipped his port. "I prefer to think of it as protecting those who would have been potential victims, rather than a personal quest for revenge. Although..." He paused. "It is personal. *Very* personal."

Peter was silent.

"Will it take long, do you think?" Viktor straightened his spine.

"No, I don't suppose that we'd need more than a week or two. Now that Lord Peter Chalmers is returning to the hallowed streets of London, it's quite natural for him to chat with old acquaintances. You know, of course, he's been involved in work for his family on the continent for some time now..."

Viktor laughed. "No, I didn't know that, actually. Busy man, that Lord Chalmers."

"Who's Lord Chalmers?"

The third voice slid through the shadows and sent both Viktor and Peter off their chairs with a curse.

The shock gave way to grins of pleasure as they turned to find Gyorgy standing just inside the door and looking at them with a mixture of curiosity and pleasure.

"Gyorgy...*szervusz*," beamed Viktor.

"Gyorgy, you sod...still creeping around like a shadow, eh?" Peter clapped his friend on the shoulder with a smile.

Gyorgy cocked his head to one side. "It appears I have missed a lot...care to fill in some blanks? And share that port while you're at it?"

A couple of hours later, the three men finally fell silent. Adventures had been shared, congratulations offered, and ideas tossed around like the third bottle of port they'd required.

"So, we are decided then?" Viktor's hair was tousled, and his cravat long gone.

"'Twould seem so," nodded Peter sleepily.

Gyorgy added his assent. "Information is going to be our most valuable weapon in this small war of ours." He stared moodily at the dying fire. "I need everything I can lay my hands on about the Kirkwood family. Especially one Dowager Duchess..."

Peter and Viktor shared a glance—*our friend has fallen too.*

"And there's no reason I can't begin to pull some gossip or rumors about Hucknall while I'm at it. Shouldn't be hard. His name isn't unknown to some of my acquaintances." His mouth tightened.

Viktor straightened. "So be it. While you are digging with your sources, Peter and I will tighten the noose around Eventyde's neck. Will you stay here, Gyorgy? There's plenty of room, and that way the others will find us all together when they return to London."

"Any news of Lukasz or Matyas?" Peter glanced at Gyorgy.

"Not a word. What of Fabyan?"

Both Viktor and Peter shook their heads. "Nothing." Viktor rose. "But I'm not worried. God knows we've proved we can take care of ourselves. After all, what could possibly happen to them that hasn't happened already in some rat-infested corner of France?"

Peter snickered. "Well, seeing as two of us are married, and one in serious lust, perhaps you might want to rethink that question, my friend."

"Um." Viktor colored slightly. "There is that."

Gyorgy rose too. "I probably should tell you...it's more than lust, you know. I intend to marry Marie-Claire. If she'll have me."

"Why on earth wouldn't she?" Viktor's eyebrows rose.

Gyorgy grinned. "My question exactly. I'm for bed. Do you have a room or shall I just curl up on that rather inviting rug in front of the fire?"

✱ ✱ ✱ ✱ ✱

Lady Chalmers untangled her legs from those of her husband and stretched contentedly in front of the fire. Lord Chalmers snuggled her close and idly ran his hand over her naked hip.

"You're plotting something, Peter." Freddie's voice held a slight accusation.

"Me?"

She snorted. If he thought she couldn't tell, well hell. His life was about to get interesting. "Yes, you. You have that thoughtful look about you."

"Perhaps I'm plotting some new and delightful ways to take this delicious body of yours," he answered.

Freddie smiled. "You're always doing that. And don't think I'm unappreciative." She shivered as he gently ran his moustache over one soft nipple. "Especially of *that*…"

She sighed. "But you're plotting something with Viktor. And now you tell me that Gyorgy is here. The forces are gathering, aren't they?" She pulled herself up on one elbow and brushed Peter's hair away from his face. "Is it Eventyde?"

Peter stared past her into the fire. "He's a foul swine, Freddie. He and Hucknall are beyond the pale of acceptable human behavior."

Freddie swallowed. "I understand. Believe me I do. Madelyne has shared some of what she went through…and I can guess a lot of the rest." She snuggled back onto Peter's chest. "I'd be the first one in line to string him up by his balls."

Peter huffed out a laugh. "That's my Amazon warrior." He held her tight. "I'm not sure how it'll play out, Freddie. He'll be ruined, that's for sure."

Freddie was silent for a moment, enjoying being held, and still trying to accept how much she loved this man. "Good." And yet her fears still niggled at the back of her mind. "Peter…I should hate for this to result in our exile from England. You've faced that once before—is it likely to happen again?"

Peter was silent for a moment. "Freddie, with you by my side, I'll never be exiled again. Not like I was before."

Sensing that there was more to come, Freddie simply dropped a light kiss on his skin.

"Before, I turned my back on everything. My home, my family, my life. I wandered around, getting into trouble, getting out of trouble, just being a wastrel really, until I met Fabyan and Viktor and the others."

"What happened then?"

"Then? We all found we needed to do more than just idle away our days playing our music. Oh the music brought us together, but something else bound us into a group. Some need we all had to right wrongs, to help others, to thank the Heavens that we were alive, perhaps…I don't know."

He paused, as if collecting his thoughts. "It was France, it was wartime. There were so many people suffering. Not enough food, or young lads being cruelly taken to serve Napoleon, leaving women and children to fend for themselves."

Peter fidgeted, as if plagued by the memories. "There was so much pain, Freddie. Nothing can be worse than a country caught in the ravages of war. It was as if we'd all been sent to meet at that one inn at that same time. All of us needing or wanting to help. So we did. Certainly we were bosky at the time. We must have been to come up with some of our more outlandish plans."

He chuckled, and Freddie knew he wasn't seeing her now, but his past. "But the end result was a group of Gypsy musicians who loudly and noisily entertained the people we met, and then quietly and surreptitiously did what we could to help them."

"How?" Freddie encouraged Peter, wanting to hear about this time in her husband's life. A time that had made him the man he was today. The man she loved beyond reason.

"How? God, so many different ways. Food, of course, wherever we could trade for it, steal it, trap it…whatever. Clothing…you'd be surprised how many people would refuse to pay us a centime for a song, but would gladly discard old clothes as payment instead." He shook his head.

"Hiding the young men. That was a prime mission of ours. To try and see that the communities and villages we visited had a few men left to take care of things. How on earth can a village of women and children be expected to repair a broken plow? Yes, they can harvest the crops, but how can they replant for the next season without a plow? How can they roof their cottages without the tools or the strength to carry the bundles up a ladder?"

Peter choked slightly, fighting his temper. "Armies don't think, Freddie. They march. They fight. They die. No one ever thinks of the lives they leave behind."

"But you did. You and your friends."

"We tried. Fabyan was our motivator. Somehow, without words, he gathered us into a group. He makes his wishes known…sometimes he writes them down, or signals us, but it took less than no time for us to understand him. Just a look now, and we're in complete understanding. It's uncanny…"

"Has he never spoken?"

Peter paused. "I'm not sure. I thought once I heard something...Fabyan was helping a child. But there was so much going on. The army was close behind us, along with a landowner whose prize goat we'd...um...appropriated." He grinned. "And damn if that goat didn't sire about a dozen little ones. We had come back that way a few months later, and there they all were."

Freddie yawned. "I envy you in some ways, Peter. Such a close bond to have formed with such a wonderful group of men."

"You're part of it now, my love."

"That's nice..."

Lady Chalmers fell asleep wrapped in her husband's arms, totally uncaring of the fact they both lay on a rug before the fire.

✻ ✻ ✻ ✻ ✻

While the Chalmers cuddled their way off to sleep, Count Viktor Karoly was very much awake in the master suite and staring at his wife, trying to comprehend what she'd just said.

"You will have to kill him, of course."

Viktor blinked. "That's rather harsh, Madelyne darling. The man is your father."

Madelyne snorted and peeled her body away from her husband's, where it had fallen after their energetic lovemaking had ended. In a mutually satisfactory way as always.

"Since when?" She tucked the covers around them both.

"Well...I...er..."

"Exactly. He has never acted like a father, Viktor. He's seldom acted like a man. He's a beast in so many ways, and that's being unfair to the beasts of this world. At least they can claim the need to survive. Alfred Eventyde is just evil. Through and through."

Viktor sighed. "I know you're right. But kill him? I'm not sure if that's the answer."

"If you don't, I will."

Viktor turned his head on the pillow and stared at the blue-eyed angel who met his gaze determinedly.

"I'm not joking, Viktor. After what he's done to me? I can only begin to imagine what he's done with the rest of his life. I don't want to know. He may have planted a seed in my mother and given me life, but that doesn't entitle him to my affections, my loyalty or any other kind of filial feelings."

Madelyne's mouth firmed. "And I can't help thinking that he'd not miss a chance to extract revenge on me too. For thwarting his plans. For messing up his arrangement with Hucknall. I have so much more to lose now, Viktor. If he were to try and hurt *you*..."

Her voice quavered for a moment and a small hand crept across Viktor's chest.

He seized it and raised it to his lips. "Sweetheart, it won't happen. We're safe from him. He would gain nothing by attacking us but the condemnation of his peers."

"But if he *should*..."

"He won't. I have my friends, my servants, and one rather bloodthirsty little wife. I am well-protected, trust me."

"I'll feel better if you kill him."

Viktor couldn't suppress a chuckle. "We'll see, love, we'll see. If our plans go well, I can guarantee you that he'll never cross our path again."

"So you do have a plan, then?"

Viktor cursed softly beneath his breath. In Hungarian. "Madelyne, you are the most devious..."

She giggled and nipped his chest, ringing his nipple with her tongue. "Perhaps that's why you love me."

He tugged her close and kissed her thoroughly. "That and so many other reasons I've lost count."

Madelyne subsided, content.

Almost.

"So...tell me about these plans of yours?"

* * * * *

The same moonlight that shone on the face of Madelyne, Countess Karoly, as she extracted the details of his plan from an unwilling Viktor, also shone on a small caravan.

It was tucked into the depths of the forest, not far from a small stream, and its occupants were finishing off their wine and readying themselves for the night. They were still a couple of days' journey from London, but Lukasz and Matyas Eger were in no hurry.

Lukasz stretched and yawned loudly. "Lord, but I'm tired."

Matyas sluiced the empty wine bottle in a bucket of water and tossed it into a basket where it clinked against its fellows. "Why? We've done naught but amble through this forest like snails."

"Perhaps that's it. My brains are slowing down along with my body."

Matyas shrugged. "I agree it's been a little quiet of late. But admit it, Luk, the peace has been most welcome."

The two men efficiently cleared away their possessions, stowing them safely around the caravan and dousing the fire.

"Tomorrow—perhaps we should make more of an effort to get on the London road? I'm beginning to miss the others." Luk stepped up into the caravan.

Mat followed him and closed the door, sliding the bolt carefully home and locking them into their own private world. "Agreed. I look forward to seeing them once more. It's been a long time since we have been separated for more than a night or two."

Mat's words were echoing his own thoughts, in their usual way. Luk realized that in the last several years, the Gypsies had become so used to functioning as a unit, that to be apart like this was unsettling, to say the least.

Of course, it was nothing compared to what he would be feeling if he were alone. To be apart from Mat was unthinkable.

The two men shed their clothing and snuffed the single candle, unfolding the blankets and stretching out side-by-side as they had done for more years than they could recall.

This night, however, sleep would not come to Luk, and he sighed as he stared from the small window into the starry, moonlit sky.

"Can't sleep?" Mat's voice broke the silence.

Luk shifted his arm and rested his head on it. "No."

"The dreams again?"

"Not this time, no. Just...thinking. How long has it been, Mat?"

Mat chuckled. "Since what? Since we had a woman? Since we ate? Since we saw our friends?"

"Since we met."

Mat stilled. "I don't know. Twenty years at least."

Luk could hear him turn on the blanket as he too stared out into the night.

"Must be at least twenty. After the orphanage it was five years or so on the streets of Eger, then those years with the Turk...then..." Mat's voice tapered off.

"I suppose so." Luk's mind wandered over their pasts. He couldn't recall a time when Mat hadn't been there at his side. He didn't want to imagine a time when that would ever happen. "Mat...I..." He paused.

"I know."

And the funny thing was, mused Luk, Mat *did* know. He knew exactly what Luk was thinking, what he was trying to say. It had always been this way between them.

Since that first moment when two boys had confronted each other over a scrap of stale bread and their eyes had met. Instead of fighting, they'd shared. And from that tiny shared meal a friendship had sprung that had carried them through the past twenty years of their lives, enriching them, saving them from death time and time again, and bringing them to this quiet forest, as grown men.

While the world considered them brothers, only Lukasz and Matyas knew their name had been stolen from the town they'd lived in. And only they knew that the bond between them had nothing to do with blood ties, and everything to do with a meeting of their souls.

Luk sighed. "It must be the wine. Or the excessive quiet we've been experiencing."

Mat chuckled. "Perhaps it is time for our woman, Luk."

"Aha. I think you're right. It would certainly take care of some longings I confess have gone too long uneased." He grinned into the darkness. "Whose turn is it this time?"

Chapter 19
The Eger's Excitement

"Yours, I think." Mat smiled. He loved it when Luk led this game.

"Very well. Give me a moment here…"

Mat's hand fell down his body to his cock. Already it was starting to stir. It knew well what awaited it.

"Perhaps tonight is a good night for our silver angel."

Oh yes. The silver angel. An excellent choice for a soft country night such as this. Mat sensed Luk's hand moving downwards as well.

"There she is, coming towards us…" Luk began his fantasy. "She's wearing a simple wrap of silk, the color of moonlight, but it is so loose she's having to hold it to her with one hand…"

"And the other?" Mat's grasp on his cock was strengthening as his arousal grew to the picture Luk was painting for him.

"The other is pushing her hair away from her face. Her long hair…so white it's almost silver. Blowing softly now, and there…yes…"

"What?"

"It's caught…wrapped around her breast."

"Which one?"

Luk paused in his monologue and his strokes on his cock stilled. "Does it bloody *matter?*"

"Uh no. Sorry. Carry on." Mat apologized and allowed his hand to continue arousing himself. Gently at first, he stroked his length, letting his mind fill with the image of the silver angel and how she would look as she neared him.

Luk snorted and continued. "The wind is picking up now, and blowing the silk away from her body. She's naked beneath."

Of course. She always was.

Mat smiled as he tugged on the skin of his cock, gripping a little harder now. This game of theirs had begun so many years ago, when death had stared them in the face and they determined to meet it with a raised chin and a defiant attitude.

He remembered the first woman they'd created, and how they'd come together, sharing their climaxes, mingling their seed and binding themselves to each other in preparation for the next life.

They'd cheated their fate, but the 'game' had stayed with them. Neither man would ever think of giving it up, so much a part of their natures had it become.

"Tell me how she looks tonight, Luk."

"She looks lovely, but a little lost. As if she's seeking something. Someone." Luk's body was moving next to Mat's now, as he too stroked himself.

"Her breasts are bared...the silk has fallen away. Such wondrous things, breasts."

"Describe them."

Mat could hear the smile in Luk's voice as he complied. Luk knew how much Mat loved breasts. "They're full, very round and heavy, with nipples...ah...those nipples...see how they're hardening as the breeze touches them? Small, perfectly-shaped nipples, the color of...the color of ripe peaches like we used to steal from the Eger marketplace, remember?"

Mat did indeed. And in his mind, he could see those nipples. His cock was hard now, a slight bead of moisture dewing its head. He ran his thumb over the little drop and smeared it around, enjoying the feel of the cool air as it touched warm damp flesh.

"She's lifting them towards us, Mat. Offering them. She wants us to taste them."

"I think we should, don't you?"

"Yes. Just a lick. A sweet suckle perhaps."

Mat's mouth watered, and his hand moved faster. Beside him he could hear Luk's actions matching his.

"How good they taste. Fruity and womanly. Oh...she's lying down, Mat. The silk is crumpled beneath her and she's lying on it, and...and she's parting her legs for us."

Mat's forehead broke out in a sweat. "Tell me. What do you see?"

* * * * *

What do I see?

For one terrible instant, Luk saw not the silver angel of his fantasy, but the savage face of the Turk as he held a pistol to Mat's head. He drew in a sharp breath and banished the image.

To his relief the angel returned, lying in wait on her cloud of silk. "I see her cunt, Mat. She's wet. So wet. Her honey is slicked around her flesh."

"She has hair there, yes?"

"Oh yes. The most delicate downy hair, shining with her juices and just waiting for us to part it and find her heat."

"And do you think we should use our tongues this time?"

Luk considered this. "I think perhaps I shall suckle her breasts some more. You can use your tongue if you'd like."

"Well..." Mat paused. "I shall use my hands first. I want to see her. See that little cunny swelling and shining. Touch those folds of flesh that beckon us."

Luk hissed in a breath. Mat was very good at creating the details of these fantasies. Luk's cock agreed. Beneath his hand his arousal hardened to the point of pain. It wouldn't take long tonight.

"And how does she look, Mat? Tell me while I tug on these hard nipples of hers..."

Luk tugged on the other thing that was hard, and slipped a hand beneath to cradle his balls. He loved the warmth and the feeling of his seed pulsing inside the tightening pouch of skin.

"She looks...she looks...ready, Luk," breathed Mat. He was moving deliberately now, as he lay next to Luk, and his voice was rough.

Luk knew that both Mat's hands would be circling his cock. They'd compared techniques often enough. Early on, they'd tried it on each other, but as they'd gained experience with their women, they'd come to understand the subtleties that existed between one's own touch and that of another.

There were some things that could only be shared to a point. Self-pleasure was one of them.

"Then take her, Mat...take over..." Luk's balls tightened as he pictured the scene in his mind.

"She's so hot and wet...her flesh is burning me..." Mat's voice was a harsh breath, ragged as he pumped himself. "I'm sliding into her. Deep. Very deep. Her thighs are brushing my skin and parting even more."

"Thrust into her, Mat. Take her. Claim her. She's *ours*..." Luk's hips rose now, in time with his hands and his spine tingled sharply.

A groan from beside him matched the sound trapped in his throat.

"I'm there, Luk. I'm there. She's hanging on to me, pulsing around me, tugging at my cock with her hot cunt...oh *God*...we're coming..."

So was Luk.

With a muffled shout, Luk's body let go, his seed spurting over his belly and his muscles screaming out their pleasure at the release.

He vaguely heard Mat's cry beside him.

For a few seconds the world stood still, and all Luk could do was wait for his body to return. Emptied of its tensions, it finally did.

With a sigh, he let his hands fall to his side, brushing Mat's skin.

Mat's hand moved to grasp his.

"*Köszönem, testvér.*"

Thank you, my brother.

* * * * *

My little brother.

Matyas allowed himself a private chuckle the following morning as he dressed after their brief but invigorating dip in the stream. Calling Luk *little* anything was to do him an injustice.

The sun was barely rising, but they'd become accustomed to waking at dawn, and the chance to start the day clean and refreshed was always welcomed. Mat watched his friend climb into his breeches and adjust himself.

Luk was one handsome devil. They both topped six feet, but Mat knew that Luk had the shoulders and the muscles to go with it. He himself had a lean strength about him, and did not begrudge Luk his power. It had come in handy often enough, as had his own lightning-quick reflexes.

Dark as night, the two were easily assumed to be brothers. They were content to let it be so. No two brothers could have shared more, and in truth would probably have liked each other a lot less. The mere fact that they both had black hair, dark brown eyes and a similar height was a simple result of their birth.

The fact that they had found contentment and safety with each other was a blessing from God. One for which Mat privately gave thanks each and every day of his life.

As he did this morning.

Suddenly, Luk raised his head. "I hear something."

Mat heard it too. "A hunt? Seems early?"

Luk was already bustling to the caravan, locking it up tight. "Too many men, not enough dogs. Let's go and find out."

The two men silently entered the forest. Mat could sense his adrenaline rise as they headed for the commotion that disturbed the tranquility of the dawn. Many times before, they had stealthily done much the same thing, only then they'd had to worry about soldiers, scouting parties, and the occasional irate husband.

This sounded different. Louder, more raucous, as if someone was completely uncaring about whether they were heard or not.

Mat stilled Luk with a hand on his arm. "Ssshh…" He froze, straining his ears for something he thought he'd heard. As if by mutual consent, both men eased back into the undergrowth. Someone was coming their way.

Running, by the sound of things, panting hard, but running as silently as possible. Not silently enough to avoid being overheard by the sensitive ears of the Egers.

Within seconds, they saw her.

Mat sucked in a quiet breath. "Holy Mother…"

Luk's mouth opened.

A woman was running along the forest path, her gown held up in a bunch in front of her. Hair tumbled every which way, and skin showed through tears in the fabric where it had caught on brambles or branches.

She was looking over her shoulder, trying not to stumble, and sobbing for breath.

Behind her came the shouts.

"Hoorooo...gone awaaaay..." A man's voice shouted a hunting cry.

The woman tripped and cried out, slapping her hand across her mouth to stifle the sound.

"Tally ho...I hear her..."

Luk and Mat shared one quick glance, then moved.

With incredible speed they closed in on the woman, Luk behind her with a strong arm around her waist, and Mat in front of her placing a hand over her mouth.

"Mmmmppfff..."

"Hush." It was all Mat said, and he had no idea if she understood. Her eyes were wide with terror and she struggled in Luk's grip, but to no avail. He lifted her off the ground as if she weighed no more than a feather, and within seconds they all melted back into the forest.

Moving as silently as possible, Mat and Luk carried their bundle several yards from the path and then tumbled themselves into a thick patch of ferns, pulling the lacy fronds back above them to cover their bodies.

With Mat on one side of her and Luk on the other, the woman was trapped neatly. Mat brought one leg over hers to still her thrashing fear, and Luk stroked her cheek with his hand as he attempted to calm her.

Her heart pounded against Mat's chest. "Quiet, *kicsi őz*. Your hunters will not find you here. Stay still."

Surprisingly, the woman obeyed.

She froze between them as the sounds of half a dozen men thrashing through the forest drew nearer.

"Damn bitch...we should have brought the dogs." A shout from less than ten yards away sent Mat's heart into overdrive. The adrenaline coursed through him and for a moment, the English countryside disappeared and he was once again buried in a wild forest in the depths of Europe, hugging Luk close and evading the Turk's men.

All that was missing was the blood from their beatings.

And the pain.

His arms tightened around the woman, and Luk's body tensed on the other side of her, a slight shudder, no more, but one Mat felt as surely as the rock that presently dug into his ear.

He too was reliving some old memories best left buried.

"Come on, Charles. Leave her. She's not worth it." Another voice called from further away. "Besides, Eddie's casting up his accounts again…" Laughter accompanied the sound of vomiting.

"Never could hold his brandy, the stupid bastard." The man they'd called "Charles" crashed away, putting welcome distance between him and his prey. "All right lads, I suppose this party's over. Let's find ourselves some food. I have a hunger gnawing at my belly…"

More raucous comments followed, some directed at the hapless Eddie, others suggesting in graphic terms what sort of activity could assuage the hunger Charles was suffering from.

Mat couldn't have cared less. All that concerned him was that the party of drunken men was now heading away, back from whence they'd come.

For long moments, the three people lying in the undergrowth remained silent and still, waiting for the sounds of the forest to reassert themselves.

Mat felt his jacket dampen with the moisture seeping up from the ground, but ignored it. He also felt the soft breasts of the woman pressed against him. That was harder to ignore.

Her head was buried in his chest, and all but smothered by Luk's arm. She was naught but a brown shadow between them, but she was still breathing, and free. That was the most important thing, right now—keeping her free.

Finally they moved. By mutual consent, both Mat and Luk eased their hold a little and let the woman go.

Mat looked down at her as she raised her head.

Huge brown eyes stared at him, and then turned to look at Luk. She blinked.

"Good heavens. I've been rescued by two Hungarian gods."

She blushed.

* * * * *

Luk disentangled himself and rose, helping both Mat and the woman as they stood. "Who were those men? Why were they chasing you?"

"Oh, and we're not gods," added Mat.

She shook out what was left of her skirts. "You could have fooled me." With practical and business-like gestures, she straightened her clothing and attempted to tidy her hair. "What else do you call people who save a woman from a fate a *lot* worse than death?" She eyed them up and down once again. "And you're certainly handsome enough to be gods. Angels? No. Gods, yes."

Luk grinned. "We haven't been formally introduced, Ma'am. The god to your right is Matyas Eger. I am Lukasz Eger. At your service." He bowed correctly, ignoring the crumpled ferns at his feet.

"Eger? Isn't that a town in Hungary?" Interest lit her eyes. "There are some well-known wines from that area, I think?"

Luk glanced at Mat. "We have rescued ourselves a Hungarian scholar, I do believe, Mat."

Mat nodded. "Your knowledge is out of the ordinary, Ma'am...would you care to join us for a bite to eat? Our caravan is not far, and we can at least offer you the chance to tidy yourself. And tell us how you came to this...this difficulty?"

The woman tilted her head, stared at them both, and nodded. "Very well. And I must complement you on your gift for understatement. That was a great deal more than a 'difficulty', as you put it. I am in your debt, gentlemen. Shall we?"

With as much grace as a woman could manage with her gown hanging around her in tatters, she tucked her arms into theirs and allowed them to lead her back to their caravan.

As they walked, Luk took stock of her, and knew Mat was doing much the same thing.

She was short, barely reaching their shoulders, and her gown was one of the ugliest he could remember seeing in a long time. It had once been brown, not a good color choice for her, since her hair was also brown, as were her eyes.

It rendered her naught but a mouse, until one caught the sway of her ample hips. Her skin was white beneath the tears, creamy glimpses showing through as she moved. There were soft curves there, and full breasts if he did not mistake, and Luk found himself increasingly aware of her scent.

Stale sweat mingled with the unmistakable fragrance of a woman.

Her hair was a rat's nest, tangled and filled with twigs and leaves, and there was no doubt in Luk's mind that a good bath would probably be welcome.

The unlikely thought that he'd like to help her wash her back popped into his mind, and his cock hardened.

He frowned.

Reaching the clearing and their caravan, both men urged her to sit while they fetched bread and cheese and shared their morning meal.

The woman ate with gusto, whether starving or just used to eating well, she finished her plate and sighed with pleasure, blushing as a slight belch erupted from her throat. 'Thank you, Sirs. I feel much better now. Perhaps it's time I let you be on your way."

She stood, and swayed a little.

Luk and Mat were right beside her.

"I think not, *kicsi őz*," frowned Luk.

Her eyes turned to his. "What does that mean?"

"Little deer."

She snorted, even as she leaned against them. "It's been some time since anyone called me little, and I don't think I've ever been compared to a deer."

"You are exhausted. Will you not rest for a while in our caravan?" Mat's voice betrayed his concern. "We are on our way to London, but there is no hurry...we can take you to a place of safety...you have but to tell us where."

She sighed. "I have no place of safety, Mr. Eger. In truth, I don't know where I'm going."

"Then come inside and sleep." Luk's words were out of his mouth before he knew it, but Mat was nodding in agreement. "Let us move on, away from this place, and find a new campsite. When you have rested you can tell us how all this came to pass."

The woman's eyelids were drooping, whether from the warmth of the morning sun or the fact that she had a full belly, Luk could only guess. "Come, Ma'am. We will not hurt you."

She turned as they tugged on her arms. "I know that." She smiled, her full mouth curving into the first real grin Luk had seen. It struck a chord in him somewhere. "You two..." she sighed. "You two are gentle. You're...different."

Half asleep already, she made no demur as they settled her into their bed, pulling the blankets around her. She blushed as they tended to her.

"Ah, *Prioshka*," murmured Mat.

"Whassat?"

"The blushing one," whispered Luk as he tucked her hand beneath the cover.

"That's nice. Better than Priscilla..."

She slept.

Chapter 20

It was the lack of movement that finally woke Priscilla Hill.

For a second or two she lay there, aware that she was warm and safe. Two things that had been noticeably lacking in her recent experiences.

The sun seemed very low in the sky, and with a slight gasp she realized she must have slept the day away as her two Hungarian gods had driven this odd vehicle through the quiet lanes.

At least they'd be miles away from Charles Atwood and his cronies. But where to go now? What to do?

Ever practical, Priscilla untangled herself from her blankets. Time to get up, get thinking, and make some decisions.

And see the Egers again.

A little shiver of excitement ran through her. They were handsome as the gods she'd called them, but there was something…something beneath the good looks, some quality or need that appealed to her on a very fundamental level.

She wanted to find out what it was.

And apparently her curiosity was reciprocated. Within moments of her stirring, two smiling faces peered in over the half-door.

"Good day, Prioshka," grinned the one called Luk. *Shoulders*, she thought to herself.

"Did you sleep well?" asked the other. Mat. *Height*, she categorized.

Now she knew them both. It was a handy trick, especially when dealing with several new children.

"Thank you. Yes. I feel a bit guilty, actually…" She smiled back at them. "And I have to apologize for something."

Two sets of eyebrows rose simultaneously in question.

"I *stink*."

Their laughter rang out, bringing a chuckle to Priscilla's own throat. Good heavens. They were *gorgeous*.

"I believe we can help with that. Come on out and see where we are." Mat backed out as Luk helped her rise.

She stepped carefully down the wooden stairs and looked around. They'd found the perfect campsite. Shrouded by willows, the caravan rested on a grassy bank, a few yards from a quiet stream.

The horse had been hobbled a little distance away and was lazily cropping the grass beneath its feet. A small fire was burning, something delicious smelling was cooking in a pot, and the only sounds were those of the birds settling down in the dusk.

"Ooh…how lovely."

"So, Prioshka. Food first or a bath?" Mat's laughing question was accompanied by his hand, holding out a towel and—blessings above—a bar of what looked suspiciously like soap.

She glanced at them. She was hungry, yes. But a *bath*. The chance to rid herself of the stench of the schoolroom and stale sweat.

"If you don't mind…I think…a bath?"

"We don't mind at all, Prioshka," smiled Luk. He rummaged inside a container lashed to the outside of the caravan. "And I think that gown of yours needs to go. Perhaps this…"

Priscilla gasped as he held out a robe in shades of flaming scarlet. "Oh no, I couldn't…really…" Her hand reached out and stroked the fine stuff, and she sighed at the feel of it.

"Of course you could. 'Tis not for us, but for anyone who might need it. You, Prioshka, definitely need it." Luk grinned apologetically.

"Um…my name is Priscilla. Priscilla Hill. *Mrs.* Priscilla Hill."

Mat and Luk exchanged quick glances. "You are married?"

"I was. My husband was killed several years ago in Europe. I'm a widow." She swallowed down her feelings. She'd cried enough. And then moved on.

"Our sympathies, Prioshka. But to us…" Mat flicked a finger at her cheek and watched the color rise so beautifully. "You are *Prioshka*. The blushing one."

Priscilla lived up to her new name. "Yes, well, it's annoying. This silly blushing thing. Better suited for schoolgirls. Which I am most decidedly not." She sighed and took the soap and robe from Luk. "I am thirty-one years old, childless, I've been a governess for the last six years, and I smell awful. Right now, I'd kill for a good soak. So just lead me to the water and call me in about a week."

"Come, Prioshka. Your bath awaits."

And await her it did. The stream flowed lazily around the bend in its path, creating a small natural pond and the last rays of the sun flickered from its gently rippling surface.

With a sigh of pleasure, Priscilla began to unbutton what was left of her gown, then paused. "Um…" She turned to the two men interestedly watching her.

"Privacy, gentlemen?"

Luk and Mat grinned. Identically, wonderfully handsome grins. *Good heavens.*

✳ ✳ ✳ ✳ ✳

Mat was strangely loath to look away. He knew Luk felt the same. There was something so appealing about this woman and her combination of stout practicality and femininity.

"We dare not leave you alone, Prioshka. Even here, where all is quiet. It would be foolish of us to take such a chance." His words made sense to him, but his tone was low. It puzzled him. This reaction she was causing in him, making his loins stir.

She sighed. "Very well. Please turn your backs, and I'll manage somehow."

The men obeyed her request. For all of about thirty seconds.

As soon as they heard the water splash around her, they turned as one back to the river. For a second, they gasped—she was nowhere in sight.

Then she surfaced, dark hair streaming over skin as creamy and pure as milk. And arms that were mottled with bruises.

This time the gasps were of horror. Mat realized that this woman had been hurt. Perhaps it was that knowledge that spurred him on, or perhaps it was the realization that Luk had the same idea in mind.

Whatever it was, they both stripped off their clothes hurriedly, and splashed into the water without a second thought.

"Aaargh...what...what..."

"Prioshka...someone has hurt you..." Luk ran his hands gently up her arms.

"We did not do this to you this morning, did we?" Mat knew he was frowning at her. "When we pulled you from the path?"

He pushed the strands of damp hair away from her face, watching her as she realized their intent was to comfort her. He even saw the moment when the fact of their nudity dawned on her.

A slight shift in expression, perhaps, a little spark of fire behind her brown eyes. Whatever it was, it made his touch even more gentle, a caress of affection—and more. He let his hand rest on her neck.

The color flooded her cheeks. "No. It was not you. My last...charge...thought it was acceptable to pinch his governess." Her eyes closed for a moment, and Luk moved behind her.

"That is wrong, Prioshka. No one should be permitted to do such a thing. Especially not to one with skin like yours."

Luk's hand rested on her other shoulder, and Mat felt his cock swell as the water swirled around her full breasts, almost hiding them and almost revealing them with its gentle movements.

"There is nothing special about my skin, Luk," she breathed.

"Oh you're wrong, Prioshka," said Mat. He slipped his hand up her neck to cup her cheek. "You have skin like velvet. White velvet."

She snorted through her blushes. "Nicely put. But it's very grubby right now, so if you don't mind..."

"Oh we don't mind at all." Luk grabbed the soap from her hands and tossed it gaily to Mat. "Consider us your servants."

"Will Milady permit us to wash her hair?" Mat laughed out loud at the look on her face. She was clearly torn...torn between her natural modesty and the desire to be cosseted.

"I...well...I..."

"Good. Just relax." Mat lathered up the soap and swirled his hands over her head, making her close her eyes to avoid the bubbles.

From behind her, Luk's hands joined his, massaging her scalp, tugging the tangles free and scrubbing her hair thoroughly.

And, inevitably, one thing led to another.

Their laughter faded as the soapy foam traveled lower, followed by the capable touch of the Egers.

Her neck was washed, and her shoulders received the devoted attention of four hands. Her skin colored delightfully under their attentions.

As Luk's hands slid lower, she sighed, moving slightly as he massaged her spine with consummate skill.

Mat didn't need to see Luk's face. He knew its expression matched his own. His blood was heating as they washed this charming woman, who was apparently unaware of her own charms.

He let his fingers trail lightly down over the swell of her breasts, just as Luk slipped his own hands around her body, rubbing soap just beneath their fullness.

She gasped, and a little moan followed as she moved against Luk's chest.

Mat neared her, letting her nipples just brush his own firm skin. "Ah, Prioshka...so good. So soft..."

They moved nearer the bank, both Mat and Luk reading each other's thoughts as always. Kneeling in the water, they took her weight and helped her float.

One of Luk's arms was beneath her shoulders and his head neared her breast. Mat moved between her legs and let them rest on his shoulders.

Slowly...very slowly...each man washed her with loving hands.

And Priscilla sighed with pleasure.

* * * * *

She was floating. The feeling of weightlessness was strange, hypnotic almost to someone who wasn't used to the sensation.

The water supported her along with the two men who were lavishing attentions on her body, and Priscilla surrendered to the delight of the moment. It was wrong, of course, but who cared?

She was tired. Tired of being at the beck and call of children with few graces and no manners. Tired of never quite fitting into any of the families she lived with. Of being in some odd place between servant and guest, neither fish nor fowl nor good fair game, as her father would have said.

Good heavens above, what would he have thought if he could see her now? A country parson's daughter, languishing naked in a stream being caressed by two of the most handsome men she could remember seeing in a long while.

Luk's hands began to wash her breasts, and her memories faded. Mat's hands stroked up her thighs and she stopped thinking about anything at all.

She could only feel.

The luxurious slide of the soap over her skin, the warmth of their hands as they smoothed and swirled the foamy suds over all kinds of lovely places...like *that* one right *there*...

It was incredibly arousing, and to her surprise Priscilla found a heat building inside her she'd long thought dead. Her buttocks tightened as Mat began to wash her mound, and her nipples hardened to taut peaks beneath Luk's fingers.

"Oh...oh..." She couldn't stop the moan of delight.

Her hair swirled free in the water, rinsed of the grime and dirt that had turned it lank and smelly. Her skin glowed as the sweat was rinsed away, and she felt her spirit being cleansed as much as her body.

Then...oh yes...then lips replaced hands.

With eyes closed and cooling water lapping at her curves, Priscilla gave herself up to the knowing mouths and tongues of her two saviors.

Luk suckled her, gently ringing her nipple at first, then tugging on it, little teasing pulls that sent bolts of fire through her and down to her clit.

Where Mat answered their call with a skill all his own.

His head was tucked low, almost in the water, but she could feel the strength of his shoulders as he raised her a little and brought her to his mouth. Oh *God*.

His tongue found her, seeking, licking, delving between the folds of her newly-cleansed flesh. Driving her arousal higher with each touch, he too teased and suckled her, unhesitatingly finding that little bud of sensation that brought a soft cry of delight bursting from her throat.

"Yes...Prioshka, so beautiful..." murmured Luk. Or was it Mat?

She didn't know. It could have been both.

All she knew was that something was building within her, something bubbling up deep from her loins that threatened to swamp her with sensations unlike any she'd ever experienced.

All throughout her marriage, she'd enjoyed the sexual act, but *this*…this was beyond her experience.

No one had ever loved her like *this* before.

Her thighs tightened around Mat's head as Luk bent to her breast, each man an artist, intent upon creating magic with his tongue.

And goodness me, it's working.

Priscilla's breath rasped in her lungs.

"Let it go, Prioshka…let it go…"

Someone was telling her to do something. What? Who?

"Relax sweetheart. Relax…"

How could she relax? When a volcano was about to erupt inside her and turn her world upside down?

"Come for us, love, come for us…"

Yes.

That she could do.

With a scream of delight, Priscilla let it happen.

Waves of pleasure swamped her and she held Luk's head tight to her breast as her legs pulled Mat's face even closer to her clit. She could feel the spasms as they rocked her, taking her breath away and sending her muscles into rigid mounds of shuddering sensation.

The water splashed around them as she rode out the internal storm, gasping for air and losing herself for what seemed like hours in a vortex of physical chaos.

And slowly, exhaustedly, Priscilla came back to earth.

* * * * *

They sat around the fire, letting the dying flames flicker over their faces.

Luk smiled as he looked at Prioshka. No—Priscilla. *Damn.* He couldn't think of her as anything but Prioshka now, especially remembering the way her whole body had flushed with her heat as she came.

Mat was smiling too.

Neither man had reached his own climax in the water, but that was irrelevant. It would happen. They all knew it. And it was this knowledge that made Luk smile.

"You liked the meal?" Mat's question was casual, and his pose even more so.

They'd tugged on their breeches but little else, and now sprawled comfortably on blankets, leaning against the wheels of the caravan.

"Oh yes," she answered. "And everything else too."

There it was. The color rising and falling on her cheeks with her thoughts. So honest, this woman.

"Tell us your story, Prioshka," urged Luk. He had a deep need to know her. Really know her. To find out what lay behind the soft curves and wide smile. What thoughts were tumbling beneath her mass of shiny brown hair. How she had come to be who she was, and what had driven her into this forest.

"Please, Prioshka?"

Luk smothered a grin at Mat's pleading tone. Like two children begging for a fairy tale, they urged her to bare herself. To spread her life before them.

She smiled. "Very well." She glanced at them. "But I warn you, 'tis not exciting at all. Quite boring, in fact."

Luk gazed at her. "You would never bore us, love."

Prioshka snorted. "Right. Take one simple country vicar's daughter. Educate her, marry her to a local farmer, give her a few local children to teach. Take away her husband, kill him on some stupid battlefield in Europe, and then turn her out to find her own way...not the most exciting of tales, is it?"

Mat's hand tugged on a wayward lock of her hair. "Go on, sweetheart."

She sighed. "I became a governess. Since I liked to read, enjoyed teaching children, and can speak several languages..." She slanted a grin at them. "*Not* Hungarian..."

Luk laughed. "*Yet.*"

She blushed. "Yes, well...where was I? Oh yes...I became a governess. My first position was acceptable. Difficult, yes, since a governess is in an odd position in an English household. She's not a part of the family, nor a part of the 'belowstairs' community. It could be..."

"Lonely?" Mat's voice spoke the word trembling on Luk's lips.

"Yes. Unquestionably lonely. But..." She shrugged. "Survivable. Unlike my latest position."

"Ah yes. The huntsmen." Luk's mouth curled in distaste.

"Who were they, Prioshka?" Mat's question was harsh.

"Just men." Her tone was flat, expressionless. "A house party where the wine had flown too freely, and the women, apparently, not freely enough. They considered the governess...fair game."

"And you, naturally, did not."

"I certainly did not. I am not that kind of woman..." She paused. And blushed.

"No you're not." Luk reached out for her hand and held it tight. "You are a woman who needs loving. Not raping."

Mat was already holding her other hand. "Luk's right, Prioshka. Loving a woman is a totally different thing to what those animals had in mind."

She thought about that for a moment, silent beneath their gazes. Then she squared her shoulders. "You're right. There is a difference. And I must, in all honesty, confess something."

The men waited.

"I enjoyed what we did...in the stream. I enjoyed it—a *lot.*" There was a defiance to her tone that brought smiles to the faces of both Mat and Luk.

"So did we, love." Mat's grin gleamed in the firelight.

"Don't doubt that," added Luk.

She sucked in a breath. "Look, I've been married. I've experienced what happens between a man and a woman. And I can't help but think that you two...that is...that *it* didn't happen for you?"

There was the color again, flushing brightly now as the glow of the fire matched the glow in her cheeks.

"Ah, Prioshka..." Luk stroked her fingers between his. "Pleasure comes in many shapes and forms. The pleasure of watching a woman reach her peak beneath our touch...well, that is a satisfaction in and of itself."

"And as for us? There's time yet..." Mat's voice was husky, and Luk felt his cock swell beneath his breeches. There was indeed time. But it had better be soon.

She sighed, whether in anticipation or concern, Luk couldn't tell. He hoped it was the former.

"Well, enough about me. I'd much rather hear about you two. How you came to be traveling through this forest? How long you've known each other?"

Luk and Mat shared a quick glance.

"But...we're brothers," stammered Mat.

Prioshka smiled. "Indeed you are. But not blood brothers, I'm thinking. Your brotherhood is deeper by far."

The men sat, stunned. How had she known?

"Tell me, please?" She fidgeted around and settled herself more comfortably, still holding onto a hand of each of them. "'Tis your turn to tell *me* a story."

Chapter 21

And they did.

In the quiet of an English forest, dark now, and lit only by the embers of their fire, Mat and Luk told her a tale.

Haltingly at first, and then with more confidence, they bared their past. Priscilla wondered if anyone had heard this story the way she did. Listening more for what was *not* said than what was.

She sat quietly as they told of meeting in a Hungarian orphanage, lost, hungry and sharing their food. Of taking the name of their town as their own, scavenging from the streets when there was no other alternative, and sleeping beside the steps of the great Cathedral, as if to seek shelter from God himself.

She held their hands tight as they told her how they'd fled Eger, only to fall prey to the "Turk".

Here was something, she realized, as both their hands flexed beneath her fingers at the mention of his name.

They described themselves as his servants, and prepared to move on, but she stopped them. "You were more than servants to this man, weren't you?"

There was silence for a moment, as two pairs of brown eyes stared into the fire.

"Yes," said Luk.

"The Turk...he was a trader. A provider of commodities to those who needed them." Mat's voice was harsh.

Priscilla swallowed, once again intuitively reading what had been left unsaid. "And you...you two were—provided?"

"When necessary. Yes." Luk's words came out as a pained grunt.

"That explains a lot," she said, thinking the words to herself, but speaking them aloud.

"What?" asked Mat roughly.

Priscilla paused, looking for the right words to express what she'd discovered. "It explains why you two are...as you are. So close. So in tune with each other. And so comfortable...together."

Luk blinked. "I don't understand."

She gripped their hands tighter. "When young lives are threatened, by whatever horrors befall them, they instinctively seek something...*anything*...to hold on to, to trust, and to love. It's human nature." She glanced at the two men who were staring at her intently.

"You two found each other and hung on to each other. You were each other's touchstone, if you will, someone who was there, *always* there, and could understand, since you were both experiencing the same things."

They nodded in unison.

"So now I understand. How you two can seem to share a thought. How you two can also share...a woman. There is no competition between you, just a profound trust." She blushed a little. "And an extraordinary love."

Mat made as if to speak, but she continued, determined to finish her thought. "It's a love that goes beyond anything physical. It's a love born of fear and desperation and nurtured by selflessness and respect. I admire you for it. I'm amazed that you've survived, and overwhelmed by what you must have gone through together."

She raised both their hands to her lips and dropped a light kiss on their knuckles. "And I'm proud to know you."

Once again silence fell, and Priscilla listened, almost believing she could hear their hearts beating on either side of her.

Luk tugged his hand away. "I need my music." His voice was cracking.

Mat also pulled his hand away, and gulped.

Priscilla tried to ignore the sparkle of tears that glittered in their eyes as they swept around the small clearing. But her own heart was full.

Full of emotions, of desires, of needs...and full of these two men, who had their own needs. She wanted to help them. To cherish them. To give them something that perhaps they'd not known.

To give them all the love she had bottled up inside her. A love that had tried to find an outlet with her husband, and then with the children she'd tutored. But had slowly withered as her attempts had met with failure after failure. Nobody, it seemed, had needed what Priscilla had to offer.

Until now.

A sound jerked her from her thoughts, and the plaintive chords of a violin rolled softly through the night.

Another one echoed the tune, and within moments, each man was playing—in harmony, in counterpoint, but always together. Just like their lives, their music was intertwined, haunting and beautiful, yet with an undercurrent of sadness and desolation.

It brought the glitter of tears to her own eyes, and she dashed them away, fearing to miss a note of the wild Gypsy melodies that buried themselves in her soul.

Finally, they stopped, lowering their bows and looking at her.

"Oh my. So wonderful..." she breathed. "But so sad. Will you not try something more cheerful? Perhaps something English? I sing a little..."

She knew her cheeks were coloring up again, damn them, but was ready to lift this introspective mood.

Mat's lips softened and he glanced at Luk. "As Prioshka wishes..."

* * * * *

It was a simple country tune, one of the first English melodies they'd learned, but it sprang from Mat's bow with ease. Luk was right there with him.

And Prioshka was smiling.

Mat's heart smiled too. They'd found a rare treasure in the forest...a woman who seemed to be as attuned to them as they were to each other.

"Summer is a'comin' in..."

Her voice rang out over their playing, rich and true and shocking Mat to his core. He glanced at Luk, seeing his eyes widen in surprise.

Prioshka could *sing*.

This wasn't the polite voice heard over teacups at a musical soiree. It wasn't the carefully schooled sound of a girl trained to the classics. It was the pure liquid emotion of a woman whose vocal chords were her instrument.

Her range was astounding, and not a tremor marked her passage from the lower register to the upper notes of her song.

She sang from her heart.

Mat and Luk responded. They played from their hearts too.

And as the hours passed, they taught her their songs. Some in Hungarian, making her laugh, and others in English. In return, she hummed her favorite melodies, clapping her hands with pleasure as they picked up the tune and improvised their own versions.

Their music filled the night, appreciated by none but the startled creatures out hunting for a meal. Performing in a natural concert hall where the ceiling was carpeted with stars and the walls non-existent, three hearts met in a rare blend of music and joy.

It was seductive, passionate, and it left all three breathless when they finally stopped, the last notes echoing into the darkness.

"Prioshka," breathed Mat, panting slightly. "Such a voice. Such a wonderful voice..."

She blushed. "I loved to sing in my father's church."

"The Lord must have loved to hear you," said Luk, laying his bow and his violin back into its case.

"Thank you." She ran her hands down over her robe self-consciously. "I was told I was too loud."

Mat snorted. "Only by those who didn't appreciate such beauty, I'll warrant."

She glanced at him, an odd expression crossing her face. "Mat, I have no illusions. The word 'beauty' is not used in connection with me. Ever."

Mat stared at her. She genuinely believed what she was saying. She certainly didn't fit the mold of conventional loveliness, true, given her curvaceously rounded body, her lack of inches, and her overly generous mouth. Her hair was a cluster of simple brown curls, her eyes a matching plain brown, and there was nothing to mark her as anything more than "average". Unless one looked into her heart.

Mat looked into her heart.

And felt his own turn over. He held out his hand to her.

"Prioshka. Come. Let us show you how wrong you are."

Luk came up behind her and rested his hands on her shoulders. He understood.

"Beauty comes in many shapes and forms, love," said Luk softly. He dropped a kiss on her neck, and Mat watched as her nipples hardened beneath her robe. "We find yours to be beyond anything we've ever seen."

Mat closed the distance between them as she reached out to take his hand. "It's a beauty that shines, sweetheart." He stroked her cheek as Luk nibbled upwards to her ear. "A beauty from within. And we see it. We see *you*."

"Can you see *us*, Prioshka?" Luk whispered the words low, but Mat heard them. He followed them up with a gentle touch of his lips to hers.

He pressed himself to her breasts and felt her heart pounding.

"Can you *be* with us, Prioshka? Can you open your heart and find a place for two wandering Gypsies?"

He felt the breath she took as she stood so close between them. "You are already there."

Mat's cock hardened rapidly at her words. She knew what he'd asked, what he and Luk intended. And she had accepted.

One hand slid up his chest to tangle in his hair, while the other reached for Luk's head. She pulled them both even closer.

"Yes," she breathed. "I can see you. I want to be with you. I want to find the music and the love that I've lost. I want to…give…"

Mat moved closer, sensing Luk doing the same. She was pressed between their hard bodies now, their arousals solid against her hot flesh. Mat burned where his cock brushed her belly, and Luk's breath was coming faster as he pushed himself to her back.

Mat kissed her lips again, letting them part this time, and sliding his tongue within. She tasted of the dark wine they'd shared, and honey. And something else…a welcome, a heat that asked nothing but offered everything.

He pulled back and turned her into Luk's waiting embrace.

Luk's lips replaced Mat's and Mat's hands learned her body, stroking from her buttocks up her sides and around to cup her breasts and force them into Luk's chest.

His cock reminded him that it was still confined within his breeches, and he groaned. Or maybe it was Luk. He was probably suffering the same constriction.

Finally, she peeled her lips from Luk's mouth. "*Please...*"

It was a quiet word, but one that sent shivers of delight through Mat's body to his balls. As one, he and Luk offered her their hands.

"Come."

They led her into the darkness of their caravan.

* * * * *

Priscilla felt her clothes evaporate beneath the attentions of four busy hands. She could see little, but feel...oh so much.

Hot hard flesh met her fingertips as she reached out towards the two men who would become her lovers. Their breaths mingled, and she knew not whose lips kissed hers, nor did she care.

She cared only that they touch her, caress her, and bring moans of pleasure to her throat.

And *that* they did. Very well indeed.

While her head was held firmly and her mouth plundered by a hungry tongue, another tongue investigated the curves of her belly, tickled her navel and moved lower. With an uncanny coordination, both men delved into her softest tissues, driving her practically mad with their movements.

She writhed beneath the firm grasp, and found herself lifted bodily onto the bed. Gasping as their skin separated, she sighed once more as two bodies tipped the mattress with their weight.

A pair of lips found her breast, tugging on the nipple and making her moan. A mouth took light nibbles from her hips, her thighs, and ran teeth down towards her knee and back up, finally finding the sweet moisture of her pussy.

She was wet, running with tears of pleasure now, and ready to experience whatever these two had to offer. Her hands were everywhere. She could feel hot skin, soft hair, a tiny budded nipple on a firm chest.

She wanted more.

"Let me touch you...both..." She whispered the words and felt the two bodies next to her shiver.

They moved, in concert as always, and she became aware of their weight near her shoulders. Two cocks rested on her breasts.

Carefully, she reached for them, letting each hand find the solid smoothness and learn the similarities and differences between them. One was ridged just *here*...the other...*there*...

She slipped her hands around them, finding their balls tucked into hardening sacs beneath. It was a fascinating voyage of discovery for Priscilla and she enjoyed every single minute of it.

They allowed her to rove wherever she wanted, silently telling her with little sighs and caresses how much they enjoyed her touch.

When twin droplets of moisture beaded both heads, they finally moved.

"We will not get you with child, love," whispered a voice. Mat?

"Nor will we hurt you, Prioshka," murmured another. Luk?

She couldn't distinguish the two of them now, and had no desire to try. They were as one, loving her to distraction, and she needed them. Both. Now.

"Don't worry about children." Her brain forced itself up from her pussy and struggled to respond. It was important they know something. "I am barren. I lost three babes during my marriage and can have no more."

Their tenderness knew no bounds.

Tongues slithered over her now, leaving no inch of skin untouched. They turned her onto her side and nibbled at her buttocks, parting the firm flesh and teasing at the rosy ring of muscles they revealed.

They rolled her onto her stomach and straddled her, one dragging his cock sensually over her spine as the other buried his head between her legs and drove her to distraction with his tongue.

She burned.

Her body took on a life of its own, legs parting, muscles tightening in anticipation of what was yet to come, and her mouth kissing and suckling whatever came near it. She reached for whoever was closest, and lost herself in their loving.

Like a well-choreographed minuet, Luk and Mat took her to the limits of her mind. Her thoughts vaporized as they touched her, teasingly, then insistently, finding the most sensitive places and working them skillfully until she was ready to scream.

While one mouth suckled her nipples and fingers kneaded her breasts, another tongue plunged deep into her cunt, lapping away her juices and forcing her legs to open wider—and wider still.

She was sobbing with delight, gasping words she didn't understand and couldn't hear.

But they could.

They moved. She was raised by strong arms and felt one man slide beneath her. Her legs dangled over the edge of the bed, and slowly—oh so slowly, she was lowered onto a firm cock.

There were hands guiding it home. They were helping each other.

With a little sigh of relief, Priscilla let it fill her cunt. Stretching her, completing her—almost.

One was in front of her now, and blindly she reached out, feeling the heat burning from him before she touched his flesh. His cock was there.

Ready for her.

As hands slipped around her to her breasts, pinching the nipples and pulling them to even greater hardness, she opened her mouth and leaned towards the cock she now held tight in her grasp.

With a sound of pleasure, she sucked it between her lips.

Now she was filled.

One cock began to move at the urging of the strong hips beneath her and the other slid from her mouth and back in again in a matching rhythm. A hand slipped between her legs and found her clit, smearing the juices over her already soaked flesh and teasing her to the heights of pleasure.

As her arousal swamped her, Priscilla reached for a hand. She pulled it past her and made sure it touched the man behind her.

Together, the three became one.

Holding on to each other, moving, rocking, thrusting and suckling, they let themselves go—blindly taking the path to oblivion, side by side by side.

Priscilla's heart pounded as she felt the beginnings of her orgasm stirring deep in her cunt.

Within her mouth, the cock she sucked began to tremble and the veins to pulse, and the thighs beneath hers tightened to marble.

It was going to happen. To all of them. Together they were going to fall into some universe where life would change forever.

The cock in her mouth tried to pull back, but she grabbed onto it, refusing to let go. She wanted this. Wanted her cunt to explode around one cock as another flooded her throat.

She dug her fingernails into a firm buttock and sucked hard, just as the first waves of her orgasm broke.

Her cries were muffled, but the shout that broke from the men was not. Inside her cunt hot jets of seed filled her, and inside her mouth spurts flowed down her throat. Muscles clenched, bodies trembled, and they reached for the soul of madness.

Together.

* * * * *

They woke her twice more during the night.

Once so that Luk could avail himself of the delights offered by her snug cunt. He'd let Mat take her there first, being very content to have her mouth draw his seed from someplace around his armpits.

She'd not been skilled, but her enthusiasm and delight in what they did had made that particular climax memorable. Luk couldn't believe it when she'd taken his hand and made sure he was touching Mat as they came.

In some way it had lent a sense of spiritual completion to the act that had shaken Luk to his soul. Coming together inside this woman, no matter how it was accomplished, felt...*right*.

Luk's arousal had hardened in his sleep, and he awoke to find Mat in similar straits. They'd gently begun touching the soft woman who lay between them, stroking and caressing her, relishing the warmth of her skin and her welcome as she, too, awoke.

No words had been spoken—none were necessary.

She'd opened her arms to them and welcomed them once more, without shame or hesitation.

Lips had mingled, sighs were the only sounds within the caravan, and this time, Luk had settled between her rounded thighs, seeking her heat with his cock. Mat knelt by her head and she took him into her mouth willingly, his sigh of pleasure echoing Luk's.

As talented on the flesh of a woman as he was on the strings of his violin, Luk strummed her clit as he thrust into her, feeling her vibrate beneath him as he found all her sensitive folds.

She was all boiling hot wetness, clasping his cock with muscles she probably didn't even know she was using. The thought flashed through Luk's mind that she'd been made just for this—for them. He offered up a quick prayer of thanks to whatever guardian angel had sent her fleeing through the forest and into their arms.

Then she lifted her hips slightly and moaned, and Luk's mind blanked out. Mat panted now as she sucked him vigorously, and he reached out, finding Luk's shoulder and gripping it hard.

Once again, the three became one. Mat growled in the back of his throat as Luk's cock plunged deeper, hammering into her, balls slapping her flesh in time to the movements of her head as she took Mat deeply into her mouth.

It was a rhythm none could have consciously sought, but one that their bodies demanded. A syncopation of movement played by a trio of lovers intent on finding that final moment of perfection.

And it came. Mat's cock muffled Prioshka's strangled cry, but her shudders were unmistakable. Luk thrust deep and let her cunt squeeze him—almost to the point of pain.

Mat's trembling hand dug into his shoulder as his own release neared, and Luk's balls hardened into a knot as his buttocks clenched hard.

Mat let go. With a roar he came, and the sound of his orgasm and Prioshka's mouth taking it all tipped Luk over the edge.

Buried deep in her cunt, Luk exploded, fireworks detonating behind his eyeballs and his arm linked with Mat's. He cried out as his body shook with the force of it, an elemental sound that came from somewhere deep inside him...a place he'd not known about until tonight.

As they tumbled into a tangle of exhausted limbs, Luk wondered if perhaps it was his heart.

Dawn was nearing the second time they awoke.

Prioshka was dreaming, muttering and murmuring in her sleep. Exchanging brief glances in the dim early light, both Luk and Mat touched her. This time, it would be for her alone. Their thank-you to her.

Still slick and slippery from their loving, her body was soft and relaxed as they began their voyage of exploration. Not an inch of skin went unexamined, or unkissed. She woke gradually beneath their hands, sighing and groaning with delight as they once more aroused her sleepy body to awareness.

They discovered sensitive spots beneath her arms, licked their way up beneath her breasts to her nipples and back down again, and dueled with their tongues around her navel, making her squirm with delight.

Luk slipped his fingers between her legs and lazily spread the hot wetness he found there over her skin. He let his fingers slide lower, between her buttocks, into the dark cleft and over the tight puckered flesh of her anus.

She jerked upwards, which pleased Mat since her breast was already in his mouth.

"Ssshhh...Prioshka. This will heighten your pleasure," breathed Luk.

"I'm not sure...I can take no more..." Her voice was cracked and rough with sleep.

"Yes you can. Let us show you."

They continued to arouse her, playing gently with her body, as Luk's fingers continued his sensual massage. Her body was completely fluid to their touch, ebbing and flowing to each man's caress.

Luk gently slid one slick finger into her anus, past the snug muscles, and let it rest there as Mat continued to cherish her nipples with his mouth.

She sighed and relaxed, and Luk shuddered at the pleasure of knowing this was a first for her. That they were giving her back something precious and special. He continued his subtle pressure, tugging on her folds of flesh at the same time and abrading her clit with his thumb.

Her hips moved restlessly and she found their heads with her hands and held on tight.

"Oh God…"

"Come for us, Prioshka," breathed Mat.

Luk could hear his breath as he gently blew onto her wet and gleaming nipples. Her muscles were starting to tremble around his fingers. She was indeed coming.

"Now, Mat," he urged.

Mat's head dropped once more and he suckled her strongly into his mouth as Luk pressed upwards into her clit.

She cried out and her whole body arched as the spasms of her climax began. She rolled and bucked beneath them, sobbing out their names, and shaking like a leaf in a storm.

Her body gripped Luk's fingers tight enough to bruise, and her hands pulled on his hair as she exploded.

Mat's head rose from her breast and they both watched this amazing woman riding the incredible peaks of her orgasm.

Their eyes met across her body, and as if with one mind they leaned to each other, resting their foreheads together. Joining. Becoming one with Prioshka and her body that held them both captive.

Slowly, she relaxed and Luk eased his hand from her buttocks.

"I want you to come too," she breathed. "Please."

She glanced down at their cocks, once more harder than iron and resting hot against her skin.

"You can't take us again, love," said Luk. "It would be too much for this night."

"Then come *on* me, not in me." With hands that still shook from the aftermath of her orgasm, Prioshka took a cock in each hand and brought them to her breasts. "Bathe me in your seed. Let me watch…let me share."

Chapter 22

Something in Priscilla's mind was telling her she was a wicked and wanton woman. She ignored it. This night had expanded her horizons, taking her into a dream world where love was shared selflessly, passion was boundless and pleasure just a touch away.

She was greedy. She wanted more.

Mat and Luk had given her so much, and yet she sensed there was more that could be experienced. She wanted to know—them.

She'd been thoroughly pleasured by them in the darkness, but now, with the dawn breaking, it was her time to watch.

They exchanged a look when she spoke, then moved to her sides, cocks rigid and already beading with a tiny drop of moisture.

Obeying some instinct, she stretched and rested her arms behind her head, offering her breasts to their gaze and her body to their hearts.

I am yours. Always and forever.

She pushed aside the thought that forever might only last a few more hours. She was determined to experience every drop of delight she could wring from these two wonderful men.

Her breath caught as they reached for themselves, and with slow strokes began the journey to their releases.

A cock would dip slightly, brushing her breast, and her mouth watered with the remembered taste of their skin—their seed. Each salty and tangy, they were different, and Priscilla smiled a little as she realized she could probably tell them apart now just from the taste of them.

Mat's eyes were closing as his grip tightened, and Luk's breath was coming faster. He kept his eyes open, focusing now on Mat's hand, and then on her breasts as they rose and fell beneath him.

The sound of their hands on their skin was an arousal in itself, the slipping of flesh on flesh providing the music to their actions and an accompaniment to the song their cocks were singing. A song of desire and heat and all the passion denied Priscilla for so long.

She smiled. Her life would never be the same after this night, and she had no regrets. No regrets at all.

Mat's rhythm grew jerky and Luk's thighs hardened against her body. They were coming, she just knew it.

With a matching moan, both men erupted, spewing their seed across her until it mingled into a pool on her breasts. It was hot, burning its way through her skin and into her heart.

They shuddered in spasms of pleasure, sagging as their balls emptied their precious cargo onto her willing flesh. Their seed. Magic life-containing liquid resting hotly on her body.

She moved her arms and reached out to them once more, running her hands gently over their shoulders. Their muscles were loosening now as they fell from the peak, and she rubbed them, soothing them and murmuring their names.

Mat reached for a cloth and delicately wiped away the warm stickiness as Luk reached for the covers they'd kicked aside.

For the third time they settled themselves together, like puppies exhausted from play.

And as the dawn rose, three hearts slowed, three minds eased, and three bodies fell asleep.

✷ ✷ ✷ ✷ ✷

"Stay with us, Prioshka."

Mat's words fell into the quiet morning light as they shared a light meal, and Priscilla felt her heart stop for a second as their import dawned on her.

"What?"

"Stay with us, love." Luk stared at her intently. "We want you. Beside us as we travel, beneath us and around us as we love, and between us as we sleep."

Her eyes filled with the sting of tears. "How...I mean...where..." Her mind spun out of control.

"Does it matter?" Mat's voice was quiet. "You need a place to call home. We need a heart to call ours. Is there a better match?"

Priscilla looked at them. So handsome, so strong, and yet needing something she, little plain Priscilla Hill, could offer.

"Travel with us, sweetheart. See the world at our side. We are on our way to London to meet up with our friends, but after that we're free. The world awaits us."

"I…I…" The words stuck in her throat as she allowed herself the luxury of imagining such a life.

"With our music and your voice we can make our own way. We'll be dependent on no one, except ourselves. It's a free life, Prioshka, not elegant or easy…but free."

Priscilla snorted. "I never wanted elegance."

"Yet you deserve it. And so much more. More than we can give you. All we have to offer is this humble caravan and…ourselves."

Mat's eyes were pleading as she faced him and Luk.

"It's more riches than you can possibly imagine, Mat. But…are you sure?"

"We are sure." Luk's voice was firm. "There is much we have yet to see, love. Now that the war is over, Europe beckons. Come wander a while with us. Practice some of your language skills. Learn Hungarian the right way. In bed with us." A wicked grin curved his lips.

Priscilla sighed. Good lord, these two were…wonderful.

"How I would like to. But…" She paused. "A time will come when you'll both want to wed. To settle down with families of your own. I don't think I could bear it. And yet I know it must happen."

Two frowns crossed two faces. "Never, Prioshka. Children of our hearts? Perhaps. Children of our flesh—no."

"I don't understand."

Mat drew in a breath. "Prioshka, we do not know who we are. As orphans, there were no records of our parentage. We made a promise to each other a long time ago that we'd never father children who might, through no fault of ours or theirs, end up in the same situation."

She opened her mouth to speak, but Luk forestalled her. "You see, love, we have a very small piece of land, not far from Eger, that we quietly bought a few years ago. It's covered with untended vineyards right now, but eventually we shall return to it. The war got in the way of our plans, but it didn't really matter."

"It's not large, but there is potential there. We intend to go back soon. And once there…"

"What?" Priscilla couldn't help the question

"Once there," continued Mat, "We shall open our own orphanage, but this time there will be food. And love."

Priscilla blinked as the pieces fell into place. They were going to give other children the chance they never had. To make some kind of sense of their past. Use their experiences to better other lives. And they wanted her to be a part of it.

"It sounds…like heaven."

And indeed it did. To live in Hungary, to love these men, all the while tending to children desperate for affection, with minds crying out for knowledge and a helping hand…Priscilla's eyes filled with tears once more.

"Then come and be a part of our heaven. We need an angel. And…truthfully neither Mat nor I can imagine it now without you."

Luk held out his hand, as did Mat.

They were offering so much. Did they realize it? Had they any idea that their simple plans had opened up a new world for this sheltered governess? That their loving had opened her heart and their passion had opened her soul?

There was only one answer she could make.

She placed her hands in theirs. "Yes."

* * * * *

Their newfound partnership lasted all of two hours.

"You haven't thought this through," complained Priscilla as she clambered onto the seat of the caravan between Luk and Mat.

Mat gritted his teeth. "There is nothing to think through, Prioshka. You are with us now. End of story."

"But…what will people think? You're going to London. There might be people there who could help fund your project. They're not going to want to come anywhere near you if they think you're…we're…well…if I'm…"

"If you're what?" snapped Luk. "Our lover?"

Mat couldn't help the grin as once more the hot color flooded Prioshka's cheeks.

"Exactly." She may have been blushing but she wasn't about to back down from her arguments.

"Who cares? We don't." Luk clicked up the horses.

Priscilla sighed gustily. "It's just that I don't want my presence to be a hindrance. I love you both too much to want to harm you in any way."

Luk's severe countenance relaxed. "Sweetheart, we love you too. It took no time at all for you to climb into our hearts. You're there now. Permanently."

"Say goodbye, Prioshka." Mat grasped her hand and folded it into his.

"Goodbye?"

"Goodbye to Mistress Priscilla Hill, governess. She is no more. Behold a new person—Prioshka Eger. Beloved woman of the Eger brothers. Lover, friend, playmate, teacher…all that and more."

"But what of your friends?" Prioshka's voice was weakening under the touch of his hand and the press of Luk's shoulder on her other side.

"Our friends?" Both men shared a chuckle.

"They'll love you as we do, darling. Never worry your head on that score. We've been through too much together to ever be critical of each other at this date." Luk nodded at Mat's words.

"We spent several years in France, Prioshka…" His voice tapered off.

"You did?"

Mat heard the curiosity. "We did."

And over the next few hours he and Luk shared some of their stories, bringing a gasp to her lips as they told of missions accomplished, lives saved—and occasionally lost.

"You mean you actually…"

A sharp lurch interrupted Prioshka, and both men swore sibilantly.

Reining in the horse, Luk clambered down as Mat leaped to the ground from his side. Further curses echoed along the lane.

"Damned linchpin," muttered Mat.

Prioshka scrambled down into the road and joined them, staring at the cracked wood. "Oh dear."

"'Oh dear' is right," growled Luke. "The damn wheel will have to come off."

Shortly thereafter, the wheel lay prone at the side of the road, while two shirtless gods muttered and mumbled to themselves as they attempted a repair. Prioshka looked on, helpfully passing a tool when needed.

Mat couldn't resist the opportunity to tease her. "Enjoying the show, love?"

She grinned back. "Indeed I am. I have the best seat in the house too."

"I can think of a better one," added Luk. His hips slanted forward slightly, showing a nice bulge in his breeches.

Prioshka hid her smile and pursed her lips. "Work first, play later."

Mat gave a theatrical sigh and returned to his task, shaping a new pin from a convenient branch with his knife.

The sound of a jingling harness made them all look up to see a large traveling carriage approaching. The driver reined in the horses at a command from its occupant.

The door opened and a woman stepped out. She surveyed the scene, letting her eyes linger on the two shirtless men.

"May we be of assistance?"

Her voice was cool, her demeanor even more so, and she glanced at her driver, who climbed down and moved over to the group looking at the damaged wheel.

"Thank you, Ma'am, but I believe we have things well in hand." Prioshka's voice was brisk.

Mat suppressed a grin of amusement. Their Prioshka was a possessive one, all right. He was profoundly glad of it too.

The woman turned, and then paused. "I am traveling to London. There's a...friend there I am seeking. Might either of you gentlemen know a Gyorgy Vargas?"

She turned into the sunlight and three mouths dropped as the rays hit a pair of pure china blue eyes.

Mat gulped. "Indeed, Ma'am. He's a good friend of ours."

The lips curved up into a small smile as she took one more look at the honed and sweaty bodies. "Somehow, I had a feeling that might be the case."

Luk straightened his shoulders. "You are a friend of Gyorgy's? He is well?"

The elegant head tilted slightly. "Indeed yes. And probably in London by now. Which is where I intend to find him. I must suppose that you two are his companions in your musical group?"

Both men bowed gracefully, ignoring their bare chests. "We are the Egers, Ma'am, Lukasz and Matyas. And this..." Mat held out his hand to Prioshka. "This is Prioshka Eger."

Prioshka dropped a polite curtsey as her cheeks colored up.

"A pleasure to meet you all," said the woman. "I am the Dowager Duchess Kirkwood. Marie-Claire to my friends." She nodded towards her carriage. "Why don't you let me take you to London, and my footman will see to the repair of your caravan? You can tell me where I may find Mr. Vargas in exchange for the lift."

The three exchanged glances.

"You may rely on my man. He's very knowledgeable about such things. If you'll give him a direction in London, he'll see that your belongings are kept safe."

Mat sighed. "I don't see that we have much choice. Other than stay here for several more hours trying to do it ourselves."

Luk agreed. "I don't relish spending the night here by this road, that's for sure. And there are no guarantees we'll be finished before dark."

"Will we not be taking you out of your way, Ma'am?" Prioshka's hesitancy was evident in her voice.

"Not at all. Other than finding Mr. Vargas, I only have one task to accomplish in town."

"And that would be..." Prioshka's question hung in the sunlight between them and Mat held his breath, wondering if this woman with the strange eyes would answer.

She gazed at them contemplatively then took a breath. "I'm going to kill a man."

✳ ✳ ✳ ✳ ✳

The carriage swayed as it lumbered its way along the London road. Prioshka nervously smoothed the skirts of the colorful outfit Mat and Luk had insisted she wear, and glanced at the woman next to her.

How could anyone be so composed? So cool? And what did she think about a woman traveling with two such handsome men?

The Duchess caught her gaze. "You are very lucky, Miss Eger."

"I am?"

"Indeed. To be so loved by such men."

Prioshka's jaw dropped and she looked over at Mat and Luk. They were grinning at her as if they hadn't a care in the world.

"I...I...we..."

Marie-Claire smiled, and with a gesture that seemed strangely awkward for her, she touched Prioshka's hand. "A blind man could see the affection between you. I envy you. If these two are anything like Gyorgy..." Her voice tailed off.

"He is special to you?" She couldn't hold the question back.

"Oh yes." Marie-Claire's amazingly blue eyes drifted to the window. "I didn't realize how special. Just one night, Prioshka, that's all it took."

Stunned by the fact that she was holding hands with a Dowager Duchess who had just casually used her first name, Prioshka gulped. Then a slow smile began. "It only takes one night with men such as these."

A laugh was surprised from Marie-Claire and she too glanced over at their companions. "Hush now. Any more of this and their heads will swell."

"Agreed." Prioshka rested her head against the cushions and felt the tension seep out of her. This woman understood. She was in love with Gyorgy Vargas, friend to Mat and Luk. She knew the power of

197

such a man's touch. It made them sisters of a sort, women who shared a knowledge few were privileged to possess.

A thought came to her, and comfortable with her surroundings, she dared voice it. "I take it then, you are not going to London to kill Gyorgy?"

Marie-Claire blinked. "Good God, no."

Luk leaned forward. "May we ask who you intend as your target, Marie-Claire? Killing a man is a difficult thing. Not something to be undertaken lightly."

Marie-Claire's expression firmed into a mask. "Believe me, friend Luk, I do not take it lightly. It is a man who deserves to die. But perhaps the less you know of that, the better."

Silence fell between them as they sensed Marie-Claire's reluctance to tell them more.

"Well, if you need help, just let us know." Prioshka folded her hands complacently on her lap. "From what I understand, these men look upon themselves as family. And now that I..." She blushed. "...I am one of the family, I'll stand by them. And you."

Luk and Mat seared her with their gazes as her little speech concluded. They knew exactly what she meant.

Her decision was made, her objections overcome. She was theirs.

Forever.

Chapter 23
Fabyan Finds His Fate

As the Dowager Duchess of Kirkwood's carriage rolled into the outskirts of London, Viktor, Peter and Gyorgy were hard at work on their investigations. Viktor and Peter used their contacts and their acquaintances to solidify their picture of the financial disaster looming over the head of Lord Alfred Eventyde.

Gyorgy was focused on learning about one particular woman...and to his surprise, he found an interesting trail. One that led to a name he was not pleased to hear used in connection with her—Sir Francis Hucknall.

They gathered in the evening by the fire in Viktor's study, seizing the opportunity afforded them for a little privacy. Madelyne and Freddie were doing their social duties and busily encouraging an assortment of gullibly rich ladies to donate to their favorite charity.

The building had been hurriedly completed, the servants installed, and there were now a dozen or so women temporarily seeking shelter within its walls. Madelyne had named it "The Zentaily House", which was as close to the Hungarian word for "sanctuary" as she could come.

"After all, Viktor," she'd said when he tried to get her to pronounce it correctly. "I doubt that too many of our guests will be Hungarians. Most will be English women desperate for a roof over their heads and a start in a new direction. They're not going to care what it's called."

Faced with such irrefutable logic, Viktor had done the only thing possible. He'd kissed her.

His eyes warmed at the memory as he sat with his friends.

"So it looks as if Eventyde's affairs are getting shakier by the second," said Peter. "He's moving money around, pulling out of some ventures, calling in his debts, even selling off a couple of his hunters. He's sinking everything he's got into the shipping line. I can't see the sense in it myself, but others have made big killings that way."

Viktor nodded. "It's a foolish man's way to make a fortune...worse than putting it all on the turn of a card, in my opinion."

"But..." said Gyorgy thoughtfully. "It does make it a hell of a lot easier to destroy the man. If that's what you want to do."

"Oh I do." Viktor's words were emphatic. "Nothing less will suffice."

Peter nodded. "We're in agreement then."

Viktor straightened his shoulders and looked at the two men. "It will take but a few words in the right ears. The company will totter. Other investors will probably pull out leaving Eventyde with a handful of worthless stock."

"What about the people who work for them? Are we going to be putting a few hundred honest men out of a job?" Gyorgy's concern was merited given the course they were intent upon pursuing.

"Not if we time it right," answered Peter. "That's the beauty of this little scheme. The ships of this line are at sea right now—there's only one cargo vessel in port and it's scheduled to leave tomorrow at high tide. By starting our campaign after it leaves, we can be over and done with before any ships make landfall. The crews will be completely unaware of what's happening to their company until it's all over."

"And, of course, after Eventyde's destroyed, we'll pull it back up to financial solidity with a few more choice rumors." Viktor's tone was satisfied. "No harm, no foul. If everything works according to plan, it'll take less than forty-eight hours to ruin him."

"And then what?"

"Good question, Gyorgy," answered Viktor thoughtfully. "I think *that* will be up to my wife." He shrugged. "So have you learned anything about your mysterious Duchess?"

Gyorgy stroked his chin. "Several things...none of which I like, and more than a few concerning our old friend, Francis Hucknall."

Two heads swiveled rapidly at Gyorgy's words.

"Really?" Viktor's drawl was cool, but his expression intense. "How the hell does he fit in with the Kirkwood family?"

"Good question. And one to which I don't yet have all the answers. But there's something unpleasant going on there. I'll let you know as soon as I have the truth of the matter."

Peter's lip curled. "If Hucknall's involved, there's bound to be something unpleasant. 'Tis rumored he was involved in the death of two prostitutes recently. But of course, there's no proof. Money buys silence."

"Well, perhaps we'll end up killing two birds with one stone," mused Viktor.

"Not until I find out how Marie-Claire is involved," cautioned Gyorgy. "I won't have her tainted or hurt by anything we do."

Peter grinned and looked at Viktor. "He's got it bad."

Gyorgy snorted. "This from a man who runs when his wife simply blinks in his direction?"

Peter held up his hands in the classic fencing gesture of a man acknowledging a hit. "You're right. One flash of those green eyes and I'm lost. I admit it." He grinned at Gyorgy. "And it's wonderful."

Gyorgy looked at his friends. "You are both lucky men. I envy you. But after this is done, I'll give you fair warning. She is going to be mine. The next wedding you attend will be that of Gyorgy Vargas and Marie-Claire Devereaux."

The sound of quiet applause echoed through the room.

As one, the three men turned to see a fourth standing in the shadows.

He was tall, held himself proudly, and there was a touch of silver in the black hair above his ears. It dappled his neatly trimmed beard and twinkled in the lush moustache over his mouth.

He was smiling.

The three men nearly stumbled over themselves as they rushed to their feet, one name on their lips.

"*Fabyan.*"

* * * * *

Fabyan Szabo felt his smile spreading from ear to ear.

His friends clustered around him, hugging him, clapping him on the shoulders, wringing his hands with theirs and generally making affectionate nuisances of themselves.

He loved it.

Finally, he held up his hand and motioned them all back to their chairs, pulling up one of his own. Anyone would think they'd been parted for years instead of a couple of weeks.

With simple gestures, he encouraged them to talk, and listened intently as they took turns imparting their news.

So Viktor had married, as had Pyotr. And both happily by the looks of them. Not to mention the fact that Pyotr had finally accepted his heritage and become Lord Peter Chalmers once again. That was good. A man should face his past demons some time and lay them to rest.

Peter had shared his secrets with Fabyan one drunken night, and Fabyan knew it was only a matter of time before Peter's nature forced him to deal with the pain that lurked in his heart. Apparently falling in love with Freddie had done the trick. And Gyorgy?

Well, there was a man in the throes of passion if ever Fabyan had seen one. He had that "look" about him that told the world he was on a mission, and wouldn't rest until he had his woman where she belonged. In his bed.

Fabyan hid a private smile with his hand as he stroked his moustache.

He listened to their stories, their adventures and their embarrassed explanation of how it came to be that in such a short time all three had succumbed to a particular woman.

He just shook his head and let his eyes tell them of his happiness for them.

He held up two fingers.

"Lukasz and Matyas?" said Viktor. "I don't know. Haven't heard from them. But I'm sure they'll arrive soon."

Peter chuckled. "Probably busy enjoying the favors of a variety of country lasses across the home counties."

Fabyan nodded and raised one eyebrow.

None of the men present missed the question.

"Yes, we're plotting." Peter looked apologetic. "Not like we did in Europe, but plotting just the same."

Fabyan leaned forward and rested his arms on his knees, folding his hands together and waiting. He was very good at waiting.

"There are two men, Fabyan. Two men who have shown themselves to be beneath reproach. Both names are known to you...Lord Alfred Eventyde is one."

Fabyan's jaw tightened.

"Yes indeed," continued Viktor. "Our host on that eventful night. And the other is his guest...Francis Hucknall."

Fabyan gave one short nod. These were indeed men whose existence soiled the ground they walked on. Viktor and the others could have no idea how much Fabyan wanted Eventyde dead.

It was his secret—his alone, and had remained his secret for many years.

He turned his attention back to his friends and listened as they detailed their plans. They were sound. Efficient, lethal and effective. At least where Eventyde was concerned.

He rested his hand inquiringly on Gyorgy's arm as the conversation turned to Hucknall.

"I don't know, Fabyan," sighed Gyorgy. "I don't know about Hucknall yet. We can't touch him financially—he's too shrewd to let himself fall into that trap. And the man has no reputation left to destroy. I do know that he holds a great deal of power over a number of people. He makes a habit of buying up their vowels, calling them in and accepting their properties in exchange for the debt." Gyorgy's expression was one of distaste.

Fabyan made a light motion with his fingers, as if holding a hand of cards.

"Maybe..." said Viktor thoughtfully. "The clubs he frequents are not reputable gaming houses, that's for sure. He seems to know when someone has lost heavily at the tables...but whether he plays or not himself...Gyorgy?"

Gyorgy pondered the question. "I don't know. I can find out."

Fabyan nodded.

"And you, Fabyan...will you stay here?" Peter looked at his friend.

Fabyan shook his head and pulled out a small card bearing a nearby address.

"Oooh. Very nice, my friend. This would have impressed the hell out of Napoleon's troops." Peter grinned.

Fabyan punched him in the shoulder.

"Good. You are near enough to keep in touch. We need your counsel, Fabyan," said Viktor as he glanced at the card. "And I know you'll want to meet Freddie and Madelyne."

Fabyan smiled again at the warmth in his friend's voice. He did indeed want to meet these two women who had knocked two such confirmed bachelors off their feet and into matrimony.

They made plans to rendezvous once more the following evening, and parted, Fabyan enjoying the hugs and handshakes as he left Viktor's home. Truly he was blessed to have such friends.

As his steps took him through the shadows and down the few short streets to his own apartments, his mind wandered back over their acquaintance and to that fateful night when he'd stumbled on the very drunken group of discontented and angry young men.

He'd seen their strengths, heard them sob out their weaknesses over their brandy, and watched as the scars had surfaced—some physical, some mental. He knew his own soul bore scars that matched theirs, and somehow he had forged a partnership between them all that had transcended his silence and given each of them a chance to repair their damaged lives.

And it seemed they were continuing to do so. "Zentaily House". He grinned to himself. "*Szentély*". Sanctuary. A good name for a good project. God knew women needed it.

His mind slid back to a night in Paris so many years ago, when a young and handsome blue-eyed Hungarian had stumbled over a battered and bleeding woman in an alleyway.

His Annabelle would have benefited from a sanctuary. Somewhere to hide from the brute who'd savaged her. As it was, she'd found her sanctuary with Fabyan. And he'd found his heart, only to lose it when she left him. Revolutions were painful and calling this one "The Terror" was accurate and precise. And Annabelle would have been trapped...possibly guillotined. Every little fraction of her body screamed out "aristocracy", from the delicate line of her neck, to her fragile wrists. Her golden hair had been shorn, but nothing could hide her breeding.

And the mob didn't care about anything but ridding themselves of the hated *aristos*.

He understood her need to flee. He also knew he couldn't accompany her. But when she left, she'd taken his heart with her. His silence had fallen upon him, as if her departure had robbed him of the desire to communicate with his fellows. He'd not spoken more than a word or two since.

He had no heart for it.

He'd had women in the intervening years, of course, even stayed with one or two, but none had replaced Annabelle. No one could ever replace Annabelle. No one had her rare combination of strength and beauty. No one could make his cock hard with just a brush of their hands or his balls ache with a mere kiss.

He'd fucked since then, but he admitted to himself—he'd never loved.

And the two just weren't the same.

Fabyan sighed as he approached his front door. Tomorrow, perhaps, he'd visit this Zentaily House of Madelyne's…perhaps there was something he could do to help. A friendly smile, an hour spent just holding the hand of a woman in need—Fabyan knew well how these things could make a difference in a life filled with pain.

He'd done it before.

With Annabelle.

* * * * *

"I must request a favor from you all."

Marie-Claire Devereaux spoke to the three occupants of the carriage as it made its way through the London streets towards the town house of Count Viktor Karoly.

"Please do not mention my presence to Gyorgy."

Mat and Luk raised their eyebrows. "But surely…" began Mat.

"He's going to want to see you…" said Luk.

"And I shall want to see him. But not yet." She made as if to reach out her hand. "Please. Not yet. Not until I am ready."

Prioshka nodded. "I understand."

China-blue eyes met hers. "I knew you would."

Luk and Mat glanced at each other in confusion.

"There are things I need to do. Matters I need to settle. I will not seek Gyorgy out until those matters are concluded to my satisfaction. The next time we meet, I need...I need to be free." She looked down at her hands. "I must be free."

Prioshka moved her hand and covered Marie-Claire's. "You know where we can be found. All you have to do is send word. I promise that we won't tell Gyorgy you are in town, but you must promise us to keep us informed of how...how you are? How things are going?"

"Marie-Claire," said Luk. "We can help you. We will stand by you. It's what we do."

Mat nodded in agreement. "Do not mistake our abilities for those of simple musicians, Marie-Claire. We have spent time doing things in Europe that have given us skills that might be of use to you. Please...call on us immediately if you need us."

"I will. And thank you." Her lips curved up into a smile of more warmth than usual. "It would seem that Gyorgy chooses his friends well."

"As do we, Marie-Claire."

Prioshka's words were followed by a quick hug, and for a moment the low light from the carriage lantern sparkled on something like tears in Marie-Claire's eyes. They were gone in an instant.

"You will stay safe?" Mat's question was more of an insistent demand.

"I will, Mat. As much as possible. I should have done this business years ago. But I let things slip...time passes...it took Gyorgy to make me realize what I had lost and what I could find again. Please do not worry about me."

"We can't help it," muttered Luk, looking less than pleased.

Marie-Claire chuckled softly. "I am glad. It has been a long time since anyone worried about me. But truly, there is no need."

"I'm more worried about my hide when Gyorgy finds out that we knew you were in town and didn't tell him," said Mat bluntly.

Prioshka laughed at that. "He's your friend. He'll understand."

Luk snorted. "No he won't."

"He will. I will explain all to him, never fear." Marie-Claire's words were followed by the sounds of the carriage drawing to a standstill in front of the steps leading to the Karoly house.

"Thank you, Marie-Claire," said Prioshka. "I look forward to our next meeting."

"As do I."

Luk and Mat helped Prioshka from the carriage and accepted their small bags from the driver as he tossed them down.

Marie-Claire was about to pull the door shut, when Luk leaned in. "Remember. We're here for you." He grinned at her. "Good hunting."

Good hunting indeed.

Marie-Claire tapped on the roof of the carriage and left the three people to make their way into the large house.

Chapter 24

As was his custom, Fabyan rose early. It had been a necessity in France and had become part of his nature. Consequently it was scarcely past eight o'clock in the morning when he ventured out to pay a visit to Zentaily House.

Correctly deducing that there would be plenty of activity, since this was not the sort of establishment housing women who danced 'til dawn and then slept away the following day, he knocked and was welcomed by a matronly woman.

"Good day, sir. What may we do for you?"

It took a few moments for him to make himself understood with hand movements, smiles and his card.

"Oh I see, sir. A friend of Lady Chalmers and Countess Karoly, are you?" The woman beamed at him. "Right fine ladies they are too, sir. Please come in. Would you be wishful to look around?"

He nodded, eyes already noting the fresh paint, the smell of breakfast cooking, and the overall cleanliness. This was a good place. Welcoming.

"Why don't you take a quick peek into our kitchens, then...our guests are just finishing up now..."

He followed the bustling skirts of the housekeeper, who informed him she was Mabel Branston, and had been with "the dear Countess" from the beginning of the whole project.

While she nattered on happily about how much good they were doing, Fabyan saw for himself the handful of small rooms where fabric was piled, or paper and pens set ready at small desks that might have been rescued from some schoolroom.

The kitchen was redolent with the fragrance of bacon and fresh bread, and his mouth watered.

Mrs. Branston obviously noticed, since she pulled him to an empty chair, sat him down without ceremony and plunked a plate in front of him containing several slices of fresh bread and pats of butter.

"Help yourself, Mr. Zaboo. There's plenty for all."

Several pairs of eyes widened as he reached for the bread.

"Mr. Zaboo here is a friend of the Countess's come to pay a visit, ladies. He don't...um that is, he can't..."

Fabyan smiled and gestured delicately at his throat, shaking his head at the same time.

Murmurs of sympathy swept around the table as the half-dozen women took a good look at the extraordinarily handsome man sharing their meal.

Fabyan chuckled to himself. If nothing else, he'd brought a little something different to their breakfast table. He wondered if they'd survive seeing all six of the Gypsy musicians together.

Mrs. Branston continued her work, shepherding off those women who had finished their food to various activities, and chatting knowledgeably about possible jobs, different parts of the country, and all the positive things that could lie ahead for her "guests".

Finally Fabyan was alone, finishing up his bread and butter, and washing it down with an excellent cup of tea.

"Well, I don't mind telling you, Mr. Zaboo, it's certainly lifted my heart to be able to help these women like this," said Mrs. Branston. She pulled over a cup and poured herself the last of the tea.

"Of course, these are the healthy ones. We've a couple that aren't doing so good." She shook her head on a frown. "I just can't understand what makes people think they can hurt other people."

He nodded in agreement. He'd never understood it either.

"Why don't you come upstairs and look in on our patients? They'd probably appreciate a nice smile and a minute of your time..." She glanced at him. "That is, if you don't mind being in the sickroom?"

He snorted. Given some of the things he'd seen, a sickroom was the least of his concerns. He just smiled and gestured for her to lead the way.

She led him up a flight of stairs and along a hallway. "We try and keep it to two guests per room...a lot of these women need companionship, but crowding them in isn't always the answer. One woman can become a friend—too many can be intimidating."

She stopped at a door near the end and turned. "This is Mrs. Carstairs. Her husband died, and her brother-in-law threw her out into the streets. She has no family, and wasn't well at the time. A good shower of rain, a couple of nights without food or shelter and...you know..."

Fabyan's mouth firmed. He understood. Inflammation of the lungs was common under such circumstances, and had claimed too many people who lacked the strength and the resources to fight it.

The woman lay restlessly on her bed, tossing her head and muttering. A servant was with her, cooling her forehead with a damp cloth, and keeping a pot of water steaming on the hearth.

The room was warm and the atmosphere cloying, but Fabyan knew it was the best thing to relieve the congestion that rattled every breath the sick woman drew.

"Here, now, Mrs. Carstairs. You've a guest come to visit you."

The woman's eyes opened, and for a moment fear screamed loud behind them. But one look at Fabyan's comforting smile and she relaxed.

He took her hand. Dry and hot, it betrayed the fever that was wracking her body, and he stroked it gently.

"Who are you?" She pushed the words out and coughed.

He touched his fingers to her lips to hush her, and held her other hand against his jacket.

"A friend, Mrs. Carstairs, just a friend. Come to see how you're feeling today." Mrs. Branston leaned over and rested her hand worriedly on the woman's forehead.

"Very well..." Her breath rasped in her lungs.

The housekeeper frowned. "You'll do better in a day or so, mark my words." She ladled out some weak broth into a cup. "Perhaps Mr. Zaboo can persuade you to drink a little of this. You need to keep your strength up."

Fabyan eased his arm around the woman's shoulders and helped her up, taking the cup from Mrs. Branston. With muttered words of thanks, the woman did manage a few sips.

"Good girl." Nodding at him, Mrs. Branston let him lay the patient back down and take his leave. Elegantly, he raised her hand to his lips and kissed it, bringing a smile to the wan face on the pillow.

"Thank you, Mr. Zaboo. I'll warrant that'll do the poor lass a world of good. She'll get better, but there's a long road ahead of her." Moving to the last door, she paused. "Now in here is Mrs. Smith. I'm not so sure about this one. Her illness seems more of the spirit than of the body. She's weak, but doesn't have a fever. It's as though she's lost her will to live. Sad thing, really. But understandable. She was tossed out on her ear by her husband, had to struggle to survive for the last several years, and has been steadily going downhill. She's a lady, make no mistake about it, but more than that, she won't say."

Quietly, Mrs. Branston opened the door.

The room was darkened by curtains drawn over the windows, and Fabyan's eyes took a moment to make out the slight figure lying beneath the covers. Then he caught sight of unruly blonde hair tumbled over the pillows.

He blinked and moved closer to the bed.

"Mrs. Smith…wake up dear. You've got a visitor."

The woman turned her head to the wall. "Please go away." It was a whisper, but Fabyan heard it.

His heart started to pound fiercely and he stepped to the side of the bed. With a shaking hand he reached to the woman's chin and gripped it, turning it toward the light.

His pulse pounded like cannon fire in his ears as he stared at her and for the first time in recent memory his throat struggled with a sound.

"Annabelle."

* * * * *

"Fabyan."

The cry was wrung from her throat like the last breath of a dying animal.

"You *know* each other?" Mrs. Branston was thunderstruck.

His arms were already reaching for her, lifting her from the bed and gathering her close.

"Yes…yes…oh God." She sighed weakly. "If I'm going to die, I can't think of anywhere better than with him…" Her thoughts were incoherent, and her mind whirled as she felt herself lifted against his heart, bedclothes trailing off her like the shrouds she truly believed they would be.

"*Not…die…*" he rasped. "*Not going to die.*"

"Well…goodness…I don't know…" Mrs. Branston wrung her hands, but stopped as Fabyan looked over at her.

"*Carriage…*"

"But…she…I…"

One more glance from his blue eyes told Mrs. Branston he'd brook no arguments, and in spite of her frail state, Annabelle wanted to laugh. She knew that look of old. He still had the ability to command people with a single glance.

"I'll summon you a hackney right away, sir." Mrs. Branston hurried from the room.

"Fabyan…" breathed Annabelle. "Oh Fabyan…"

She raised her hand and stroked his cheek just to make sure he was real. Firm skin met her touch, raspy where he'd shaved and hairy where his beard met his cheek. "It's been so long…so very long…"

His eyes burned her face, traveling from her hair to her chin and then back to meet her gaze. His arms tightened around her.

"Your voice…you don't speak…Fabyan?"

He sucked in air. "*Nothing to say. After you left…nothing to say.*"

She gasped. It had been more than twenty years. He hadn't spoken in all that time. And *she* was responsible. Tears flooded her eyes and spilled from their corners.

"Oh God, Fabyan…I've missed you so."

The room spun as he wrapped her in the blankets, and the excitement of the moment overwhelmed her. "Fabyan…I don't feel too well…"

The last thing she saw as her world darkened to blackness was the tender gaze of the man she'd loved so long ago and had never stopped loving. Her Fabyan.

When she opened her eyes again, he was still there.

But she was no longer in the small sickroom at Zentaily House.

She blinked at him, reaching towards him in a gesture of need and reassurance. "Am I dead?"

He grinned and shook his head. "No, love."

His voice sounded scratchy and harsh, but she could understand him perfectly. She remembered. "Fabyan, you stopped speaking...because of *me*?"

He brushed her hair away from her face. "Hungry?"

She sniffed and realized the scent of croissants filled the room. He'd remembered. She'd developed a passion for the bread when she'd been with him in Paris. It had been so long and yet he'd not forgotten.

"Oh yes..." Her mouth watered as she watched him spread butter on the hot roll.

"Eat."

She did. Just seeing him there, looking at her with those unforgettable blue eyes was enough to make her hungry, and she realized it wasn't just food she wanted. Although more years had passed than she cared to count, the spark was still there.

Fabyan could still stir her body like no other man ever could. And several had tried. She pushed the thought away and finished the roll with delight. Nothing had ever tasted so good. Or perhaps it was just the fact that she was sitting up in bed and Fabyan was less than two feet away.

Which brought another thought to her mind. "Where am I?"

"My apartments."

"Oh. You brought me here?"

He nodded, passing her a second roll. She could only finish half of it, in spite of his frown. "I cannot, Fabyan. Too rich. It's been a while..."

She leaned back tiredly onto the pillows.

Fabyan moved to a small side table and clinked glass as he poured two small drinks. He returned to the bed carrying them and offered her one.

She cautiously took it and sniffed. "Brandy?"

"Just a little. For your health."

He put his glass down and shrugged out of his jacket, tossing his cravat after it. His shirt followed.

Annabelle was wide-eyed, watching him as he stripped. She absently sipped the fiery liquid, sputtering a little as it burned her throat. But a warmth seeped into her after she'd swallowed, although whether it was from the liquor or the man disrobing in front of her, she wasn't quite sure.

His body hadn't changed much. Other than the few silver hairs, he was still lean and sculpted, muscles in all the right places...

He shucked off his boots and breeches, unconcerned that he was now quite naked. Oh yes. He still had muscles in *all* the right places.

She'd know his cock anywhere. It had haunted her dreams, plagued her memories and she'd awoken more times than she could recall yearning to feel it inside her once more. She'd thought they would remain only dreams.

Now she wasn't so sure.

He picked up his glass, rounded the bed and casually slipped beneath the covers beside her, pulling her into his warmth.

"Now, *kedves* Annabelle. Tell me."

Where to start?

Annabelle took a last sip of her glass and put it aside. She was too intent on cuddling into Fabyan's chest to want more brandy. He was intoxicating enough. She let herself enjoy the feel of his hair as it curled over his skin, and idly slid her fingertips through the whorls she found around his small nipples.

He caught her wandering hand, raised it to his lips, kissed it and pulled her even closer. "Tell me."

She sighed. He always had been a determined man.

"It's been so long, Fabyan. I don't know where to start."

"You left me."

"Yes." She shivered. "I had no choice. The mob was coming, Fabyan. They were searching house to house. I couldn't let them take me and run the risk of them taking you as well for helping me. I just couldn't." Her fingers tightened against his skin.

"There was another reason too."

She felt him drop a kiss on her hair and swallowed as she fought for the next words she knew would strike deep into his heart.

"I was expecting your child."

* * * * *

Fabyan's world shifted on its axis.

"Our child?"

Annabelle snuggled into his arms as if she'd only left them yesterday. Her body still fit his, her curves were more womanly now, but still a perfect match for his hands, his mouth...there was only the thin flannel of her nightdress between them, and he cursed it silently for a moment as his brain struggled to come to terms with what she'd just said.

"You were pregnant?"

She nodded against him, breath rapid. "I'd only just found out. The day before. I was going to tell you that night...but..."

"They were coming. *Les enragés.*"

Annabelle shivered, remembering the mobs of self-styled soldiers, rabidly intent on guillotining anyone who might have had an aristocratic heritage.

"I managed to get onto one of the last wagons out of Paris that night...I dared not leave anything behind that would link us in case I was captured. Luck was with me and I connected with a packet from Calais to Dover. I went home."

"Home?"

"What passed for home. He took me back, of course. He had no idea where I'd been or what I'd done. He assumed the child was his, and for my sins I let him believe it." She turned her face away. "I let him take me, Fabyan. It was the only way to protect our child. To make him truly think he'd fathered an infant on me."

Fabyan's muscles tensed beneath her trembling body. "I understand. You did what you had to do."

Annabelle couldn't begin to guess at his feelings. Even now, after all these years, the horror of what she'd had to do still made her sick at heart. But their child had lived. "I had hoped to be able to find you after the Revolution settled down. To let you know that I...that we...had a child. But Paris was in chaos, and my baby needed me. I had to stay, Fabyan...please understand. I was so torn. I wanted nothing more than to be with you, but now I had a little person relying on me for everything. A little part of you and me. It was all I had left."

Fabyan said nothing, but still held her tight. He'd not pushed her away in disgust. It was something. Deep inside a little flicker of hope kindled inside Annabelle. Perhaps he could forgive her for what she'd done.

"Anyway, the years passed. Our child grew and thrived. I was able to take the occasional trip to France, when peace seemed imminent, but I could never find you. And I did try, Fabyan, I *swear*. Every time I was in Paris I made enquiries. But you'd gone. Long gone."

She sighed. It hadn't been easy. Asking about a faceless Hungarian soldier. A nobody without connections. She'd received blank looks, and the occasional sneer. Insinuations that a lover had left her and she was seeking him. They hadn't known how close to the truth they were.

"Go on." Fabyan's voice was quiet but insistent.

"Our child grew up, Fabyan. There was…trouble. An incident took place, and events were taken out of my hands. I was sent away. For good this time. We were separated forever. And my heart broke." Her voice caught in her throat. "It's been several years now. I was given a pittance to survive on, and it ran out. I've had no money for the last year."

"What did you do?" His tone was harsh, but whether with anger or emotion, she couldn't tell.

"I worked. I taught French. I did whatever I could to keep a roof over my head and food in my belly. Once I even considered…"

"No."

She smiled. "No. I didn't. But hunger is a fierce motivator."

"I know." He paused. "So you are still married?"

"In name only. And my heart has always been yours. I gave it to you, Fabyan, all those years ago. You shared it with me in our child, and no one else has ever—*ever*—taken your place."

He turned to her and cupped her head, turning her face to his. "I never stopped loving you either, Annabelle. Never."

Gently he lowered his lips to hers and Annabelle closed her eyes, blinded by the joy she saw shining from his heart. There was an answering joy blooming in her own and it threatened to swamp her as their mouths met.

What started as a soft kiss quickly turned hot.

The heat that had been ignited so many years ago still smoldered, and it took but the briefest touch to fan the flames. Her lips parted and his tongue entered, relearning her and teasing her with its familiar yet strange taste. As if she'd rediscovered a flavor that had been long forgotten.

Brandy and man and passion filled her mouth and she answered with her own, letting the teasing curl and parry of her tongue against his tell him of her undying love for him.

She sighed a breath and he inhaled it, taking her essence deep into his lungs. Then he pulled their bodies apart.

"You are tired," he rasped, chest heaving.

"No...never with you, Fabyan..." It was a plaintive cry. She'd lost him for so long and now he was here. Naked. Next to her in bed.

"Sshhh..." His hands stroked her, soothing her. "I'm not leaving you. Nor are you leaving me." Fabyan's voice cracked. "Ever again."

He tugged her down against the pillows and quickly stripped her nightdress from her. "Just let me touch you."

She sighed. As if she'd object. She'd been starved for his love for too long and now the banquet was before her.

Annabelle willingly bared herself for him, unafraid that he'd find her aged beyond the young girl he'd loved, unafraid that he'd find her undesirable...knowing only that she loved him beyond anything on this earth.

With the possible exception of their child.

Chapter 25

Fabyan's heart was so full that his silence was not, for once, self-imposed. He was choked with emotions and couldn't have spoken a word if he'd tried.

Not that he wanted to. He just wanted to touch her. To reassure himself that she was here, next to him, lying naked and welcoming as she always had. How well he remembered.

Her body had changed, as had his, but he saw only the firm breasts of the woman he'd loved for most of his life. He saw the nipples tighten as he delicately ringed them with his fingertips. He watched her legs move as his hand traced a path down to her rounded navel and back again to cup a full weight in his hand.

He heard her soft intake of breath as he bent his head and suckled her, finally filling his mouth with that heat that only Annabelle could provide. She still fit perfectly.

She tasted—right. She smelled as he recalled, a bloom of moist warmth beginning to rise from her mound as he aroused her slowly and carefully. He reminded himself that she was exhausted, and made a mental promise to give her as much pleasure as she could take without tiring.

He had many years to make up for, but he didn't have to do it all in one hour's time, much as he wanted to.

Their future was uncertain, but Fabyan was assured of one thing—he'd never lose her again.

He slid a hand down to her pussy, and his thoughts evaporated. Hot, wet folds of flesh met his touch, and she moaned as he found her with his fingers. Her hand touched his head, holding him close to her breast as she moved beneath him, sighing with delight.

"So long, Fabyan...it's been so *long*..." Her whisper was a breath of joy in his ear.

And it had been. His fingers sought entrance and found her tight, yet opening to his intrusion with all the delicacy of a rosebud unfurling its petals to the sun. She still responded to him, craved his touch as much as he craved hers…the intervening years disappeared in the blink of an eye and Fabyan gave himself up to the thrill of learning her all over again.

He tugged on her nipples, making them stand high and proud, and then moved downwards, following the scent of her arousal to its source. Her curly hair glistened with moisture now, and his mouth watered at the sight.

Annabelle's skin had always been the softest he could ever remember touching, and so it was still, her thighs parting to permit him access to her secrets, and caressing his shoulders with the lightest brush of their creamy velvet surface.

Infinitely slowly, and with infinite care, Fabyan lowered his face to her cunt. He breathed in her essence, and extended his tongue, just flicking the swollen folds in anticipation.

She sighed. "*Fabyan…*"

"Yes…" he answered. "*Yes.*"

He nuzzled his mouth into her heat. There she was. That little bud right where he remembered it, tucked amongst her hidden secrets, waiting for his touch to bring it to trembling arousal.

She moaned as he probed delicately around it, finding all the places that had been burned into his mind from the very first night he'd loved her like this. He loved the taste of her, the scent of her…and he'd never banished either from his memories. He knew where to stroke, where to press and where to caress.

He'd relived this moment in his dreams for so many years. Her honey was flowing over his tongue, telling him how quickly she responded. She always had. The first time he'd buried his head between her legs he'd known exactly what to do, some instinct, some primal urge driving him to touch her in the ways that would send shivers through her body—and it was still happening to her.

Her hands were clutching at his head, the linens, anything she could find, as if she was anchoring herself to the bed lest his tongue send her flying. And that was what he wanted to do. Send her flying.

Then catch her again, hold her tight, and *never* let her go.

Her muscles clenched and released around his body, and he gently slipped his tongue from her clit into her cunt, bringing it out again and stroking it around, lapping at her and listening to her breaths.

Raspy and harsh, her lungs were heaving now, her cunt open to his loving, her body quivering. He slid his hands beneath her buttocks and lifted her, positioning her in the perfect spot.

Her legs rose to his shoulders, and he trembled as she clasped him tight. Did she know she wasn't just touching his skin, but so much more? Did she know that his cock might have been rock-hard, but his heart was the part of his body that was about to overflow?

Did she have any idea how much he had loved her in the past and how much he loved her now?

Did *he*?

He bent his head to her again, letting his eyes drift up over her mound and along her length to her face.

He watched her as he claimed her with his tongue, each flutter of an eyelid, each parting of her lips as she moaned.

Her nipples were tight buds and her breasts rose and fell as she panted with deepening arousal. Her belly fluttered and he felt her thighs harden and her buttocks firm beneath his hands.

She was close now, so close. He wanted to keep her like this—trembling on the brink of her peak, sobbing his name as she fought for more. Watch her cheeks flush and the chords in her neck stand out as she threw her head back, gasping with pleasure.

But he felt her tremors and knew she didn't have the strength. And neither did he. Blinded for a moment by the desire to plunge into her and sink his cock into that boiling cunt that wept for him, he closed his eyes.

And pressed hard with his tongue, upwards, around, down and over once more, finally suckling her hardened clit between his lips.

She exploded against him.

Wracked with spasms, her body jerked, and he thrust his tongue into her, moving it around, sharing her orgasm, feeling her muscles as they tugged at him. He let her roll through it, groaning against her flesh and humming with pleasure as she came once more.

Her breath was a whisper but he heard. "*Fabyan. My Fabyan.*"

His cock surrendered. Hearing his name on her lips as she climaxed sent him over the edge, and he came, long hot spurts of seed shooting from him as his balls emptied themselves along with his heart.

The pain of their separation vanished as his come seeped into the linens between her legs and he stunned himself by crying out her name.

"Annabelle."

His voice, so long unused, came back strong and firm as he shouted the only word that had ever mattered. The name of the only woman he had ever loved.

Annabelle.

* * * * *

She woke much later. The fire was lighting the room and for a few moments Annabelle fought her muddled brain to remember where she was. Then the memories flooded back and she moved.

He was there. Next to her. Lying boneless on his back with one hand reaching towards her. Even in sleep it seemed he was not about to let her go.

She smiled.

The rest had done her good, her appetite was sharp, and her heart light for the first time in years. He still loved her. And God knew she had never stopped loving him. Unable to resist the temptation, she let her hand drift to his chest and lower, following the trail of hair down to his navel.

She noticed touches of silver there, dappling the formerly jet-black curls. She didn't care. He was her Fabyan, now and forever. They were older and had lived a lifetime apart, but finally they were reunited, and the world had shifted back to where it was supposed to be.

Fate had taken a hand and brought two hearts together. And two bodies. One of which was sleeping soundly and the other awakening.

Annabelle let her hand slip lower. She shifted to her knees, and explored him, pushing back the covers to reveal his cock as it lay on its bed of dark springy curls. Again, she noticed the silver threads, and smiled. He was still gorgeous. He'd be gorgeous at any age.

Cautiously, she let her hand rest at the base of his cock and it stirred, lengthening a little as the warmth of her palm seeped into his body. She danced her fingertips over it, grinning as it hardened beneath her touch. She was having fun.

For the first time in more years than she could remember, Annabelle was having fun in bed with a man. And that man was Fabyan. Her heart.

Once, long ago, she'd tried to recapture this passion, this—ecstasy that she'd known with Fabyan. A nice man, one who took care of his body, and made love with gentle expertise. It was expected that married women entertain themselves with lovers, and for a certainty she wanted nothing to do with her husband. Nor he her.

But she'd felt awkward, embarrassed, and unsatisfied. It hadn't happened again.

Until now.

She ran her hands over Fabyan's thighs. His muscles were as strong as ever, and his scent stirred her. She'd know that scent even if she was blindfolded and in total darkness.

And to think he'd not spoken. He'd had nothing to say to the world since they'd parted. She caressed his balls, just barely skimming her fingertips over the sac holding such precious cargo.

He moved a little, parting his legs, as if to give her greater access. She glanced up, but his eyes were still closed and his breathing even. Perhaps he was feigning sleep. She didn't know. Neither, at this moment, did she care. She had him where she wanted him.

His cock grew as she continued her exploration, until its expanding length could no longer be resisted. She bent her head and took him into her mouth.

He moaned. "Annabelle…" His hand drifted to her head, touching her hair gently.

She pulled back a little, administering a swift lick to the head as it left her lips. "Shhh."

Sucking him back in, she grasped him more firmly, no longer afraid of disturbing him. He was very much awake. His legs moved a little, and his breath caught as she worked him with her mouth and her tongue, loving every inch of him she could find and caressing his balls with her free hand.

She rolled them in her palm, feeling his cock jump as she did so. The room was silent, the only sound coming from her mouth as she devoured Fabyan. His length, his taste, the little salty drop her tongue drew from him—it was all as erotically arousing as anything she could ever remember.

To be able to love him like this. To tell him with her actions how she felt about him. To give back to him the pleasure he'd given her and to make up for the years they'd been apart.

Her head spun with delight as she felt the long vein pulse against her lips, and she intensified her efforts, letting his cock brush against the roof of her mouth all the way back to her throat.

"Annabelle...I..."

She ignored him. She wanted this so badly. She wanted to take him inside her in so many different ways—each one cementing their love for each other. Each one obliterating the havoc their separation had brought to their lives.

She got her wish.

He groaned and his body tightened with a shudder. "I can't..."

She didn't want him to. With a strong suckling movement, Annabelle urged him to let go. And he did.

Groaning with pleasure, Fabyan came, filling her mouth and throat with his sweet-salty come. She swallowed and continued sucking him, milking each and every drop of his seed until his balls lay limp and empty and his cock softened on her tongue.

He sighed. "Annabelle...you didn't have to..."

His hand tugged gently on her hair and he pulled her away from his belly and up into his arms.

"Yes I did, Fabyan. I've never wanted anything so much before. And I'll want it again too."

"You shall have it, love. But not right now. You must rest."

She cuddled close to his chest and listened to his heart as it slowed down to its regular rhythm. "Now I think I can. *At last.*"

Within moments, they were both asleep.

* * * * *

Breakfast the next morning was a riotous affair at Count Karoly's home, where Luk, Mat and Prioshka were welcomed with all the enthusiasm of troops returning home from the wars.

The servants simply shrugged and served extra food. They'd settled the visitors the night before, obeying their request that they not disturb their host.

So Peter, Gyorgy and Viktor were ecstatic to see their two friends smiling at them in the breakfast room, and Freddie and Madelyne made haste to welcome Prioshka.

Once again, stories were told, and adventures exchanged, and during a lull in the conversation, Madelyne leaned back and gazed in awe at Prioshka.

"I am dumbfounded. *Two* of them. I can barely handle *one*."

Ever true to her nature, Prioshka blushed. Then grinned.

All three women shared a companionable burst of laughter.

"I'm in awe, too, Prioshka," giggled Freddie. "And perhaps later...you can give me a few tips?"

Another round of chuckles erupted from the teacups, making the men break off their conversation and glance over.

"Care to share the humor, love?" asked Viktor of Madelyne.

She shook her head.

Peter and Gyorgy raised their eyebrows. Mat and Luk, glancing at Prioshka's bright cheeks, simply smiled.

Peter rose. "Well, Freddie and I are going to drop over to Zentaily House this morning. What are you folks doing?"

Viktor tugged on his lip thoughtfully. "I have a couple of contacts I should try and pin down. Madelyne and I will join you and then we can go on from there." He glanced over at Gyorgy. "Perhaps Fabyan will be by...he said he'd visit sometime today?"

Plans were made, appointments set, and shortly thereafter, Mat, Luk, Gyorgy and Prioshka remained at the table as the others took their leave.

Luk sighed. "It is good to be together again, my friend." He smiled at Gyorgy. "And to see those two wed...well, it's a surprise, but a pleasant one."

Gyorgy stared at his teacup. "I intend to wed too."

Prioshka jumped. "But Marie-Claire never said—"

"*What?*"

Gyorgy was out of his seat and standing in front of Prioshka before the words had finished spilling from her mouth.

She clapped her hand across her lips to stifle a curse.

Luk and Mat rushed to her side and faced Gyorgy.

"What do you know of Marie-Claire?" Gyorgy's voice was harsh and his expression forbidding.

"She asked us not to tell you. It was a mistake." Luk glared at Gyorgy.

Prioshka dropped her hands and looked up at the undeniably riled man before her. "Gyorgy, I should not have spoken as I did. We made her a promise and I have foolishly broken it."

Gyorgy ran his hand over his face. "It's all right. I'm sorry too. I didn't mean to snap at you. But please...this is more important to me than anything. Tell me what you know? How do you know her?" His eyes remained fixed on Prioshka's. "*Please?*"

The three conspirators exchanged glances. "It will mean betraying a confidence, Gyorgy." Mat stood tall and met the other man's gaze.

Prioshka put her arm on Mat's and tugged. "You're right, but I have to confess that I'm worried about her, Mat."

Gyorgy sat down with a thump. "I think you'd better tell me the whole story, and we can decide afterwards if you've broken your word or not."

Luk and Mat nodded.

"She's a damned independent woman, Gyorgy, I'll say that for her. But before you bite my head off, let me assure you she knows where we are...and that we're here to help her should she need it. We certainly wouldn't leave her at loose ends."

The story tumbled out as Luk, Mat and Prioshka related the tale of their eventful journey to London.

"And I like her, Gyorgy. She's not only beautiful, she has...a certain something about her. She's shy."

Gyorgy choked over his tea. Shyness wasn't part of the woman who'd offered herself to him and his whip.

Luk frowned. "But she's here on a mission, Gyorgy. And we don't like the sound of it."

Gyorgy stared at him. "A mission?"

Three pairs of eyes looked worriedly back. "Yes, a mission," said Prioshka.

"What kind of mission?"

Nervously, Prioshka pleated the tablecloth beneath her fingers. "She said...she said she was here to kill a man."

Gyorgy gulped. "*Kill* a man?"

"Don't worry, Gyorgy. Not you." Prioshka's hand reached out and smoothed his sleeve. "We asked if she was going to kill you and she said no."

In spite of his inner turmoil, Gyorgy couldn't help but grin. "Well, thank you for relieving my mind on that matter, anyway." Of course, Marie-Claire probably would be the death of him, but not in the way that the others meant. She'd kill him with her passion. And his. And he'd die a happy man.

He shook his head to clear it of images he didn't need to remember right now. "Did she say who?"

"No. She keeps her counsel very well indeed." Mat frowned too. "I got the impression it was someone from her past perhaps. Something that she should have done...what did she say 'years ago' or words to that effect."

A number of pieces of a puzzle fell into place in Gyorgy's mind and he leaped from his chair with an oath on his lips.

"*Az anyad.*"

"What?" His three friends stared at him.

"I know who she's come to kill." Gyorgy started for the door. "And I've reserved that privilege for myself."

"Who, Gyorgy?" Luk moved to intercept him, but Gyorgy shook off his hand.

"*Francis bloody Hucknall.*"

Luk and Mat turned as one to Prioshka. "Stay here. Wait for us." The words tumbled from their mouths as they hurried after Gyorgy.

She nodded. "Of course."

As soon as they'd left, she rushed to the door.

Chapter 26

Gyorgy's heart was in his throat as he waited impatiently for the carriage he'd summoned at the top of his lungs. The servants had run to do his bidding without a second glance.

A jangling of harnesses heralded its arrival and as Gyorgy leaped for the door, he found two men right behind him, shouldering him into the seat and making themselves at home beside him.

"Didn't think you'd get to do this on your own, did you?" grinned Mat.

"We're not about to miss out on *this*, Gyorgy." Luk's excitement radiated from him. "After all, we've met Marie-Claire too. And liked her."

Gyorgy's temper abated and he smiled back at his friends. "I'm glad."

A frown crossed all three faces as a small hand reached in and opened the carriage door again.

"Oh no you don't," said Prioshka, tumbling in on top of them and hanging on as the horses were whipped up by the driver. "Not without me."

"Damn it, Prioshka..." sputtered Luk.

"Good grief sweetheart," said Mat, holding her close and setting her between them. "Didn't we tell you to wait?"

She snorted. "Don't even consider it. We're together. In this and everything. Besides," she glared at them. "You might well remember that Marie-Claire might need the presence of another woman. For...for..."

Gyorgy bit down on his frustration. "Look, Prioshka. I appreciate your wanting to help, but this is not a task for a woman. It could be dangerous."

Mat and Luk moved closer to her, protectively.

She reached over and took Gyorgy's hand. "I know that. And I'm not a fool. But where they go—I go. Is that clear?"

Gyorgy blinked. "Um. Well. When you put it like that..." He glanced up at the two men who stared back at him with a mixture of defiance and concern.

He grinned. "She's a fine woman, my friends. You have chosen well."

They relaxed and Prioshka settled herself more comfortably between them. "As have I." A smile curved her lips as she released Gyorgy's hand and found her own clasped by the men next to her.

Luk reached for the side of the carriage as it lurched around a corner. "So tell us, Gyorgy, where are we going in such a hurry and why does Marie-Claire want to kill Hucknall? What *is* all this about?"

* * * * *

"The Dowager Duchess of Kirkwood, my Lord."

The butler's voice rang impressively through the breakfast room of Kirkwood House. The rest of the elegant Mayfair neighborhood was probably still sleeping, but Marie-Claire had hoped that her nephew-by-marriage would be up early. Her hopes were answered.

"*Marie-Claire!*" A young, sandy-haired man rose in surprise as she entered the room. "You're the last person I expected to see this morning."

She smiled. "Forgive me, Dennis. I had to come. It was time."

The Duke of Kirkwood looked awkwardly around, and then gestured to a chair. "Have you breakfasted? Would you care for tea?"

"None for me, thank you. I just wanted to tell you that I was in town, and that I am going to be taking care of some unfinished business. You have a right to know."

Dennis's face paled. "Don't...don't tell me you're here to deal with...with *Hucknall*?"

"Look, Dennis. It's gone on long enough. I need to be free of it all. You're well established now. There can be no threat to you or Delphine, or the children."

"But...there *is*. I mean there *could* be..." He stopped and hung his head. "I...you see..."

Marie-Claire clenched her teeth, but held on to her temper, allowing nothing of her inner furor to reveal itself. "Dennis...what has happened?"

He raised miserable eyes to hers. "It was the cards, you see. I really believed I could win the hand." His gaze fell. "I didn't."

Marie-Claire fought for composure. "You're telling me you played cards *with*, and lost *to*, Francis Hucknall?"

His head came up at that. "No, of course not. What kind of fool d'you take me for?"

She bit her response back, waiting for the rest of the story.

"I just...I...it was at my club. I lost a lot, Marie-Claire. *A lot.* And then when I went to make arrangements to settle, I was told that my vouchers had been 'transferred' to Hucknall."

She drew in a shaky breath and expelled it again as she absorbed these new developments. "So. Now he owns you too."

Dennis couldn't meet her eyes. "Yes. And I've been paying him back, plus interest of course, for the last six months or so."

"You couldn't meet the debt?"

He swallowed and named a sum that made even Marie-Claire blink. "Good God, Dennis...what were you thinking?"

"I couldn't begin selling off my estates...they're entailed. And what was mine and Delphine's has to be protected for the children. For Eric and Rose's dowry...and..."

Marie-Claire held up her hand. "Don't explain. Not to me. I understand."

Dennis had the grace to look embarrassed. "Of course you do. I'm sorry. You've protected us with your absence, exiled yourself from London, done more than I had any right to expect, just to protect us. I don't know what to say..." He shifted uncomfortably in his chair. "I can only assume that you're here to tell him he can no longer..."

"Keep me buried in the country? Yes." She stood and moved to the window. "I plan on leaving England. Soon, I hope...if things go according to plan."

If things go...according to Gyorgy.

She turned. "It has to end, Dennis. This family has had enough of the stranglehold Hucknall's put on us. I refused to let you and Delphine suffer for my husband's mistakes, and I'll find a way to make sure your children don't suffer for yours."

Dennis Kirkwood sighed. "Look, Marie-Claire, I truly appreciate your help…but I just don't see what can be done."

No—he wouldn't.

She looked at him. The Kirkwoods were fundamentally weak. The old Duke hadn't thought twice about marrying a nameless bastard French girl. The young Duke hadn't considered the consequences of gambling away a good portion of the Kirkwood fortune on the turn of a card.

The old Duke had spilled the shameful secret of his young wife's birth one night over his brandy and given a foul and evil man the tools to wring money out of him for the rest of his life, mercifully short though it was.

Marie-Claire had soon found that Hucknall liked the income. With her husband's death, he'd appeared at her door, announced that he knew the truth of her origins and demanded she continued to pay him or he'd make it known far and wide through London, bringing disgrace on the Kirkwood name.

Dennis had been so young. Newly married, ill-equipped to face the duties that went along with being Duke. And—yes, weak. She'd been forced to protect him, and pay. Her town home had gone, most of her fortune, her jewels, all she had was her house in the country, and Hucknall had generously allowed her to keep that. And of course he'd had an ulterior motive.

The last time they'd met he'd warned her.

"I'm a patient man, Duchess. I'll take your money. I'll wait. Because soon you'll want to come back to London. A woman like you won't like life buried in the country." Marie-Claire suppressed a shiver of disgust as she remembered his words. And his expression. "And when you come back, it'll be as my mistress."

He'd run his eyes lasciviously up and down her body. "I'll have you. Maybe not right at this moment. Maybe not this year. But I'll wait. With you on my arm I'll have the entrée back into society where I belong. So I'll take my time and do it right. You'll have to give in. And when you do…" He'd licked his lips. "I'll take great pleasure in fucking you, Duchess. Great pleasure."

So she'd left London. And never returned, preferring to pay whatever it took to keep Hucknall quiet than accept life as his mistress.

She'd protected the young Duke, kept her bed empty, and been in financial bondage to Hucknall ever since. He hadn't guessed how much she'd enjoy the quiet of country life, but his interests had apparently fulfilled his needs. Thankfully, she'd not had to deal with him in person.

But she knew he had not lied. He was indeed a patient man. Like a giant spider lurking in the shadows, he spun his web, biding his time and waiting for his victims to make that one mistake that would land them fair and square in his trap.

Enough was enough.

She no longer cared that she was a base-born bastard. Neither would society. Dennis had found his feet as Duke, and could withstand the small scandal better now than he would have done several years ago. She needed the freedom to go to Gyorgy, tell him the truth about her past, and see where they would go from there. For the first time there was something she wanted, and she wasn't about to let Hucknall get in her way.

But the added complication of Dennis's gambling debts certainly made her task more difficult. She'd hoped to avoid what had seemed like the only solution. But now...the world would definitely be a better place if Francis Hucknall wasn't in it.

She squared her shoulders. "Dennis...I would appreciate it if you would not mention that I've been here. I shall attempt to resolve this problem. The fewer people who know about it, the better."

"What are you going to do?" His expression held a germ of hope as he stared at her.

"I shall see if I can talk some sense into Hucknall." She cradled her reticule in her hand and took comfort from the weight within. "If I can't, then perhaps there is another way to deal with him."

Dennis swallowed. "Do you want me to come with you?"

Brave words from a trembling man. "No. Your duties are to your wife and children and the Kirkwood estate."

He was so young, realized Marie-Claire. He was titled her nephew, and was almost her age, but still...he was so *young*.

"But Dennis...one word of warning. No more gambling."

He coughed. "You have my word on that...Aunt."

She smiled calmly. "Silly isn't it? We're of an age, yet I'm your aunt." She moved to the door. "Goodbye Dennis. And my best wishes for your future. I doubt that our paths will cross again, but I will let you know where I go, so that we can take care of any estate business that might crop up."

He nodded. "Thank you, Marie-Claire. Thank you for not...not making me feel stupid."

She patted his arm. "Live an honorable life, Dennis. Be an honorable man." *Like Gyorgy.*

* * * * *

"So Hucknall's been *blackmailing* her?" Prioshka's shocked voice echoed through the carriage.

Gyorgy ran a hand over his face. "Yes, from what I could find out. Regular sums of money have worked their way into his bank from the Kirkwood estate. They started just after she wed the old Duke. It wasn't hard to dig up information on her if one knows where to look." His face turned hard. "As if anyone would care about the circumstances of her birth."

Prioshka's face twisted. "But they do, Gyorgy. It's sad and pretty disgusting, but that sort of thing can destroy someone in less than twenty-four hours. Especially here in London."

Mat nodded. "It makes sense. The young lad who became Duke...her nephew I suppose...he'd have been in a bad situation if the word had gotten out."

"So she pays up and stays in the country—" began Luk.

"—slashing everything she has to the bone to protect some weakling Duke. It's not like it was her fault to start with." Gyorgy's voice was harsh. "And Hucknall milks her dry. Along with an assortment of other poor fish he's hooked. She's not the only victim of his filthy plans."

Prioshka's hands clenched. "I understand why she intends to kill him. I think I'd like to help."

Gyorgy glanced at her. "*You* will stay in the carriage."

Mutinous eyes gazed back at him. "*I* will go with Mat and Luk."

"Gyorgy has a point, Prioshka-love. This is no place for you." Mat held her hand tightly. "We will not put you in danger."

"You're too important." Luk put his arm around her.

She snorted. "It's not a subject that is up for discussion."

Three men sighed.

Gyorgy opened his mouth to resume the argument when the carriage pulled up in front of a quiet house, set back from the street and apart from its neighbors. Even though Hucknall's reputation stank to the heavens, his money had still managed to buy him an excellent property in a respectable location.

Theirs was not the first carriage to arrive.

"She's here."

The words were barely out of Gyorgy's mouth when he pushed his way past his friends and hurried up the neat pathway to Hucknall's front door.

He didn't care now whether Mat, Luk, Prioshka or the devil himself was standing behind him. All he could think about was Marie-Claire. And that scum she was dealing with. Alone.

The door was half-open and a maid peered around it.

"Let me in, girl," said Gyorgy. "I need to see Hucknall."

"He's…uh…he's…there's someone…"

"I know. Trust me. It will be all right." Gyorgy summoned his best smile and aimed it full force at the poor maid. He realized she bore a nasty bruise on one side of her face. "Did he do that?"

The words slipped out in spite of his rising temper, and Gyorgy's heart hardened even more when the girl nodded. "There's only three of us left. The butler left yesterday. I'd go too but I have nowhere else…"

The others gathered close behind him. "I have a friend who can help. This lady…" Gyorgy turned, knowing Prioshka would be there. "This lady can tell you where to go. Leave this place. Take the others. There is nothing for you here now."

She opened the door wide and let him in. "Thank you sir. He's in his study. Please…"

The tone of her voice and the distress in her eyes added to Gyorgy's fury. If that vermin had lain a hand on Marie-Claire…

They started down the long hall towards the room the maid had indicated.

They jumped as the sound of a gunshot rang out.

Chapter 27

Marie-Claire stared at the man behind the desk.

She'd *shot* him.

And yet he rose, glancing down at the blood oozing through his jacket from his arm. "Well, well...the bitch has claws. Didn't think you had the stomach for it." His teeth flashed. "You'll be fine bedsport, that's for sure. Bring that passion to our fucking and I'll make sure you're well taken care of."

Her lips curled back from her teeth. "You are lower than dirt, Hucknall. As if I'd let filth like you touch me."

He moved around the desk, and in spite of her resolve, Marie-Claire backed up a step, the now-useless gun dangling from her hand. How could she have known it would throw to the left? She'd aimed right for his heart too.

She cursed inwardly, but held her chin high. "You have taken enough. Stolen enough. It ends now."

He laughed, a raspy sound that made his jowls quiver. "Oh I haven't begun to *take*. I'm going to start with those tits of yours." He stared at her breasts, covered by the delicate lace of her gown.

"Nice and full they are. Just right for a bit of sucking and pinching, eh? And I'll wager your cunt will heat right up too. And your arse. Oh yes. I'm going to enjoy shoving my cock right into that tight arse of yours."

She fought back nausea and let her eyes drift around the room seeking any kind of weapon. For once, her anger might have overridden her common sense. She should have brought another gun.

He was getting closer, but she refused to back away, preferring to meet his eyes with her own and pour all the hatred and contempt she felt for him into her gaze.

He sneered. "Looking at me like that isn't going to help. Remember you're a French bastard. A whore who got lucky and married a Duke. You're not fit to lick my boots, bitch. But I'll let you lick something else. You Frenchies are good at that."

His hand dropped to his breeches.

"*I think not.*"

A hard voice interrupted Hucknall and he turned with an oath.

"*Gyorgy.*" Marie-Claire breathed his name and her heart soared as she saw him standing so tall and handsome in the doorway. His dark gaze flashed to her and he smiled briefly, then returned his attention to the man menacing her.

Hucknall snorted. "Filthy gypsy, huh? I should have known someone like her would find a champion in the gutters. Like to like, I always say."

Gyorgy opened his hand and the coils of his whip unfurled. "You say a lot, Hucknall. I don't care to hear any of it. Neither does the Duchess."

"Duchess? This whore? She may have the title, but she was born in the slums. Looks like she fooled you too. Of course, you probably don't care..." Hucknall's confidence in his own superiority was astounding.

And, Marie-Claire realized, very foolish.

Gyorgy's face creased into a smile. It was not a pleasant one, and in spite of herself, she shivered.

He moved his hand slightly, and the whip flew across the space between the two men, making Hucknall jump as it sliced open his cheek. "What the *fuck*..."

He backed away.

Gyorgy moved forward, flicking his wrist again and slicing the other cheek. Without moving his eyes from Hucknall, he spoke to her. "Marie-Claire, you might want to leave now."

"I think not, Gyorgy. I need to see this." Her heart was light, singing with the knowledge that Gyorgy had come to save her. He *cared*.

"Very well."

Hucknall was blustering now, confused by the incessantly flicking whip and trying to dodge the lashes that were bringing more blood from his skin.

"I see you shot him," said Gyorgy casually, raising a nasty weal on the man's neck and making him gasp.

"Yes I did. But the damn gun threw to the left. I missed his heart."

"Pity." Gyorgy sliced the stained shirtfront and slashed into the skin beneath.

Hucknall was backed up against a wall now, eyes darting around, looking for a way to avoid the unavoidable. Gyorgy's whip.

"The house is empty, Gyorgy."

Marie-Claire heard a voice behind her. *Mat*. Which meant Luk was here too. Some of the tension drained out of her. With such reinforcements, there was no need for fear anymore. Hucknall was finished.

Hucknall's face was draining of color as Mat's words sank home. He darted for his desk, reaching for a drawer.

"Gyorgy..." warned Marie-Claire.

"No...no, Hucknall. I don't think so." Gyorgy's whip latched on to the man's wrist and he pulled back sharply, making Hucknall scream as the leather bit through his flesh to the bone.

The drawer clattered to the floor and the gun hidden within fell with it.

"Tsk, tsk." Gyorgy continued his attack, ignoring the blood and the whimpers from Hucknall as he clutched his mangled wrist.

"You are scum, Hucknall. You're not a man, you're vermin. You don't deserve to share this earth with your fellows. You do know that, don't you?"

Hucknall bared his teeth. "You'll pay for this, you gypsy bastard. How dare you think you can come in here and do this..."

"Oh I dare." Gyorgy's words were cold as ice. "I dare even more."

His whip flicked to the man's throat and sliced across it, not deeply but enough to scare Hucknall into immobility.

Gyorgy moved closer. "I dare to suggest that this world will be a damn sight better place to live without you in it."

He reached for the gun and Hucknall lunged.

Marie-Claire bit back a cry of terror as the two men grappled, but Hucknall had the disadvantage of anger and confusion, while Gyorgy was cool and in control. He lightly avoided the bigger man's attack, and flicked his whip, catching Hucknall's boots and hobbling him.

Hucknall fell—heavily…hitting his head on the side of his desk and going down with a mighty crash.

He didn't move again.

"Everybody all right?" Prioshka's practical tones filled the silence in the room, and like a magician breaking a spell, everyone breathed once more.

"Yes," said Gyorgy, bending over Hucknall's body. "Except for this trash, of course."

"Is he dead?" Marie-Claire was shocked that her voice was so steady. Even now she could see him reaching for Gyorgy…feel the terror in her heart that Hucknall would hurt him.

"Looks like it. Can't feel a pulse, anyway."

Luk walked to the desk and opened the drawers. "He hit his head pretty hard on the corner. Probably snapped his neck."

"Find anything?" Mat was running his hands over the bookshelves.

"Aha." Luk pulled out a sheaf of papers. "Here. This looks interesting." The three men ignored the bleeding mess on the floor and bent over to read.

"His records." Gyorgy's voice was hard. "There's a lot of people on this list who will not mourn his passing."

"Good God." Mat's eyes opened wide. "Look at these figures…"

"He did very well for himself with his nasty blackmailing schemes, didn't he?" Luk shook his head.

Marie-Claire felt Prioshka's hand slide into hers. The warmth was welcome, since a chill was beginning to flood her limbs.

"What do we do now?" Prioshka's voice was matter-of-fact, and gave Marie-Claire something to hold on to.

"Yes…" she croaked, her voice failing her now that the adrenaline was draining from her body. "What do we do now?"

Gyorgy's head jerked up and he stared at her. He dropped the papers, ignored everyone and strode to her. "We go home."

"Home?" She couldn't drag her eyes away from his.

"Yes. Home. To Viktor's right now, then home." His gaze softened. "Our home."

Marie-Claire's vision blurred, and she felt strong arms gather her close.

"Take care of things will you?" Gyorgy tossed the words over his shoulder as he picked Marie-Claire up.

"The usual way?"

"It will serve best, I think."

"Wait…" She had to know. Gyorgy was attempting to carry her away from it all. She had to know it was finished. She *had* to. "What's 'the usual way'?"

Gyorgy glanced over at his two friends, and they nodded.

He turned back to her. "There will be a sad accident, Marie-Claire. Francis Hucknall will knock over a lamp and set fire to his study. The house will burn before he can be rescued, since he was overcome by smoke and unable to summon help soon enough."

She swallowed. "Will it suffice?"

Gyorgy snorted. "For one such as him? There'd be a line to strike the first match." He headed for the door cradling her in his arms. "We'll await you in the carriage."

Marie-Claire let her head rest on his shoulders and closed her eyes, feeling the warmth of the sunshine on her cheeks as he carried her from the house. "Silly girl," he whispered, dropping a kiss on her hair.

"Gyorgy…" she began.

He stopped her lips with another kiss, this one hot and passionate. "Hush, love. It can all wait. We have time now."

He settled her into the carriage on his lap and arranged them both into one cuddled lump. It was as if he couldn't hold her close enough. And it met with her complete approval.

"I would have come back for you, Marie-Claire. I never would have left you. You know that don't you?" His voice was a low murmur.

"I had to come to you, Gyorgy. I'd sent you away. You'd been honorable and obeyed. It was up to me to come to you. I never would have left *you*." She raised a hand to his cheek. "I never *could* leave you."

"You're not going to. I'm not a rich man, love, but all I have is yours. Be with me. Marry me. Share my life the way you already share my heart."

Marie-Claire felt the last drop of ice in her veins melt and evaporate. She let her heart show in her smile. "Willingly. With all that I am. I want to spend my life playing your games, Gyorgy. I don't care what you have or don't have. I'm nothing but a base-born French—"

He stopped her words with his lips, sucking them into nothingness and replacing them with his tongue. He tasted sweet and hot, and Marie-Claire moaned into his mouth as his arms pulled her hard against him.

"*Excuse* me…"

Luk was casually surveying the lovers with an elbow resting on the carriage door.

Gyorgy raised his head and frowned. "What?"

Mat's head popped into sight, grinning at the two of them. "I hate to disturb you, but I think there's going to be a spot of trouble here soon. Might well be a nasty fire or something."

"Oh…yes…" Gyorgy's eyes refocused on his surroundings, and Marie-Claire laughed.

Then she stopped, astonished at herself. She'd actually *laughed*.

And it felt…wonderful. She looked at the faces around her, and breathed in the first breath of her new life. Then she turned to Gyorgy.

"Let's go home."

* * * * *

The sound of a distant fire bell clanging across London went unnoticed in the darkened apartments of Fabyan Szabo, as did the smoke that appeared as a vague cloud in the sky.

All he knew was that he was lost. Lost in the heat of Annabelle and in her loving. They'd slept, awoken, touched and slept again. And when the morning light had peeked between the drawn draperies, they'd finally surrendered to their needs.

He needed to be inside her. And she needed him there.

And so he was. Her hot slick cunt welcomed him, clinging to his cock as he gently stroked into her sleep-warmed body.

Her legs had risen to encase him and her hands were even now gripping his forearms. He had no idea that it could be such exquisite bliss.

They'd loved each other to the edge of exhaustion during the night, but this final claiming set the seal on their passion. As one, they moved towards their final moments, his cock sliding within her, touching every inch of her core, and her cunt helping him with honey and heat.

He wanted to take it slowly, give her time to regain her strength, but he'd been overwhelmed by her touches, and lured by her obvious arousal all over again.

Neither could hold back—neither wanted to.

Annabelle panted beneath him, moaning with each thrust and pushing back, urging him with her body to even greater depths.

Her breasts swayed as she moved, and he could feel her pulse through the walls of her slick passage, echoing the throb of his own heart as he took her with him.

Neither could last very long.

Annabelle's moans turned to whimpers and her fingers dug into his skin. She was coming.

And so was he. Fire spread from his balls through his groin and his buttocks clenched as he thrust into her soul.

With a roar, he emptied himself, letting his seed spurt freely into this body...this woman. She spasmed beneath him, massaging his cock, sucking him dry and locking him to her with her thighs.

It was beyond anything he could ever remember, and in that moment, Fabyan knew he could not survive without this woman at his side.

Not again. Not ever.

As his shudders eased, he slid from her, sighing as his cock fell away from her with a soft rush of moisture. "Annabelle," he sighed, more from the pleasure of speaking her name than any great need to say anything.

"I love you, Fabyan," she whispered.

"And I love you," he answered. "We must settle this, Annabelle. I shall not let you go again."

"I shall never leave you again." She turned her head on his shoulder. "But what shall we do?"

"Leave it to me. And my friends."

He smiled as he thought of Viktor, Peter, Mat, Luk and Gyorgy. Between them, they had changed so many lives and helped so many people.

Surely they could work out how to help one more.

Him.

Chapter 28

Viktor and Peter stood on the pavement outside Zentaily House with identical expressions of irritation on their faces.

Their wives, completely unintimidated, stared right back.

"No."

"Yes, Viktor. I'm going with you. It's my right. It's my father we're talking about here, not some stranger." Madelyne put her hands firmly on her hips.

The 'discussion' had begun as a messenger had rushed up to Viktor and handed him a note. He'd glanced at Peter and nodded. "All is set."

Then they'd tried to dismiss the two women who were adamantly refusing to be sent home.

And Madelyne knew she was right. "You can't win, here, Viktor. Admit it. I'm the one who has suffered the most from his actions, and I deserve to be there when he's ruined."

"And she's not going to be there without me at her side," chimed in Freddie, moving closer to Madelyne. "What affects one, affects us all. Isn't that right?"

Peter looked sideways at Viktor. Viktor looked back helplessly.

"Accept it, Viktor. We're with you. Like it or not. We love you, we married you, and we're *not* going to be excluded—especially from this. You wouldn't be doing any of this if it wasn't for me. Don't you think I deserve this much?" Madelyne pleaded with him. "Don't I deserve the chance to see retribution finally catch up with that...that...*beast*?"

Peter shrugged. "I don't see we have a choice, Viktor. Madelyne's right."

"I don't like it," muttered Viktor. "Supposing the man turns ugly?"

Freddie snorted. "It sounds as if he's been ugly all his life. I doubt he'll change now. But you'll be there. It's not as if we're going in by ourselves." She looked at Madelyne and smiled wickedly. "Besides, we have a vested interest in keeping you both whole."

Madelyne chuckled back, ignoring her husband's breathy sigh of resignation. "Yes we do, Freddie. Indeed we do."

"Very well." Viktor bowed to the inevitable. "But you will both stay quiet and remain behind us at all times. Is that understood?"

"Yes, milord," teased Madelyne, dropping him a little curtsey.

"As you wish, milord," echoed Freddie politely.

"They're going to be the death of me," groaned Viktor, grabbing his wife's hand.

"Yes, but what a way to go," grinned Peter, slipping his arm around Freddie's waist. "What a way to go."

"Eventyde House," said Viktor to the driver. "And you'd better hurry."

All four scrambled into the carriage and silence fell as they traveled the busy London streets.

Finally Peter spoke. "Does he know?"

Viktor looked over. "That his financial empire has fallen? Maybe. I'm not sure how fast word of this kind of thing travels in his circles."

"If not, I want to be the one to tell him." Madelyne's voice was surprisingly hard. "I want to look into his face and watch him crumple. I want…revenge, I suppose. I want to know that he is hurting. Perhaps not as much as he hurt me, but it will be something."

Viktor stroked her hand. "Sweetheart, revenge is not often worth the effort we put into it. It can't heal. It can't obliterate the past. It's a temporary pleasure that can leave more damage behind."

Madelyne's heart turned over once again as she saw the love and concern in his eyes. "*You* have obliterated the past, Viktor. I don't need revenge for that. This will be pure pleasure. Simply a chance to see the wrong a man has done catch up with him. I need this, Viktor. I need to know that evil does not go unpunished."

"I know, love," he answered. "I know."

The carriage slowed to a standstill outside Eventyde House.

Peter and Viktor exchanged glances. "Are we ready?" Peter's question was firm.

"We're ready." Viktor's answer equally certain.

"Then let's do it," said Freddie, gathering her skirts.

"Let's finish it." Madelyne spoke the words with finality.

* * * * *

"The Count and Countess Karoly. Lord and Lady Chalmers."

The butler intoned their titles as he stepped through an impressive door leading from the hall of Eventyde House. Viktor could feel the slight shiver in Madelyne's arm, and he pulled her close to him.

"Who the devil are they? I don't know anyone by that name..."

The huffily outraged tones of Lord Alfred Eventyde were quite audible to the group awaiting him.

Viktor calmly eased past the butler. "Oh but you do, Lord Eventyde. *I* am Count Viktor Karoly. I believe you know the Countess?"

To say that Lord Eventyde was surprised would be an understatement. Viktor watched with a great deal of pleasure as the man's eyes bulged and his jaw dropped.

"However, I don't believe you've had the pleasure of meeting Lady Chalmers?" Peter's voice dripped icicles as he correctly presented his wife.

"I...uh..."

"Lord Eventyde. My wife and I felt it appropriate to call on you since you were in town." Viktor was enjoying this. Every single moment of it. The man deserved all this and more for what he'd put Madelyne through. She stood straight and proud beside him, and his heart warmed at the sight of her.

"I...uh...well..."

Good. Words were beginning to form in Eventyde's brain.

"I fear we do not, however, bring good tidings."

Eventyde blinked. Viktor bit back a smile of triumph. The man had no idea his world was about to come crashing down around his ears.

"My man of business informs me that a recent business enterprise I had considered as an investment is now on the brink of bankruptcy. I believe you are familiar with the name...Fair Seas Trading?"

Eventyde sat down in his chair with a thud. "What? *Fair Seas*? Nonsense. Sound as a bell."

Peter stepped to Viktor's side. "Sadly, Eventyde, that is not the case. My man of affairs also confirmed that fact this morning. It seems your investors have withdrawn their support. I have no idea why, of course, something must be in the wind—as it were."

Eventyde's expression hardened as he gazed at the two men before him. Not once did he acknowledge Madelyne's presence. "You are quite incorrect. Why only yesterday—"

"That was yesterday, Eventyde." Viktor's voice snapped coldly through the room. "Today, it is finished. Over. The company has failed. And taken with it a sizeable amount of your personal fortune. Almost all of it, in fact."

Now Eventyde's eyes found Madelyne. "You...*bitch*."

Viktor's body tensed, but he felt Madelyne's arm holding him back. "Why, *Father*, how unpleasant of you. And in front of my husband too. I'm quite surprised, since you always took care to insult me in private...up to now."

Eventyde's fists clenched angrily on his desk. "It was you, wasn't it? Spiteful little whore that you are."

Viktor shook off Madelyne's hand, stalked to the desk and with a solid swing punched Eventyde.

"Don't *ever* use that word to my wife again."

Eventyde pulled himself together and reached for a handkerchief to stem the blood that poured from his nose.

"How distasteful you are," said Freddie haughtily. "Certainly no gentleman."

Eventyde ignored her, his eyes fixed on his daughter. "Does this fine husband of yours know all about you, Missy? Did you tell him of your whorish ways? Does he know he bought damaged goods?"

Viktor was ready to repeat his earlier actions, but Madelyne held on tightly to his arm this time, stopping him. "He knows, Father. And he really doesn't care. But he has quite a temper you know. I suggest you not provoke him further. You have your own concerns now. Since your business ventures have failed, wouldn't your efforts be better put into selling up the Eventyde estate to make good on your debts, hmm?"

Her smile was sweet, but her eyes were cold. Eventyde clearly saw the emotions within them, and he curled his lip. "Well, he may *think* he knows everything about you, but he's wrong." He took a final swipe at his nose. "How do you think your fancy Count is going to feel when he learns he's married nothing more than a bastard? A nameless chit whose mother was a whore?"

Madelyne froze, and Viktor's brows snapped together. "What are you talking about?"

Eventyde chuckled noisily. "Oh yes. It's quite true you know. She's no get of mine."

Madelyne turned to Viktor, a look of puzzlement on her face. Viktor smiled down at her. "Well, thank God for that."

"How dare you?" Eventyde stood, outraged. "The Eventyde name has been handed down for generations with never a touch of scandal. It's a proud and ancient heritage, passed through the centuries, which is why..."

"Why you claimed another man's daughter as your own?"

The cool voice cut through the tension in the room like a knife, and as one all heads turned to the door.

"Mama?" Madelyne blinked uncertainly.

"Fabyan?" Peter and Viktor stared.

"*Annabelle*?" Eventyde's voice was outraged.

With a great deal of aplomb, given the circumstances, Fabyan and Annabelle strolled into the room.

* * * * *

Madelyne was completely confused. "Mama?" She knew she was repeating herself, but as she stared at the woman walking toward her, it seemed her brain wouldn't let her say anything else.

"Hello my darling. I'm so *very* happy to see you." Annabelle opened her arms and hugged Madelyne as hard as she could.

"Mama...I..."

Viktor stepped to her side. "Lady Eventyde? I'm Viktor Karoly. I'm married to your daughter."

Ignoring Eventyde snorting noisily behind them, Annabelle smiled up at Viktor. "I know, dear man. Fabyan has told me all about you." Her grin passed on to Peter and Freddie. "*All* about you."

"He has?" Peter raised his eyebrows at Fabyan who grinned back.

"Mama, I'm confused..." Madelyne struggled for breath.

"Darling, I'm sorry." Annabelle hugged her daughter once more. "Sorry for the years that I haven't spent with you..."

"You should be damn glad I kept you apart," snarled Eventyde, interrupting her.

"Shut. Up." Viktor and Peter turned on him, and he subsided.

"And sorry for all the things I never told you." Annabelle continued. "The most important of which is that you're the child of my heart, Madelyne. A child conceived in love. And although I hate to say it, *he*..." she nodded at Eventyde. "He is right, for once in his miserable life. You're not his daughter."

"Well. I can't say I'm sorry about that part of it," said Madelyne. "So then who..."

Her eyes turned to Fabyan. Deep blue eyes met deep blue eyes, and somebody in the room gasped. Madelyne had no idea who, since her brain was spinning.

"Oh my God..." Viktor breathed the words.

"Madelyne...I'd like you to meet your father. Fabyan..." Annabelle held out her hand. "This is our daughter."

"Hello." Fabyan's deep voice broke the stunned silence, bringing gasps of surprise to both Viktor and Peter.

Madelyne reached out a hand tentatively to this amazingly handsome man. And one of the *Gypsies* too. "Hello...*Papa.*"

It was a poignant moment, but Madelyne was blind to the tears falling from Annabelle's eyes or the fact that Freddie was unashamedly sniffling. All she knew was that the man who had given her life was standing in front of her, looking at her with so much love in his face her heart felt like bursting.

"My daughter..." His voice broke and he took her into his embrace. Madelyne gave up the fight and sobbed.

"Well this is quite sickening." Eventyde's exclamation of disgust drew everyone's attention back to him and away from Madelyne and Fabyan.

Viktor's eyes narrowed. "Really? More sickening than a man who tries to foist his daughter off on the highest bidder? A man who cares nothing about her wishes, only his own advancement? A man who keeps the daughter apart from her mother and tells her nothing about her own life? Her own birth? Not because he cares about her at all but because he sees in her a chance to buy himself a title perhaps?"

"Well...I...housed and fed the brat, didn't I?"

"Only when it served your purpose." Madelyne pulled her face from Fabyan's hug. "You were no father to me. You were a jailer."

"As he was no husband to me, either, sweetheart," added Annabelle.

"And as he is now no longer possessor of the Eventyde fortune," threw in Peter wryly. "He's finished."

Eventyde blanched. "Utter rubbish."

Peter pulled a piece of paper from his pocket. "I received this today, Eventyde. It confirms our suspicions. Your shipping company has foundered, if you'll pardon my pun. You're ruined. Financially...and therefore also socially."

He leaned menacingly over the table. "Your name will no longer guarantee your admittance to your clubs. Your creditors are being notified as we speak. Arrangements are being made for several of your vouchers to be called in." An elegant finger poked Eventyde hard in the chest. "Do I make myself clear? It's over. You're *finished*."

"Good riddance to bad rubbish," added the irrepressible Freddie.

Eventyde slumped, staring at the document Peter had spread before him.

Madelyne turned to her father. "I think we should leave. I can take no more of his presence. And I have questions..."

Fabyan's smile was gentle and loving. "And I have answers, little one."

Viktor cleared his throat. "Uh...Fabyan? When did you find your voice?"

Fabyan glanced at Annabelle. "When I found my heart."

Freddie sighed. "Oh, that's *so* lovely."

"Get out. All of you—get out." Eventyde snarled at them. "Take your simpering sniveling stupidities and get the fuck *out*."

It was about the only thing Eventyde could have said that all six people present were willing to do. Within moments they'd left the room. And not one of them glanced back.

Not even when the sound of a single shot followed them through the house to the steps.

* * * * *

"I categorically refuse to call you 'Father'." Viktor's voice was firm as he stared at Fabyan.

The older man chuckled. "I'd plant you a facer the first time you did."

"She's your daughter. I can't believe it." Viktor shook his head. "Well, I can, of course…seeing the two of you together. She has your eyes."

Gyorgy was smiling at them. "And so Fabyan speaks at last. To threaten his new son-in-law."

Mat and Luk grinned as well.

Peter brooded. "Hell. I'm not related to anyone."

Luk passed the brandy and Peter cheered up.

The six Gypsies were sprawled around the dining table, having been most properly left at the end of the meal by their women. They were disconsolate, a little drunk, and had quite rightly guessed that the conversation taking place over the teacups was probably about them.

"We've come a long way," mused Viktor, staring at his brandy.

"Hell, yes," agreed Gyorgy.

"Who would have imagined it?" smiled Luk.

"Not me," answered Mat.

"Nor me," added Peter.

Fabyan smiled. He was enjoying the chance to share his opinions with his friends. To finally speak his thoughts. Annabelle had truly given him a most precious gift, in addition to a daughter. "I am not surprised."

Five heads turned.

He sipped his drink and contemplated them. "You are all men of intelligence. Men of honor. No matter your backgrounds, your secrets, your skills. There are some things that matter more than all the superficial trappings of a man's life."

"There are?" Peter squinted at him.

"Yes." Fabyan paused, gathering his thoughts. "Give me a minute or so and I'll think of them."

The others laughed. "You're drunk," teased Mat.

"A little," smiled Fabyan. "And are you surprised? I gain a beautiful daughter and a disreputable son-in-law practically all in one day."

"Not to mention your voice," chimed in Luk. "Um...Fabyan?" He saluted him with a sloshy swirl of brandy. "It's damn fine to hear you talking, but do us all a favor. Don't sing."

Fabyan nodded through his laughter. "I won't."

"Leave that to our Prioshka." Mat and Luk beamed proudly.

"You should hear her," said Mat. "An angel couldn't sound better. A voice like a flute and a nightingale combined."

"Really?" Viktor's eyebrows rose.

"Yes *really*." Luk raised his chin. "You doubt our word?"

Viktor sighed. "Of course not. Leave it to you two to find the right woman for you both, and it turns out she *sings* too."

Fabyan watched the byplay with affection.

His feelings for these men had deepened over time from friendship to a deep and abiding camaraderie. They shared so many fundamental values, their beliefs matched like pieces of a child's puzzle, and their thoughts echoed one another as their music played counterpoint.

"So..." He tapped his glass lightly with his fingers, interrupting the current exchange of affectionate insults. "Do we all have plans for our future?" He paused. "'Tis much different now than just a few short weeks ago when we left London for a simple country weekend."

The others nodded in agreement.

"I confess I find myself lacking in enthusiasm for a return to France," admitted Peter. "Now that I'm getting used to the idea of being Lord Chalmers again...and of course there's Freddie to consider..."

Good-natured grins answered this comment, and Fabyan realized each man now carried the additional burden of love deep in his heart. They would be no good as warriors working undercover for the cause of freedom anymore.

He said so. "Our jobs are done in France. We've helped many, saved a few, and can be proud of what we've accomplished. But our paths lie in different directions now. "

"Agreed." Viktor put his glass down on the table. "I find I enjoy London. There is much to offer here, and even a chance to continue what our work in France began. With Zentaily House, we've met a need...I'd like to see it continue."

"Shall you not return to Karoly?" asked Gyorgy.

"Oh yes, I shall. Definitely. I'd like for Madelyne to see it. But not yet. Things are still too uncertain over there to risk such a trip. And besides, she and Freddie...well, they're head-over-heels with the whole Zentaily venture."

Peter nodded. "And God help anyone who gets in their way." He grinned at Fabyan. "I wonder where Madelyne gets *that* particular characteristic from?"

Fabyan made a rather ungentlemanly gesture back at Peter.

"Well," said Luk, interrupting the byplay. "Mat and I are taking Prioshka back to Eger."

Mat smiled. "We have some plans of our own. Zentaily House might help women in need, but there's another group of people who also need a lot of assistance." He looked grave. "The children."

Faces turned to Mat and Luk.

"We're going to work on our vineyard. See if we can make it pay. Turn the old winery into an orphanage while we're at it." Luk raised his chin, as if waiting for comments or criticism.

He received nothing but smiles and raised glasses.

"We can help, Luk. You'll need startup capital..." Peter frowned thoughtfully.

"And certainly some local contacts..." added Viktor.

Mat bit his lip. "I...we..."

Fabyan held up his hand. "Don't say it, Mat. We're a unit. We work together, as one. Where one has a need, the others meet it. Where another could use our help, he gets it." He raised his glass. "To your wines and your orphanage. May they both produce the best vintage."

The toast was drunk enthusiastically.

"And you, Gyorgy?" Viktor looked over at his friend. "Have you made plans yet?"

Gyorgy grinned wickedly. "Oh yes."

Peter snorted. "He means other than getting Marie-Claire into your bed."

Gyorgy punched Peter in the shoulder. "I'm marrying her first, you idiot." A huge smile crossed his face. "As soon as may be arranged, too. After that..." He paused. "I'm not sure. We'll have to see how this whole Hucknall thing plays out. I know she's going to want to make sure the Duke of Kirkwood is secure. But then?" He spread his arms wide. "The world awaits."

"It does indeed," agreed Fabyan. "It does indeed."

And as the conversation ranged over the variety of futures that lay ahead of them all, Fabyan sat back and gave some thought to his own situation. And Annabelle.

They'd face it together, he and Annabelle. Of that, there was no question. The suicide of her husband, however, had solved one problem and created another. She was now free to wed, but to do so within days of his death would be unseemly in the extreme. Even Fabyan, in his haste to make her his, knew that.

"Problems, Fabyan?" Peter's voice interrupted his reverie.

"Not really. Just thinking about..."

"Annabelle?" guessed Gyorgy.

Fabyan smiled. "Always. Always have, always will."

Viktor ran his hands through his hair. "You'll marry her, of course?"

"Of course. And also claim Madelyne, privately, as my own. You'll have no objections?" Fabyan glanced over at Viktor.

His smile was answer enough, but he spoke the words anyway. "I couldn't be happier. For you both."

"Eventyde's suicide does put rather a damper on things, though. Annabelle will have to wait out her mourning..." Fabyan pursed his lips.

"Only here in England, Fabyan," said Peter. "Take her abroad. Go with Mat, Luk and Prioshka, perhaps. Travel a little. Were you two to quietly wed in Europe, none would be the wiser. By the time you return—if you choose to return—there'll be something new to talk about. You'll be old news."

Fabyan pondered this suggestion. He'd not considered taking Annabelle out of the country yet again. She'd wandered for so long that he'd wanted to settle her, make a home for her and give her some security. And perhaps give himself some as well.

Gyorgy rose. "Well, while we're thinking about it, I suggest we go and find our women. I, for one, miss them. And God only knows what they've been saying about us."

He grinned and reached over into the shadows, pulling out his violin. "Methinks it's time this house rang with some music, my friends. We have a lot to celebrate, and what better way is there?"

Amidst much laughter, the men seized their instruments and left the dining room, intent upon claiming their women.

Fabyan shook his head as he followed them. Truthfully, there was no better way to express how full his heart was than through music.

Epilogue

The small church was filled to capacity.

Friends, neighbors and even a relative or two had gathered to celebrate the occasion of the wedding of Marie-Claire, Dowager Duchess of Kirkwood, to Gyorgy Vargas, Hungarian gentleman.

Late afternoon sunlight flooded the nave, and danced across the dresses of the women sitting in the front pews. Countess Madelyne Karoly, sat next to Lady Freddie Chalmers, and giggled.

"I swear Gyorgy's trembling."

"Shh. He'll hear you," said Freddie chuckling. "But you're right. He is shaking."

Peter, on Freddie's other side, gave her a nudge.

Madelyne couldn't help smiling. To think that the wild Pyotr was now reminding his wife to behave herself in church.

And there was Mat, along with Luk, sitting so tall and handsome, with equally proud smiles on their faces as they glanced down at Prioshka seated between them.

She was a good choice for them, mused Madelyne. Having chosen a brightly colored folk outfit, Prioshka was no longer a little brown mouse, but a small blaze of fire between her men. She was possessed of a great deal of commonsense, a strong will, and more than a dash of passion.

Yes, she'd do very well for Luk and Mat.

Madelyne's gaze passed on to where Viktor stood next to Gyorgy. Their gazes brushed each other, and Madelyne felt the heat shoot straight to her core. God, how was it possible to love a man so much?

Sometimes it was almost frightening how much she loved him.

Her eyes fell to the hands of the woman seated next to her—her mother. How much worse to love a man like that and then lose him for so many years. To bear him a child he never knew he had, and to suffer under the heel of a brute, all the while knowing that the one and only man she'd ever love had gone from her life.

Her heart swelled with sympathy and affection for her mother. They'd had some interesting talks over the past few days as they'd arranged for Gyorgy's marriage. And they were growing closer as women—women who loved their Gypsies.

A slight stir at the back of the church heralded the arrival of Marie-Claire, and Madelyne joined the rest of the congregation as they stood with the first chords of the organ.

She suppressed a snicker as Gyorgy nearly tripped over Viktor. Gyorgy was so strong in so many ways, yet one look from Marie-Claire and he had melted.

And how lovely she was. Her cool beauty was set off by a bouquet of blazing red roses, tied with blue ribbons that matched her eyes. There was nothing cool about those eyes today. They danced with happiness and joy and an overwhelming love for the man she was about to wed.

And on her arm? Fabyan. Madelyne's father—a man of contradictions, quiet strength and boundless emotions.

He too had spent some time with Madelyne, and she'd quickly overcome her awkwardness with him—learning how much he loved their conversations, and answering her questions. She'd discovered so much about him that was honorable, and so much that yet remained hidden.

It probably always would, she mused, watching Marie-Claire make her way down the aisle to Gyorgy and the waiting vicar.

Fabyan had stopped speaking for many years. By choice too. A man like that would know how to hold his counsel. He'd protected these men, kept their secrets, and led them on a wild and dangerous dance through Europe. He was truly a father to be proud of.

And pride was in his eyes as they swept the full church. Madelyne couldn't miss it, nor did she miss the smile directed at her or the hot glance as his eyes brushed Annabelle's.

She looked away, unwilling to steal even a little of that passion. Her mother deserved it.

The ceremony underway, Viktor and Gyorgy performed their roles and Fabyan gave the bride away on behalf of her absent family.

It was done. Gyorgy had joined the ranks of married men. His long and passionate kiss brought cheers and applause to the church, and blushes of color to his new bride's cheeks.

Viktor returned to Madelyne's side with a smile as the wedding concluded and people began to leave the church. Peter and Freddie led the way, following Gyorgy and Marie-Claire. Then Mat and Luk carefully handed Prioshka from the pew and marched out, flanking her. Fabyan had tugged Annabelle into his arms, and then reluctantly allowed her loose to set her hand on his arm as was proper. She grinned at his reluctance to let her go.

"A moment, Madelyne..." Viktor's hand stayed her as she would have followed the throng.

She looked up at him. "Is everything all right?"

He swallowed. "It couldn't be better. I just wanted to tell you..." He stroked her hair back from her cheek. "I just wanted to tell you how much I love you. That's all."

She sighed. "Viktor, that's so much more than 'all'. That's everything. You are my life. My heart. My soul. I bless the day I found you...I've even blessed Eventyde and asked God to forgive him his sins. If it hadn't been for him, I'd never have met you. And my life...well, without you it would have been nothing."

She stood on tiptoe and pressed her lips reverently to his. "I love you so much, Viktor."

The kiss turned heated, and reluctantly Viktor pulled back. "I must stop, or I'm going to forget I'm in God's house, and do something quite inappropriate."

She flashed him a wicked grin. "Can you wait and do it when we get home?"

"Oh yes." His growl turned her body to a mass of churning excitement.

"Oh *good*."

Madelyne Karoly turned towards the door and, like her friends before her, followed her Gypsy lover into their future.

THE END

About the author:

Sahara Kelly was transplanted from old England to New England where she now lives with her husband and teenage son. Making the transition from her historical regency novels to Romantica™ has been surprisingly easy, and now Sahara can't imagine writing anything else. She is dedicated to the premise that everybody should have fantasies.

Sahara Kelly welcomes mail from readers. You can write to her c/o Ellora's Cave Publishing at 1337 Commerce Drive, Suite 13, Stow OH 44224.

Also by Sahara Kelly

A Kink In Her Tails

The Glass Stripper

Guardian's Of Time 1: Alana's Magic Lamp

Guardians of Time 2: Finding The Zero-G Spot

Hansell and Gretty

The Knights Elemental

Madam Charlie

Magnus Ravynne and Mistress Swann

Mesmerized

Mystic Visions

Partners In Passion 1: Justin and Eleanor

Persephone's Wings

Peta And The Wolfe

Sizzle

The Sun God's Woman

Tales Of The Beau Monde 1: Lying With Louisa

Tales Of Beau Monde 2: Miss Beatrice's Bottom

Tales Of Beau Monde 3: Lying With Louisa

Tales Of Beau Monde 4: Pleasuring Miss Poppy

Why an electronic book?

We live in the Information Age—an exciting time in the history of human civilization in which technology rules supreme and continues to progress in leaps and bounds every minute of every hour of every day. For a multitude of reasons, more and more avid literary fans are opting to purchase e-books instead of paperbacks. The question to those not yet initiated to the world of electronic reading is simply: *why?*

1. *Price.* An electronic title at Ellora's Cave Publishing runs anywhere from 40-75% less than the cover price of the <u>exact same title</u> in paperback format. Why? Cold mathematics. It is less expensive to publish an e-book than it is to publish a paperback, so the savings are passed along to the consumer.

2. *Space.* Running out of room to house your paperback books? That is one worry you will never have with electronic novels. For a low one-time cost, you can purchase a handheld computer designed specifically for e-reading purposes. Many e-readers are larger than the average handheld, giving you plenty of screen room. Better yet, hundreds of titles can be stored within your new library—a single microchip. (Please note that Ellora's Cave does not endorse any specific brands. You can check our website at www.ellorascave.com for customer

recommendations we make available to new consumers.)

3. *Mobility.* Because your new library now consists of only a microchip, your entire cache of books can be taken with you wherever you go.

4. *Personal preferences are accounted for.* Are the words you are currently reading too small? Too large? Too...**ANNOYING**? Paperback books cannot be modified according to personal preferences, but e-books can.

5. *Innovation.* The way you read a book is not the only advancement the Information Age has gifted the literary community with. There is also the factor of what you can read. Ellora's Cave Publishing will be introducing a new line of interactive titles that are available in e-book format only.

6. *Instant gratification.* Is it the middle of the night and all the bookstores are closed? Are you tired of waiting days—sometimes weeks—for online and offline bookstores to ship the novels you bought? Ellora's Cave Publishing sells instantaneous downloads 24 hours a day, 7 days a week, 365 days a year. Our e-book delivery system is 100% automated, meaning your order is filled as soon as you pay for it.

Those are a few of the top reasons why electronic novels are displacing paperbacks for many an avid reader. As always, Ellora's Cave Publishing welcomes your questions and comments. We invite you to email us at service@ellorascave.com or write to us directly at: 1337 Commerce Drive, Suite 13, Stow OH 44224.

Printed in the United States
24225LVS00002BA/58-408

9 781843 609537